Eve of Tomorrow

Eve of Tomorrow

Book 3 of
The Dawn of Rebellion Series

Michelle Lynn

And finally, this one's for my parents. I wouldn't be who I am without your constant love and support.

Acknowledgements

Thank you to everyone who helped this series become a reality. You never complained or tuned out as I rambled on endlessly about plot and characters, trying to get it right. I couldn't have done this without the love and support of my friends and family.

Neil and all of your editing expertise and cover design. There isn't a single other person who spent so much time working through this stories development with me. I feel like this is as much your story as it is mine and the cover is beautiful.

Mom and all of your support and patience. I'm not always the easiest person to be around, especially when I'm dealing with frustrating edits.

Sierra, my amazing proof editor. You were more wonderful than I imagined and I don't even want to think about the state this book would be in without you. You are a wonderful editor and an even better friend.

Evelyn, my niece. I can't wait until you are old enough to read this book that you inspired so much. I wrote the first draft with you by my side the entire time and it gave me plenty to write about. A big thank you to the rest of my family- Robin, Mackenzie, Doug, Colby. Life's been tough, but you're there for me and that means a lot. I'll always have plenty to write about when I'm surrounded by all of you.

And most of all, thank you God for blessing me with all of these wonderful people and the gift of stories. Thank you all for allowing me to live in worlds of my own making, if just for a little while.

The Drylands

Wastelands

St Louis

Cincinnati

REPUBLIC OF TEXAS

Rebel base

Vicksburg

FLORIDALAND

MEXICO

Baton Rouge

Chapter 1

Dawn

I flatten myself to the forest floor just in time to see a knife fly through the space where I'd been standing a second ago. "Run!" Corey's command urges me forward as I get to my feet and take off through the mess of charred and twisted trees of the unfamiliar forest.

I'm fast, but my pursuer is faster. He uses long strides to gain on me as I allow myself a moment of hesitation and a single glance back at him. That's all he needs to close the gap. Still moving, I see him hurdling forward and then blackness envelops me.

I'm only out for a minute or so. The half-naked, tattooed man has an arm around my throat and warm blood trickles from where the tip of his knife is pressed into my back.

Corey's eyes are cold as he stands with his gun trained on my captor. "Let her go," he demands.

"You are the trespassers here," the man responds.

"We don't mean any harm." Corey lowers the gun, trying to diffuse the tension.

"Why are you here?" He doesn't remove the knife from my skin.

"Let the girl go and we can talk."

For a brief moment, I think he's going to do it. Instead, his arm tightens, making it hard to breathe. I gasp for air and struggle against him.

"My tribe is hunting nearby," the big man says ominously. "If you shoot, they'll come."

One look at Corey tells me that he's already thought of that. I see his lips twitch up into a smile before he hides it with a grimace. I hear the crunch of leaves underfoot before the arm goes slack at my throat and the man jerks against me. I clench my teeth as his knife cuts into my back before he falls away. My body sways as I fight the need to, but Ryan is there to catch me.

"Where were you?" I say as loudly as my voice can manage as I inhale sharply. I step away from the dead man. Ryan's blade protrudes from the back of his head.

"Damn freedom fighters," Corey curses, holstering his gun.

"Sorry," Ryan starts. "I'd gotten pretty far ahead of you guys."

"We need to stick together," Corey states.

Ryan nods his agreement. They don't seem as shaken up as me. This is hardly the first time we've been attacked since leaving the Rebel compound weeks ago, but it's the first fight since reaching the wastelands two days ago. We're in their territory now. The freedom fighters reign supreme here. That's why most avoid this place at all costs. The tattooed warrior clans fight without abandon and no one really knows what they fight for. A long time ago, they actually were fighting for their freedom. Now, that is just a name.

"Do you think we should have questioned him?" I ask when I get my wits together.

"He wouldn't have told us anything," Corey answers gruffly. "And we aren't torturers."

"It's up to us to find my sister." Ryan steps on the dead man for leverage as he pulls his knife free and cleans it on his pant leg.

"He said his tribe is hunting near here." Corey starts to move. "We need to keep going."

I wince at the thought. My back hurts where I was cut and my shirt is sticky with blood, not all of it mine. It'll heal though and I don't want to slow us down. We can't stop until we find Emily. Ryan's kid sister was taken by the freedom fighters during the fighting in Texas. We left her outside the walls, thinking she'd be safer. We don't know what they want with a 10-year-old American girl, but it can't be good. I don't look down as I step over the dead man and follow Corey and Ryan farther into the woods.

Hours later, we're still walking, but I can't keep up anymore. We haven't had a proper sleep in days and our food supply is running low.

"Ryan," I yell, hoping he can hear me despite the distance between us. He does. He turns and jogs back.

"You okay?" he asks.

I don't know how he still has so much energy. Maybe it's the fear masking as adrenaline running through his veins, pushing him to find his sister quickly.

"We need to set up camp to get some rest," I say.

"It's still light out," he protests.

"She's right," Corey agrees. "Now that we're in the Wastelands, we want to travel at night to use the darkness to hide us. We'll rest until the sun goes down."

Ryan drops his shoulders in resignation. He knows we're right and his argument disappears. The boys set up a makeshift camp while I check the packs for what food we have left. There's half a loaf of stale bread and a bit of meat that we cooked a few days ago. It's not enough to fill us. The hunting has been sparse for week now and we've given up our expectations of regular meals. We do have plenty of water, though. Two days ago, we came upon a stream where we were able to bathe and fill our empty water bottles. I take a swig and the water slides down my dry throat and drops into my empty stomach, triggering the nausea that only the truly hungry know.

I pass out the food and scarf mine down. It's all I can do to keep from trying to pick the crumbs from the ground. I do have some dignity left. Corey takes first guard and I lay back, hoping sleep can ease my weariness.

"Dawn." Ryan lightly shakes me awake and I sit up suddenly. He pats my back to calm me, his fingers finding the blood crusted into my shirt. "Are you okay?"

"I'm fine," I say as I rub my eyes and stand. "My guard?"

"Yeah," he says, his voice is absent. "But you're hurt."

"It's just a small cut."

"Let me see it," he says.

I sigh, lacking the energy to argue, and do as he says. I lift the back of my shirt and wince as he touches the spot where my skin has been split, pouring water around the edges.

He cleans away the blood and says, "I can't do anything about the shirt."

"It's fine," I say.

"Okay," he begins. "But there's no way I can sleep. I'll sit your watch with you."

"You need rest."

"I'll rest when Emily is safe," he replies. Knowing there is no way around his stubbornness, I shrug and we sit in silence for a while before he talks again.

"Who is this guy?" He motions to Corey's sleeping figure. "I mean, we've been on the road with him for a while now and I still don't know why he came."

"Corey is a Texan," I start, unsure if I have the right to tell this story. If we're going to make it, Corey and Ryan need to trust each other more than they have. "He lived in one of the farming villages with his parents. His mom, Bria, was sympathetic to the Rebels. She'd pass on messages for them." I pause and close my eyes as a picture of Bria comes to mind. This isn't easy to talk about and my voice cracks when I keep going.

"When Gabby and I escaped Texas, we were helped by a woman named Allison. She was Bria's Rebel contact inside Texas. Corey's village was our last stop before reaching the Rebel compound. Bria hid us in her home, but we were found out by Texan soldiers. Bria got us out in time and sent Corey with us. She knew what they were going to do to her."

Ryan's silence tells me he understands. Bria and her husband were killed. Ryan had to leave his home because of his father aiding foreigners. They have a lot in common.

"That's why Corey hates the Rebels?" he asks after a while.

I grimace, wishing it were that simple.

"He also saw Gabby kill someone point blank." I look away, unable to watch that bit of information sink in.

Everyone at the Rebel base knows that Gabs killed the Texan farmer and tried to kill his son. It was only because of my intervention that Matty is alive.

Ryan laughs suddenly and I scowl at him before he explains, saying, "Aren't we quite the group? An American, a Texan, and a British Rebel."

"I feel like that's the beginning of an epic story," I say with a laugh, but I stop laughing when I feel a stab of pain radiate from the cut in my back. The heroes in epic stories always suffer and, in real life, they don't always save the day. I sigh and shake my head as I watch the last rays of light leave the woods.

We wake Corey before the moon is high and start moving again. We don't know exactly where we're going, but I feel like we're close.

So close.

Chapter 2

Dawn

The closer we get to Emily, the less Ryan talks. It's been a couple days since our guard duty chat and now he's angry and scared all at the same time. I know the feeling. When my sister was in the Floridaland slave camp, I was a mess.

As the sky darkens, a burst of chilled air moves through the trees. I shiver and pull my arms tight across my chest. I'd kill for a cuppa right now.

"I wish we could start a fire," I say.

"I wish we could find something edible," Corey says wistfully.

Ryan stays quiet. I nod as I lean back against a tree and close my eyes, trying to push all thoughts of food out of my mind. I've never felt this empty. Last night we found some kind of animal, but there was only a small amount of meat.

Instead of dreaming of food, I dream about the night my patrol was attacked by a band of freedom fighters at the river's edge. I see Lucas, Grace, and Brent fighting them off. Other members of my patrol are dead at our feet. I'm grabbed from behind by a fellow Rebel. King. We wear the same uniform, but his gun is trained on me. I hear someone yell and lunge before a bullet rips into my shoulder. I wake suddenly and sit straight up with sweat dripping down my face and breaths rasping in my chest.

"You okay?" Corey asks.

"Fine," I answer shortly. I've had that dream before, many times. I do my best to forget. "We should get going," I say as I stand and begin to erase all signs of our presence from this clearing. We don't want anyone following us. I can't get King's face out of my head. Other than a few friends and my sister, I haven't trusted the Rebels since then. King shot me on orders from Jonathan

Clarke. He was the Rebel leader. Now he's held prisoner in the very base that he controlled. I never did find out if my mother wanted me dead or if Clarke kept his second in command in the dark.

My father, General Nolan, leads the Rebels now and I don't know what to think of him. He refused to allow me to go on this mission. Well, he abandoned me to make my own choices for most of my life. I don't need him telling me what to do now. He pulled rank and ordered me to stay, but I never wanted to be a Rebel soldier anyway. He can have my uniform. I'll gladly shed that burden.

I only wish my father had told me what he knows of the Wastelands. He seems to know everything that goes on in the colonies so I doubt he's as ignorant of this place as he let on. He did warn me against coming, but all I care about right now is finding Emily.

Here's what I do know. The Wastelands are a charred mess and no one seems to know why. It happened a long time ago. It has long been thought that no one could live here. Crazy weather patterns are the norm and the land is harsh. Crops have trouble growing and animals tend to stay away. How could anyone survive?

But obviously, the Freedom Fighters can. Such a wretched place is the perfect hiding place for them. My father warned us that they're much more likely to find us than we are to find them. We came anyway. We can't let them have Emily. She's just a girl. What could they possible want with her?

Chapter 3

Gabby

This sucks. I can't believe I've been sent back to Vicksburg, the capitol. General Nolan (I refuse to call him my father) made the assignment. What's worse is that Adrian, that lying jackarse of a man, is in charge. A Texan! This is rubbish! There is an entire unit of Rebel soldiers with us so I don't know why I had to come. Nolan said it's because I distrust Adrian and will keep a better watch on him than most would. I wish the general would just treat me like any other ranker.

I walk through the streets and am amazed at how quickly most of them have been cleared of debris from the bombs. Some of the buildings are already being rebuilt and I've only been here a few weeks. These people move fast.

The fighting here wasn't as bad as in Baton Rouge which had to be abandoned after the battle. The entire city was in shambles and it was easier to let it stay that way. Most of the people that lived there were killed and the few who were lucky enough to survive, sought refuge in Vicksburg and St. Louis – the latter of which surrendered before too much damage could be done.

I wish I could be with Lee. He was sent to the Mexican front as part of a peace delegation and is due here any day now. Jeremy requested to be sent to St. Louis. He didn't want to face the capitol or me. Nothing is ever going to be right with us again. I take a deep breath and push him from my mind. It's time to move on.

I walk a little further and suddenly find myself where I always seem to end up, the steps that lead into the place that I never wanted to see again. The labs. I was held here. Drew was tortured here. Adrian killed his mother here.

I want to tear it apart, brick by brick. I've confronted Adrian about it a million times. Each time, he tells me that I just don't understand. I tell him to make me understand, but he says to forget about it. That's not very likely. If Adrian really wanted to shut it down, he could. The people here hang on his every word. I've watched their faces as he makes speech after speech about rebuilding and rejoining the world around them. He tells them that an isolated Texas is a weak Texas and they believe him. They forget Adrian's ruthless aunt Tia, "the prophet", and his uncle Darren Cole, the bastard torturer.

The Texans think that both Darren and Tia Cole are dead. They're right about Darren. Adrian shot his uncle. I was there. Tia is alive, for now. She's being held at the Rebel compound. As much as Adrian fights it, the people now see him as "the prophet". I don't believe in all that shite, but I'm in the minority. Adrian refuses to speak in church as his aunt did, but that doesn't lessen his power. These people need a prophet to tell them what to do. You can't just dissolve a cult and expect the followers to suddenly be able to think for themselves. General Nolan understood this.

"Gabby." I turn as Adrian walks towards me, his arms clasped behind his back. It hasn't been that long, but Adrian isn't the same person I knew before. He seems older; more serious; more full of himself.

"How did you find me?" I snap at his unwelcome presence.

"Where else would you be?" he responds calmly. "You're here a lot. Have you gone in?"

"No," I snap again as I turn away from him and stare up at the building. "I don't have access."

"I know, but I wasn't sure if that would stop you," he says. "There's a reason that I haven't given you access. And no, we aren't going to have this argument again."

I turn my head to glare, but, to my annoyance, he isn't bothered by my obvious hostility. "Come on. There's work to do," he says as he holds out his arm, expecting me to take it. Instead, I brush past him and he has to leg it to catch up.

"More interviews today?" I ask sullenly. For weeks, we've been interviewing people again and again. Most of our interviewees were involved in the government or the church when Tia Cole ran things. We're trying to gauge their levels of loyalty to her and the old ways. So far, we've found that most of these people easily transferred their allegiance to Adrian, but we still don't trust any of them.

"Not today," Adrian answers. "Our envoy to the Mexicans returned this morning."

"Good," I reply. I can only manage a single word as relief rushes through me. Lee is here. In this whole messed up world, Lee has become one of the only people that I can count on. I have felt so alone here over the past weeks. No one to trust. No one that I even really want to talk to.

It's not far from the labs to the government building. I reach the door first and swipe my card. I've been given a key card that can pretty much get me in anywhere, except for the labs. Adrian likes me to snoop and find things out about people. My first instinct is to distrust people and he uses that.

I don't hold the door for him, so it shuts in his face, but I don't look back. I use my card again to gain access to the upper floors of the building. Adrian catches up and we ride the elevator in silence. We stop on the top floor and the door slides open, revealing a travel weary group of people sitting around the table. They don't stand as we enter the room. That's the difference between Rebels and Texans. Texans would be fawning all over Adrian; the Rebels know better.

One man does rise from his seat and walks over.

"Gabby," he says in his serious way. "It's good to see you."

Before the words pass my lips, I reach my arms out and hug Lee tightly. He's surprised as he pats my back. Lee and I aren't exactly the hugging kind of friends. After a few uncomfortable moments, I back away.

"I'm glad you're here," I say honestly.

Chapter 4

Jeremy

St. Louis is like nothing I've ever seen before. It's a city that's centered on its port. Most of the boat crews are smugglers, but no one seems to care. Alcohol is illegal, but there are so many bars making their own hooch that it's almost impossible to avoid. No one ever gets busted. Everything here can be bought and sold and nothing is ever free. There's a Mexican controlled part of town, even though Mexicans aren't allowed in Texas. These people are under the same rule as the capitol, but they aren't blind followers of a prophet they've never seen.

During the Rebel attacks, St. Louis surrendered pretty early on so the destruction was limited. The docks took a big hit when people started lighting boats on fire, but everything seems to be back to normal, or as normal as this place gets.

As soon as I was released from the hospital, I requested my assignment here. At the time, I didn't completely understand why. I only knew that I needed to get away from the Rebel compound. After everything that happened, I didn't feel safe there. I was beaten by Jonathan Clarke and then thrown into a cell with Dawn. For days, we thought we were going to die. I don't remember much of that time because I was fading in and out of consciousness.

By the time I woke in the clinic, General Nolan was in charge and everything was different. We were no longer talking about attacks and battle plans. People were being deployed to re-stabilize the area and fix what we'd broken. Dawn was already gone on an unsanctioned mission. I shouldn't have been surprised. Gabby would come to check on me, but the awkward silence became too much.

I didn't really have anything to say to her. She already knew what I couldn't find the words to say. It was time for us both to move on.

"Catch," Drew yells as he lobs a bottle of water at me. I snatch it out of the air, uncap it, and take a swig.

"Thanks, man," I say as we move further in from the docks. This place continues to amaze me with its vast network of warehouses along the waterfront.

"We're heading for one of the Mexican houses," Drew explains. "It's not far."

"How do we get in?" I look down at my clothes. "We won't exactly blend."

"Our contact is meeting us out front," he answers. "Let me do most of the talking since I know what information we need."

I just nod. Normally, I'd want to be more involved, but he's right. I know nothing about any of this. I'm only here because I caught Drew heading out. He was going to come here alone, but there was no way I was letting that happen. To put it simply, I'm his protection. I've got a gun in the holster on my hip and another strapped to my leg. I hope that's enough.

"Rebel." A man steps out from the darkness. I slip my hand over the safety and then rest it on the gun, "You're Rebels?" he asks, his accent thick.

"Yes," Drew responds. "And you're Rafael."

"Come," Rafael orders. "We must not be late." He begins to lead us back the way we'd come.

"Where are we going?" I ask. "We're supposed to be in the Mexican blocks."

"No, no," he responds, his voice is hushed. "He can't meet you there."

"Who?" Drew asks. Rafael doesn't answer. Instead, he veers off into an empty building and we follow him downstairs to the basement.

"You're late," a short man says as he shows himself.

"I am sorry, Uncle," Rafael says as he backs out of the room.

"I am Miguel, Rafael says you Rebels need information." He keeps his voice low as he studies us.

"How do we know you have what we need?" I ask.

"You only talk to me," he responds. I'm about to say something else when Drew cuts me off.

"Jeremy," Drew snaps. "Wait for me outside."

I want to object, but Drew's face tells me to stay out of it. Reluctantly, I climb the stairs.

I scan the darkened street as I wait for what seems like hours. Finally, Drew emerges from the building, but I can't see the expression on his face as he rushes past me.

"Let's go," he says.

"What happened in there?" I ask as my feet catch up to his.

"Nothing." He sighs. "Another dead end. There's something going on in Mexico and we need to know what."

"What do you mean?" I ask. "If I'm going to help you, I need to know what's going on."

"I don't want to drag you into this. It's not a good idea."

"Drew, I'm already in it. You can't be going to these meets without backup," I respond. Drew stops walking and looks at me.

"I barely know you, Jeremy." He hesitates. "But Dawn trusts you."

He starts moving even quicker than before. When we reach the docks, I follow him to the ship tied to the very last slip. There isn't a single soul on deck so we board without any problems. We use the narrow staircase to head below deck. As soon as we enter the room, an older fellow hurries towards us.

"Drew," he says as they shake hands.

He eyes me up and down before steering Drew towards a table at the opposite end of the room. I follow them. There's a small group of people in deep conversation when we sit down.

A woman that I immediately recognize as a Rebel officer protests.

"Drew, we can't keep bringing people in, not until we know more," she says.

"Then who is supposed to watch my back with the Mexicans?" he asks. "You, Officer Mills, are leaving soon to follow your lead. The captain is old and slow, no offense."

"None taken," the old captain says before Drew continues.

"Lucas can barely stand and should probably still be in a hospital bed. So, tell me, which one of you are going to help me find the answers we need?"

"It's okay, Grace, Jeremy can be trusted," the man I know as Lucas states. "Dawn trusted him with her life."

Even though Drew had said practically the same thing, I see his face go dark for a second. Dawn loves Drew but, when it mattered the most, she trusted me over him.

"Did they tell you anything?" Lucas directs the question to Drew.

"I met with Miguel of the Carlita cartel," Drew begins. "They're searching for answers as well, but there's a rumor that the Moreno cartel is preparing for war."

"War?" Officer Mills asks. "The Moreno's don't have borderland."

"They have no interest in fighting Texas," Drew explains. "I was told that Juan Moreno is a dangerous man. If all of Mexico plunges into war, the colonies are next."

The door to the stairwell bursts open and two small boys run in. Their breathing is ragged and their faces are red.

"Dad," one of them yells. "We were chased, but I think we lost him." There's a sense of boyish pride in his voice. The captain tightens his jaw in anger.

"You left the boat?" he asks as he raises his voice. "You two know better than that."

"We were so bored here," they answer. Both boys look down at their feet.

"Captain," Officer Mills says suddenly, "I think we need to leave St. Louis."

"We weren't prepared to leave for a couple of days," he replies. The captain scratches his beard, but doesn't look worried.

"We have no choice," she responds. "I have some leads to track down, but I must speak with the General first."

The captain nods and leaves the room to order his sailors to prepare the ship.

"So, you're heading for the Rebel compound?" Drew asks, nodding his approval. "General Nolan needs to be brought up to speed. He probably has access to information that we don't. Jeremy and I will keep looking for answers here."

Drew and I hurry away from the docks and slip into the shadowed town.

Drew eventually stops and turns to me, but I can't make out his expression in the darkness as he speaks. "Someone will have to go to Mexico eventually to put an end to all of this."

Chapter 5

Dawn

The outer parts of the forested Wastelands don't look as if they'd been destroyed by the storms or natural causes as I was led to believe. They're scorched and twisted, but there are still spots where the greenery is trying to push through. I hadn't expected that. It's supposed to be a wasteland.

Everything is silent, save the sound of our footsteps moving forward. We've seen very few animals. We shot a couple birds a few days ago, but that's it. I've lost track of the days. I don't know when we last ate or when we last had more than a couple hours' rest. Our bodies and minds are weary. I worry that any attack would be the end of us because we're in no fighting state. My feet drag rather than step along the ground and my arms hang at my sides as if they are dead weight that I'm carrying.

We don't know how much longer we have to wander before we find where Emily is being kept. By the time we reach her, we may not be any good to her.

Corey and Ryan have spent their entire lives in the colonies and don't know any more about this place than I do. They say people just don't talk about it. They've both known people that have left their homes to explore the area. None of them ever returned. I'm not surprised. It's easy to get lost.

As we get deeper into the woods, we find that the trees are no longer burned, but stand tall and healthy around us. The ground is soft underneath our feet, probably because of the rains we've heard about.

I spot a group of deer up ahead and a thrill of excitement rushes through me. They're the first large animals we've seen in a while. More birds start to appear in the tree canopy overhead and we're running low on supplies so Corey decides it's a good time to hunt. He seems to have more energy and strength than Ryan and I at the moment, so we keep moving, knowing he'll catch up eventually.

"None of this is supposed to be possible," Ryan mutters.

"So much for a wasteland," I respond. Some of the birds move lower for cover and squawk as if warning us that the rain is coming. It comes out of nowhere and I'm soaked within seconds. I stop and strain to lift my eyes to look at the sky. The sun is still out and the blue is as brilliant as ever. How can it rain when the sky looks like that?

Ryan turns back towards me with a grin plastered across his face. It's good to see him smile.

"Let's keep moving," I say. The rain doesn't let up and the ground beneath our feet turns to mud. I'm trying to pull my foot free when I'm grabbed from behind. I yell for Ryan, but my voice lacks the strength to reach him through the pounding rain. I struggle against my captor, but it's no use. He pulls me behind a tree and waits as Ryan gets farther and farther away. I scream, but my voice is lost in the howling wind. There's a sharp pain on the back of my head and then nothing, nothing at all.

Chapter 6

Dawn

"Dawn, wake up," I hear her say. "Seriously Dawn, you weren't hurt that bad." Gabby? No, Gabby may as well be on the other side of the planet right now. I open my eyes slowly and Emily is sitting on the end of my bed.

"Emily," I say, relieved. We found her.

"Took you long enough to wake up. You wouldn't stop fighting them so they had to knock you out," she says.

"Who are they? Where am I?"

"They are the freedom fighters," she answers.

My pulse goes into instant panic mode. We've been captured by the freedom fighters. It's only a matter of time before we're dead. We're utterly buggered.

"Chill out," Emily snaps. "It's not what you think. They're good people."

"They've brainwashed you," I picture the fierce fighters that have killed so many people.

"I am not brainwashed," she yells.

"You're a kid. How would you know if they're good people?" I ask, regretting my word choice immediately as I see the tears form in her eyes.

"They never treat me like a kid!" She hurries from the room in a fit.

I'm such a jerk.

I don't know how long I've been here, but it's light outside so it's been at least a few hours. My head aches from being knocked out. The instant anger at the thought dissipates immediately because I don't have the will to hold onto it.

I take stock of the room I'm in. The window is open to allow air to move through and there's food next to the bed. I cram it into my mouth so fast that

I almost choke and then wash it down with the tea they've left for me. I don't even consider that there could be something wrong with the food. I'm too hungry. I eat everything and then stand on wobbly legs. The exhaustion of my journey hits me in full force and I almost fall. I catch myself and then carefully walk across the room to the door expecting it to be locked as I turn the knob. It's not. I pull it open. There's no one there. I'm not being held captive or even watched. What is going on? Where are the fighters that took me prisoner?

I step outside and people smile at me as I pass. They aren't the savage people I've come across. I don't return a single smile as confusion and distrust cloud my thoughts. There's a dirt path through the town that's lined with houses. These aren't the huts that I've seen huddled together on Texan land. It's more like the American town of Cincinnati where the homes are sturdy. Lines of clothing are strung between houses and I even spot a few gardens. As I walk, no one stares. No one tries to stop me.

I move slowly until my legs can't handle it anymore. I sit down, planning on heading back to my room after a short rest.

After a while, I hear my name. "Dawn Nolan," someone calls.

I turn my head and see a middle aged man jogging towards me. I suddenly wish I had something to protect myself with, but my weapons were taken from me. I reluctantly stay where I am until the stranger takes a seat next to me. I may not be a prisoner here, but, let's be honest, I'm still at their mercy. The man reaches me and offers me his hand to shake.

"Hello Miss Nolan, my name is Riley," he says. When I don't take his hand, he lowers it. "I tried to make it back by the time you woke. Sorry about the way you were brought here."

"What about my friends? Are Corey and Ryan here?" I ask quickly.

"No," he answers. "Our patrol made a mistake in only bringing you. We're trying to find your friends. It is hard to survive in the Wastelands unless we find you. That is how we stay hidden."

He stands and helps me to my feet before placing a hand on my back to lead me inside a nearby house. "I saw that you ate everything we gave you and figured you were probably still hungry."

As if on cue, my stomach gurgles. I'm served an overflowing plate of fresh fruit, chicken, and something white. I smell it and can't help, but dig in eagerly as if I've never had a hot meal in my life.

"It's corn," Riley explains. "We have the only fields that can still grow sweet corn."

I wait until I'm finished to ask my questions and am surprised that Riley is willing to answer every one.

"What is this place?" I ask. I haven't forgotten all my suspicions even though this man makes it very hard to dislike him.

"It is just a town, like any other in the colonies," he answers.

"How big is the town?" I ask.

"Bigger than you'd ever imagine. This section is where the current residents live. There is a much larger part that is unoccupied and waiting for future residents. Then we have the farms. Because of the rains, we can grow things that the Texan farms only dream of."

"How can you survive in the Wastelands?" I ask.

"We survive because it is called the Wastelands. At one point, it was uninhabitable. Over the course of time, that changed, but people's perceptions didn't. We keep ourselves hidden to stay out of the wars and whatnot. We burn the outer parts of the forests every year so that others think it is a harsh place. We also utilize our freedom fighters. They scare most people off." He trails off and I sense that he won't elaborate on their fighters. I move on, for now.

"Why did you kidnap Emily?" I ask. I don't mean for it to be harsh, but there isn't really a nice way to ask a question like that.

"Once again, we regret the way she was taken," he says as he runs a hand through his scraggly hair and watches my face, trying to determine if he should tell me the truth.

"Our people have long since suffered from a genetic mutation," he pauses. "Our women can't have children. It is our curse." His voice grows sad.

"So, let me get this straight, you kidnap young girls to make them have your kids? That's sick." I stand suddenly, wanting to run, but not sure where I could go or if I even have the strength to go anywhere.

"We don't make them do anything," he explains quickly, trying to get me to sit back down. "We bring them here when they're young, yes, but they usually get here and never want to leave. Most of them are orphans and life here is pretty good to them. When they get older, they marry and have children. They keep our society going."

"Emily isn't an orphan, her father is Chief Smith of Cincinnati," I say without emotion. I don't know how to feel about all of this.

"We received word that the Chief is dead," Riley states. "His wife too. So, yes, Emily is an orphan. Her brother would take her to the Rebels and she could die fighting their senseless battles. Ask her. She wants to stay."

With all of this swirling around my brain, I can only think of one more question.

"You knew my full name. Do you know who my father is?"

"General Nolan has been here a few times. The unoccupied side of town was built at his request."

Chapter 7

Gabby

CLOSED UNTIL FURTHER NOTICE.

The sign stretches across the steps leading into the church and a crowd of people mill about, confused.

"Back up!" I yell. I've been sent to dispel any mob that might appear because of the church closing. I was expecting people to tear down the sign and throw it in the dustbin. I was expecting chaos. What I find instead is just sad. It is the time of day that most of these people were required to spend in worship and, without it, they don't know what to do. They are lost without their reverend and their prophet telling them how to live their lives.

"Shite people, go back to your jobs. You should have better things to do. It's pathetic!" I yell. They finally begin to leave and when I'm no longer needed, I head for Adrian's office.

"What the hell is going on?" I ask as I burst through the double doors.

"What do you mean?" Adrian asks, distracted. It is only then that I notice the filing boxes cluttering up the floor and the piles of papers on his desk. I plop myself down into the chair across from him.

"Why is the church closed?" I ask. "I had to deal with those people."

He finally looks up and meets my eyes as he answers, "the reverend is missing."

"He was taken? By who?"

"He wasn't taken, he ran," Adrian says as he leans back and sighs. "The group that returned from Mexico brought quite a bit of intel with them."

I wait expectantly. I don't know why, but Adrian usually trusts me enough to be straight with me.

"There is a man named Juan Moreno in Mexico. He was working with my uncle and the reverend on a weapon. The Mexicans know this and are terrified of what he can do. That is why they've continued this war with Texas. We need to find Moreno to end the war and destroy the weapon and we need to do it before the weapon is used," he explains.

"Where do we start?" I ask.

"That's what I'm trying to figure out." He gestures to the files around the room. "These were my aunt and uncle's. I'm looking for any reference to Juan Moreno or a weapons project."

"Alright then, put me to work," I state. He seems relieved that I'm going to stay and help. He really could've ordered me to and I would've had to obey, but Adrian doesn't like to give orders.

Chapter 8

Gabby

"So, he told you about Moreno and the weapon?" Lee asks as he sits across from me at dinner.

"Why wouldn't he?" I snap.

"I didn't think you two got along," he says carefully. "General Nolan wanted you to keep an eye on each other because of that."

"You don't think I can be trusted with this information?" I demand, rising from my seat. "Or do you think that I can't handle it?" I shove my chair out of the way, but Lee grabs my arm before I can leave.

"I didn't mean that, okay?" His eyes search mine. "Sit back down."

I sit, but mostly because I'm starving. I don't even know why Lee is still here. The rest of his envoy left for the Rebel base already. They'll all be given new exciting and dangerous tasks. An assignment to the capitol is anything but exciting. Even Dawn is off on some adventure probably saving the world, as usual.

I don't say much for the rest of dinner; I just glare at Lee. He doesn't seem to mind because he is most comfortable with silence. I catch him laughing at me a few times and shut him up with a kick underneath the table.

After dinner, I spend most of the night holed up in Adrian's office with Adrian and now Lee. Most of the files have absolutely nothing to do with weapons. There are all sorts of reports from each factory and tons documenting the yield of every farm. It would be much quicker if we put all of those aside since they seem irrelevant. Adrian won't let us, though. He says his aunt would've only put important information in unimportant documents. That way, no one would ever find it. My eyes start to blur around midnight until I'm too tired to keep them open one second longer.

"Party too hard last night?" I recognize her voice before I open my eyes.

"Hi Allison," I say as I sit up sleepily. Someone must have moved me to the couch last night. Adrian is zonked with his head on his desk and Lee is in a reclining chair.

"I'd ask you how you are Gabby, but you slept with two hot men last night so I'm guessing you're good," she says with a laugh. I can't help but laugh along with her as she takes a seat beside me. There is a comfort to being around Allison. She has an open, easy way about her.

"I thought you were at base," I say. "What are you doing here?"

"It took your father some convincing," she answers.

"Don't call him that," I interrupt.

"Okay, well anyways, I've been trying to be assigned here for a while," she continues.

"You mean you chose this?" I ask as I gesture to the room around us. "After everything..."

"I was hoping to see this place dismantled by the Rebels, not destroyed," she explains. "By the time I realized that there would be no fighting, I had no choice. My orders were to join the occupying force in Vicksburg."

"Oh," A rush of emotions tightens my jaw, keeping me from saying more. I feel the same as Allison. If it was my choice, we would be tearing this place to the ground. Even the lab is still standing. That should have been the first to go.

"Have you seen Jack?" I ask, trying to steer my mind in a less traitorous direction.

"Yeah, I got in last night and went straight to see him," She smiles warmly. Jack and Allison love each other deeply. Along with Clay, they all helped Dawn and I escape Texas all those months ago. Allison had to leave Jack behind in order to get to Rebel base. I'm glad they've reunited. Allison ignores my sudden silence and keeps talking. "I figured that I should report here this morning."

"You were right." Adrian must have woken while we were talking. He flattens his hair and straightens his shirt before continuing. "Welcome back Allison," he says.

"Whatever," she responds.

It's going to take her some time to get over taking orders from a Cole. Adrian's family did some terrible things. I have only recently seen him for what he is not. He is not the Prophet, Tia, or the Torturer, Darren Cole. He is more like his mother, Elle, who died at his hand for helping the Rebels.

"What are my orders?" Allison snaps, ready to leave this office behind.

Adrian moves a bunch of files around until he finds what he's looking for. He hands a piece of paper to Allison and she promptly leaves.

"Who was that?" Lee asks groggily.

"Just another person under my command who hates me," Adrian sighs before continuing. "You guys should get out of the office for a bit. Why don't you do the morning perimeter security check?" he asks.

We don't argue with the chance to get outside and get our bodies moving. I'm a runner. I'm not meant for all of this sitting and waiting.

We walk in silence for a while before Lee asks, "why does Allison hate Adrian?"

"I don't really want to get into it," I sigh. "It's hard for me to think about."

"What did he do? I'm just trying to understand him," Lee responds.

I look at Lee. The wrinkle on his forehead and the way his lips are pursed make his concentration plain. He really is trying to figure it all out. He can't decide whether or not to trust Adrian. I answer him reluctantly.

"Adrian shot his own mother," I say as my voice cracks. "He thinks he did it to give her mercy, though. He says she would've been worse off if he hadn't done it."

"Then she probably would have," Lee says, looking away as we finish our final check. "Sometimes people have to do horrible things to help the ones they love."

"What's wrong?" I ask. He doesn't respond so I stop walking and grab his arm. "You can tell me," I say turning my thoughts from Adrian's deed to Lee's obvious pain. He stays silent for a while before deciding to confide in me.

"When we came to break you out of the Floridaland camp, that wasn't the first time I'd been there," he pauses. "I once told Dawn that I'd been in love with a girl who was sent there. That was true. I wanted to save her," he chokes on the last word.

I take his hand in mine and squeeze as he continues. "By the time I got there, she had been in the hot box for almost a week. I tried, I tried really hard, but there was no way to get her out. There was a tiny door near the floor that we could talk through, but she wasn't as strong as you Gabby. She asked me to…"

He wipes a single tear from his cheek, the first tear I've ever seen this man shed. I don't speak. I give him time.

"She wanted to be free. She couldn't take it any longer. I slid a knife through the door and she…" his voice trails off.

"Shh." I whisper, "You don't have to say it."

For the second time ever, I wrap my arms around him in a hug. This time he holds on tight. Killing someone out of mercy might end their pain, but then the person holding the knife or the gun has a new torture of their own.

Memories from my time in Floridaland are sharp in that moment. I would've welcomed death. It would've been a better fate than living life as a slave. I wanted to die in that hot box, but there was no one there to end my pain. I picture General Nolan sliding food and water through that door, not a knife. That door was my salvation. It was her death.

Chapter 9

Jeremy

Drew and I are no closer to finding anything useful. Every avenue brings us to another dead end. We've been warned about entering the Mexican side of town so we have steered clear. We can't avoid it forever. For now though, we go about our assignments.

Both Drew and I have been tasked with dealing with the refugees. Baton Rouge was completely destroyed and now the survivors trickle in to St. Louis. We also have people coming in from the farms that were destroyed.

Our food stores are running low and everyone blames Jonathan. He set fire to most of the farms and equipment and now Texans must live off rations. This is a society that has always had enough. They used to be safe behind their walls, with full stomachs and a ton of other luxuries. Sometimes, I can't help but despise them and their complaining. I was raised on nothing in a Floridaland slave camp. After my mom died, all I had was my little sister, Claire. Now I don't even have her.

I shake my head to clear it of those thoughts and focus more on what is happening right now. Drew and I are walking across town to the tents that have been set up for refugee intake.

"Tell me if I'm crossing the line," Drew is saying, "but you and Gabby didn't look so chummy the last time we saw her."

"She's not an easy person to get along with sometimes," I say looking away.

"Don't I know it?" he responds. "So are you two…"

"No," I snap, cutting him off. "We were only together because of the circumstances. We both needed someone and we were there for each other."

"Because of your sister?" he asks.

"That and just because of where we were. We went through a lot together and that made us close," he answers.

"Why aren't you together now?" he asks.

I almost tell him that he's crossed that line he mentioned, but it feels good to talk about it. "I'm not what Gabby needs anymore. She's lost her sense of what is right. She is angry and broken and she needs someone who will put her back together. Someone to pull her back from the ledge. That isn't me," I respond.

"Gabby was broken long before she came to the colonies," he says. "She was held together by the fact that her sister needed her. Dawn doesn't need her protection anymore."

When he says Dawn's name, the corners of his mouth twitch up, but his eyes give away his fear.

"Are you scared that Dawn doesn't need you anymore either?" I ask.

He hesitates before speaking, "Let's keep moving."

After a few moments of silence, I say, "she still needs you. It may not be in the way that you want, but the need is there."

We've reached the tents and the crowd milling around takes immediate notice. If looks could kill, we'd be dead a hundred times over. It must be the uniform. These people's lives have been destroyed; their loved ones killed by soldiers that looked just like us. We relieve the soldiers on duty inside the main tent and they can't get away fast enough. We're in for a long day.

The incessant noise and searing heat is making me miserable. People scream about their homes being destroyed and everything they've lost. They think we owe them and maybe we do, but that isn't how war works. You don't make up for winning a fight and you sure as hell don't apologize. Yes, the Rebels made a mess of things, a grueling, blood soaked mess, but if we give these people an inch, they'll take the whole damn city.

Along with a few other soldiers, Drew handles the intake. Every newcomer must answer a routine set of questions about their skills and the like. Eventually they'll be given jobs and integrated into St. Louis society. Not yet, though. I'm in charge of relocation. That pretty much means distributing goods such as clothing and assigning tents. The battle here was short, but there are still some badly damaged parts of the city and we don't have much room for all of these people.

"Name?" Drew asks repeatedly.

The man who stands at the front of the line is older and he wears just a white robe.

"Joseph Kearn," he responds. I watch him as he talks to Drew. He shrinks into himself and hunches his shoulders forward. Occasionally he stands straighter and I realize that he is trying to look weak. Why? He walks over towards me and his voice is hushed. For some unknown reason, this old man unsettles me. He is one to keep an eye on.

Chapter 10

The General

"Dammit Miranda, we're not going to discuss this again!" I yell. "It isn't time."

"Will it ever be time?" she retorts. "We are British Rebels. We are not American. We need to deal with the real threat. Floridaland is vulnerable right now as things in England spin out of control. This is our chance to rid ourselves of that problem."

"They aren't the real threat here," I say as I lower my voice. All of the officers left the strategy meeting as soon as Miranda started baiting me.

"Do you want our people to be able to leave England and settle in the colonies?" She too has lowered her voice, but I know that tone all too well. Our discussion is heading into dangerous territory.

"Commander Crawford's troops in Floridaland can't stop that from happening. When I left, they were already splintering. We need to focus on creating a peace between the other groups before settlement here is a possibility. We need to rebuild Texas and stabilize Mexico. Our people shouldn't have to escape the war in England only to find that we're also at war. Don't you want the fighting to end?" I ask.

"I'll keep fighting as long as I have to," she says as she walks towards the door.

"That's the point!" I yell after her. "You shouldn't have to."

I sit down at the table just as there is a knock on the door. A scrawny kid in uniform walks in tentatively. When I get angry, my face gets red. Everyone knows to stay away from me when that happens and this boy looks like he wishes he had that choice. His eyes widen as he looks at me.

"What is it?" I ask, trying to sound calm.

"Sir," he stutters, "I was sent to tell you that the prisoner is awake."

"Thank you," I reply as I stand and run my hands down my uniform to get rid of the creases. "You may go." The kid practically sprints from the room.

Normally, I'd send for Miranda before meeting with the prisoner, but she needs time to cool down. I decide to go alone. I'll use the guards as backup if need be. I doubt I'll need them though. We've been using enhanced interrogation methods on Tia Cole, the supposed Texan prophet. She has information and we need it. The problem is that she has a tendency to pass out and then she's no good to us for a few days. In between our discussions she is subjected to sleep deprivation techniques. So far, she hasn't caved.

I open the door to her cell and find her slumped in the corner. She looks at me and there is still defiance in her eyes. We need to rid her of that. I walk towards her and yank her to her feet before dropping her in the center of the room.

"Hello General," she croaks through parched lips.

"Prophet," I spit. The venom in my voice makes her cringe away from me. She then starts on the very same questions she asks every day. The very same questions I refuse to answer.

"How is Adrian, my nephew?" she asks. "He killed his own mother you know, can't be trusted. How did it feel to kill all those people in the attacks?"

She knows I wasn't with the Rebels yet so the last question is pointless.

"Have you found the information you've been seeking?" she asks, babbling on. "The Mexicans. Bad folk."

My fury rises with every word she speaks. The information I need about the Mexicans could come from her, but she refuses to cooperate. I storm from the room before she is finished. The last question is a clue; I've known it since she first asked. It tells me that she knows something and it's big. I nod to the guards to go in and do their thing. I can't stomach the torture, even though I despise that woman. Her screams echo down the hall and seem to bounce off the walls, amplifying them. When they finally stop, I go back in.

"Sir," one of the guards says, "she says she'll talk."

"Okay. You may leave us," I reply.

When they are gone, I take a seat on the floor directly across from Tia Cole's huddled form. Miranda always says a general shouldn't sit on the floor, but I prefer to look into a person's eyes as they speak to me.

"Tia," I say gently, coaxing her out of her scared and painful state. She starts to rock back and forth.

"Weapons in the wrong hands. Kill us all," she mutters repeatedly.

"What weapons, Tia?" I ask. "Explain. What are you talking about?"

Right here I make two classic mistakes. I raise my voice and I reach out to touch her. She falls away from me and then she passes out yet again.

Chapter 11

The General

The weapons are more than just a rumor, then. What did she mean about them being in the wrong hands? Who has this weapon? Is it really strong enough to kill us all? She hadn't spoken of the weapon before today so I know very little about it.

That interrogation left me with more questions than answers and that just irritates me. I hurry straight to Jonathan Clarke's cell. We had no choice but to lock him up after he showed his true colors. The anger had eaten away at him and given way to near insanity. There would never be peace with him free.

Every time I look at him, I see the boy from London. I was a high ranking Rebel as well as a high ranking soldier so I was privy to a lot of information. Jonathan's father died and his mother had an affair with the district commander. That made it possible for Jonathan to be seen as his son. The amount of information he passed on to the Rebels was amazing, but he was just a kid. He was a sweet kid. I never agreed with the use of children in our war.

When the commander found out the truth, Jonathan was sent to Floridaland to work in the orange groves. At the time, the Rebels in the colonies were falling apart and needed a strong leader. No one had done as much for our cause as Jonathan so I helped him escape. I couldn't go myself because the Rebels were better served having me as the general in Floridaland. I failed to see what would become of Jonathan and it saddens me. I look into his eyes and no longer see the young boy who I befriended in England.

"Nolan," Jonathan says as he stares at me.

Leaving out my rank is just another sign that Jonathan thinks he should still be in command. In that moment, I see that any love for me that he ever possessed is gone.

"Hello, Jonathan," I reply.

"What do you want today? Need to talk about that ex-wife of yours?" he asks as he pretends to be thinking hard. "No, no the great General doesn't have feelings. Are you finally going to torture me like you've been doing to my neighbor in the next room? I don't think that's it either. You still care about me and you're not sure I have any information of value. Well, you're wrong on that count, but I don't respond well to pain. I tend to keep my mouth shut."

"You've been a Rebel your whole life," I begin. "I have known you almost as long. You still have loyalty in there among all the anger and the hate. You're a loyal man, Jonathan."

"Loyalty gets you nowhere," he says harshly before laughing. "It just gets you a prisoner's ration and a screaming neighbor. Thrown out with the trash, that's what's been done with me."

He cocks his head as I decide what to say next.

"I need to know if you've heard about some kind of weapon in Mexico," I say. I'm tired of these games so I try directness.

"That's what you want to know?" He asks. "Well, you're in for a surprise then." He pauses. "The Texas that you're using all of our resources to rebuild, they built the weapon."

As the information clicks in my brain along with everything else I know, a sense of dread fills me. It must show on my face because Jonathan laughs again.

"You're just now thinking about those labs and the experiments, aren't you?" Jonathan asks. "That's right, Nolan, the Texans developed a biological weapon."

"You're lying," I state, unsure if a word he says is true. Can I afford not to trust him?

"That's okay," he starts. "Go and take your time finding out if I'm right." He leans back against the concrete wall and sighs. "I'll still be here when you come back to tell me I was."

I turn to leave and, with my back to him, I say, "It wasn't loyalty that got you thrown in this cell. Remember that."

Chapter 12

Dawn

Ryan and Corey were brought in a few days ago and I was so relieved that I couldn't wait for them to wake up to see them. Emily and I sat by Ryan's bed each day. They were half dead from starvation and exhaustion, but they regained their strength and woke up. They had been searching for me for days when a group of Freedom Fighters came upon them. They had no strength left to fight and they doubted that I was even still alive.

Ryan looked as if a burden had been lifted when he saw his sister. His eyes became clear again. That was four nights ago. Today he's been told that his parents have been killed back home and the sadness returns. He has too much on his mind to be curious about this place. He's even been kicking himself for not knowing this was here. I tell him that the town was built to stay hidden, but that doesn't help. He's already mapping out escape plans. I let him since it keeps him busy, but I know that there is no way we'd make it out of the wastelands without a guide.

The name of this town is New Penn and I still know very little about it. I know the water is plentiful and warm so the showers are pleasant. I know that there are more acres of farmland than anywhere else. I know that much of the fuel comes from some kind of corn. The people here are friendly and helpful. Their leader, Riley, seems okay, but I've been fooled before.

What I don't understand is why my father would want the town expanded immensely even though no one occupies over two thirds of the homes. Riley is the only person who seems to know the purpose of that, but his lips are sealed.

I'm headed back to check on Ryan when I run into a large man with a bare chest and an eagle tattoo. My pulse quickens immediately as I stare up at him. These men are the stuff of nightmares and here they are, just walking through town. Riley says they live on the outskirts and provide protection for the town.

"Sorry," he says.

I startle because I've only ever heard them speak once and that time I was being yelled at and attacked.

"It's okay," I say as I lower my eyes and walk around him. I practically sprint the rest of the way.

Once inside Ryan's room, I shut the door and lean against it.

"You alright, Dawn?" he asks.

I squeeze my eyes shut and when I open them, my breathing has steadied.

"Yeah," I respond. "But I think it's time for us to get out of here."

"It's past time," he says. "I think I've come up with a plan."

"We can't just run," I groan. "We'd never make it back to base."

"We have to try," he replies.

"No, we don't," I pause. "I think Riley will let us go. I even think he might help us."

"Are you kidding me?" he asks harshly. "The guy kidnapped my sister."

"That's not how they see it," I say. "She was alone near a battle. They probably thought they were saving her. Most of these women are so much better off here than anywhere else."

"I never thought you were dumb enough to believe them," he snaps.

"Ryan, even if you can't trust these people, you can trust me," I reply. "You know that right?"

"She's right Ryan," Corey says as he opens the door and joins us. "I've been checking out the perimeter for days now and I wouldn't even know which way to go. We aren't getting out of the Wastelands by ourselves. If Dawn thinks we can trust Riley, then that may be the only option."

Corey and I leave Ryan to stew and walk outside.

"You're sure we can trust him?" he asks me.

"Not totally, no," I answer honestly.

"I think we can," he says almost to himself.

I find Riley in one of the uninhabited sectors of town. A clip board rests on his forearm and he is writing furiously as he walks.

"What are you doing?" I ask as I fall into step beside him.

"Finishing a report for your father," he says without looking up.

"Why is he so interested in the Wastelands?"

"That is a question you should ask him. It's classified," he answers.

"Oh, okay," I mumble. I don't know what else to say.

"You are leaving." Riley states when he finally looks at me and sees the startled expression on my face. "That is what you want, right?"

"Yes, but…" I stammer.

"You didn't think we'd just let you go," he says, finishing my sentence. "I know much of what you've been through, Dawn. This isn't Floridaland or Texas. The people here are good people. One day you will need to trust us. Everything might depend on it."

"What do you mean?" I ask.

"You'll find out in due time. Now, get prepared, you leave this afternoon. The cooks already know to prepare supplies for you and your escorts are ready to go. They'll stay with you until you reach the Rebel base."

"You're letting us go?" I ask.

"We'll be joining forces soon enough," he answers cryptically.

"What about Emily?" I ask.

"Dawn, we don't hold people against their will. If she wants to go, she can, although, the Rebel base is no place for a young girl. Your companion Corey has decided to stay and that might make her decision much easier," Riley answers as he hands me a packet of papers before he continues to walk and leaves me behind, stunned that Corey didn't tell me he wasn't coming back to base.

Maybe I shouldn't be surprised. He's been wanting out since the second we walked through his door. We were responsible for the death of his parents. He must have been talking escape just to satisfy Ryan.

I look down at the document I have been left with. The front page says classified in big red letters and my father's name in smaller letters.

Chapter 13

Dawn

"Do I have to go?" Emily asks me once Ryan has gone to pick up our supplies.

"It's your decision Em, not Ryan's," I answer.

"It's just that, I like it here. I have friends and it's really a good place to live," she says as she tries to justify the hardest decision of her life.

"You should be saying all of this to your brother," I chide.

"He's going to hate me," She starts to cry and I wrap my arm around her shoulders.

"He could never hate you," I soothe.

"He could stay here too, right?" she asks. The tiny bit of hope in her voice is enough to bring tears to my eyes.

"You know he'd never do that," I say. "The peace here won't last if the rest of the colonies are at war. He needs to be a part of it all. As do I. You, on the other hand, can stay here and experience the peace that we're all fighting for."

"So you're trying to convince her to stay now?" I hadn't seen Ryan come in and now his face is contorted into a mask of rage.

"Ryan, I–" I start, but I don't get the chance to finish because Emily gets up and hugs her brother. His face softens.

"For so long, I've been so scared. In Cincinnati. In Texas. I don't want to be scared anymore," Emily says. He strokes her hair in silence for a few minutes.

"You know I love you, little sis," he whispers.

"I love you too, big brother," she responds.

And just like that, we're leaving Emily behind.

The escorts Riley mentioned are a group of freedom fighters. If I could, I'd stay here just so I didn't have to travel with these people. A tall, half-naked, man with graying hair walks towards me.

"Dawn?" he asks, his voice gruff.

"That's me," I respond, trying to sound like he doesn't scare the shite out of me.

"My name is Hunter and these are my men. We will take you to the Rebels."

I nod and keep my distance from them. I'm still terrified every time I look at them. I'd feel much safer if Corey was around. He's not though, and Ryan refuses to even look at me. He needs someone to blame for leaving his sister behind.

We head out into the maze of trees and charred earth and I don't recognize a thing. I shudder to think how long we would be lost in the Wastelands without the help of our terrifying new friends.

38

Chapter 14

Gabby

I couldn't sleep tonight and my walls felt like they were closing in on me. I just needed some air and this is where my feet took me. This is always where my feet take me. In uniform, I no longer have to worry about curfew because most people just assume I'm on duty. With the influx of Rebel soldiers and troops that have been pulled back from the Mexican front, no one really knows what anyone else is doing, meaning many of the rules go out the window.

I run my hands along the exterior bricks of the lab building as if they too call out for help. None of the screams can be heard from out here, but they still fill my head. I can't think of anything else.

Adrian assures me that all experiments have stopped and the labs are now a place to house the very sick. They can't get out for fear of causing some sort of contagion. I haven't been able to see that for myself, but tonight may be the night. I spent most of the day wading through more files in Adrian's office and I spotted a delivery schedule on his desk. Any minute now, a truck is going to pull up to the back door of this building. The door will then be open for about ten minutes. I've seen enough of these deliveries to know how they work. If Tia were still in charge, I'm sure they wouldn't be so sloppy as to leave the door open, but Adrian is their leader now and they don't worship him or fear him. They respect him, sure, but fear is a much bigger motivator.

When the delivery men have gone inside, I slip through behind them. The supplies go in the last room so I can easily make it to the cell block door before they come back this way. As soon as I step through, I'm bombarded with moans and pleas for help. Are these the sounds of the sick? Or the sounds of people that have been part of the experiments? I'd like to believe Adrian when he says that he's put a stop to those experiments, but I don't trust anyone. I'll probably never completely trust Adrian after watching what he did in this very room.

I skirt the place on the floor where I saw Elle's body drop and I can almost see Adrian throwing his gun to the floor. As I enter the cell block, I see the place where I was dragged across the room. It is also the place where two Rebels saved me. I quicken my pace to get out of this room as soon as possible. I stop when I reach the cell I was kept in. It has a new occupant.

The prisoner is a round man with blood soaked hair and a bruised face. He turns over and I get a better look. I close my eyes in horror. It's Landon. The happy man with the illegal hooch. The man who risked everything to get me and my sister out of town. I hit the glass to catch his attention.

"Landon!" I yell. He looks at me with no sign of recognition. His eyes are cloudy as he rolls over to get a better look. "Landon!" I yell again. Before I can say anything else, the door at the end of the hall slams open and a security guard walks through. I hadn't even thought about the cameras.

"No one is supposed to be in here Miss Nolan," he says.

Of course he knows who I am. I ignore him and turn back to Landon who has moved closer to the door.

"Listen to me Landon, I will get you out of here. Do you understand me?" I ask. "I'm coming back for you."

He shows no sign of hearing me so I yell louder, "Do you understand me?"

As the security guard grabs my arm, I see Landon nod once and lay back down.

I let the security guard escort me out of the building where, to my surprise, Adrian is waiting. He must have been called before I was apprehended.

"What the hell do you think you were doing in there?" he asks, trying hard not to yell.

"You don't really think I'm going to trust everything you say, do you? I had to see it for myself."

"I told you the experiments were over. Do you believe me now?" he asks.

"Sort of," I respond. I didn't see much beside the cell block so I have no idea if the experiments are continuing. I don't want to fight about that right now, though. I have other things on my mind.

"Well, then can we go back to bed? Are you finished?" he asks.

"No," I say defiantly.

He turns away, exasperated, but I grab his arm and he faces me.

"Did you know Landon was in there?" I ask.

I see a flash of pain cross his face. He knew. He knew that his own friend was in there and didn't do anything about it. Adrian introduced me to Landon. How can he think about his friend and not hate himself every second of every day?

"I don't even want to look at you," I growl as I try to get away from him.

"He was already sick when I took over," Adrian tries to explain as if that changes anything. "My uncle had already infected him with a disease they were experimenting on."

Unable to untangle my hatred of Darren Cole and my disappointment in Adrian, I keep walking.

"There was nothing I could do!" he yells after me.

"There is always something you can do when you care about someone enough!" I yell back.

Chapter 15

Gabby

I round the corner of my building and almost run right into someone.

"Shite!" I yell, not in the mood to be nice. "Watch where you're going."

"Sorry Gabby," Allison says as she tries to make sure I'm okay.

"Don't touch me!" I snap. "I'm fine. Just leave me alone."

I try to move past her, but she steps in front of me yet again.

"Gabby, what's wrong? Are you sure you're okay?" she asks.

I can't see her face in the dark, but I can imagine the sympathetic look and just want to get away.

"I'm just peachy," I say, my voice lower, and she takes a step back.

"You finally went into the labs." She isn't asking. She already knows.

"Were you following me?" I ask.

"Yes," she answers.

"Just leave me the hell alone," I say as I shove her into the building and speed by, but she catches up in no time.

"You're angry. Good. I am too. There are quite a few of us that are." She stops when I look at her.

"What do you mean?" I ask. "Like a resistance?"

"Sort of," she answers as she looks around suddenly. "We can't talk here. Can we go to your place?"

"Yeah," I say, but I don't know why I agree. Maybe out of curiosity. Maybe out of anger. Maybe out of some crazy sense of loyalty to Allison. She is the one who helped us escape Texas and join the Rebels. Do I owe her?

We shut the door behind us and she immediately goes to the window to lower the shade. All this cloak and dagger shite is starting to irritate me. My sister is the one who could deal with secret meetings and spy crap. I'm more of the run into the chaos screaming and shooting kind of girl.

"What is it Allison?" I ask. I'm suddenly tired and wish she'd leave so I could sleep. It is the middle of the night after all.

"We need your help Gabby," she says. "We want to destroy the labs."

My ears perk up immediately.

"I'm in," I say suddenly.

Dawn would tell me to think about it. That maybe I shouldn't be so quick to ally myself with a resistance that I know nothing about. Sorry Dawn, you aren't here. You didn't ask me to come on your mission so you don't get a say in mine.

"Okay then," Allison says as if she was expecting more of a fight from me. "You spend a lot of time in Adrian's office," she states.

I nod because she isn't asking. Once again, she just knows.

"We need his key card and pass code to get into the lab building," she continues.

"And that's where I come in," I say, beginning to understand. "You want me to steal it."

"You're quick. Will you do it?"

"Yes," I answer.

"Good. Do it soon." She opens the door to leave, but I have one more question.

"You're going to get all those people out of the building, right?" I ask. "Even the sick ones?"

"Of course we are," she says before hurrying away.

Chapter 16

Jeremy

As soon as the sun went down, I saw Joseph Kearn leave the refugee camp. I don't know why but I have this feeling about him. He's up to something, I just know it.

I guess I'm really starting to fit in here in St. Louis. It's a place where everyone is suspicious of everyone else. The only thing that is trusted here is money. Unlike most of the refugees, Joseph Kearn seems to have plenty of money.

I didn't tell Drew where I was going because he already thinks I'm crazy for being suspicious of a man that I only talked to once. I hope I'm wrong, but I doubt I will be.

I manage to stay hidden as I follow him across town. Where is he going? We cross into the Mexican controlled area of town and I suddenly wish I had back up. I've only ever heard bits and pieces about Mexico, but growing up in a slave camp in Floridaland didn't exactly make me worldly. I used to make up stories about foreign lands to entertain my little sister Claire. I smile at the thought of her.

I'm preoccupied by my own thoughts for only a second, but I lose track of Kearn. The street that stretches before me is devoid of people as is the alley on the left. Where else could he have gone? Most of the buildings are locked and he's a refugee so he doesn't have a key card.

I hear the clang of metal up ahead and then something flashes. The fire escape. He's headed to the roof. I wait a few minutes to allow him to reach the top before I start up. I move slowly, trying to avoid making any noise with my steps. When I step onto the roof, I immediately duck behind the generator and take a look around the corner.

Joseph Kearn greets a Mexican man and their voices carry over to me.

"Where is your boss?" the man asks.

"Dead," Joseph answers.

"Then we have no deal and nothing more to discuss," the man replies as he tries to leave, Joseph puts a hand on his shoulder to stop him. "Get your hands off me, you Texan filth," the man growls.

"Then don't disrespect me. You will regret it," Joseph says as his free hand brushes against the gun that I'm sure the Mexican man doesn't even know is there. The only way he'd probably agree to this meet is if there was an understanding about leaving weapons at home. The two men glare at each other for a few confrontational moments.

"Everything is set down there," the Mexican man says, being the first one to blink. "Los Condenados is ready."

"Very good," Joseph says. "I think it is time I took charge of the project."

"Have you found a way into Mexico without being seen?" the man asks.

"I have," Joseph answers. "Will your boss be ready with the support I need?"

"You forget yourself Mr. Kearn," the Mexican says as his voice turns hard. "Don't question his preparedness."

I throw myself back behind the generator as the Mexican man rushes past me and hurries down the steps. Joseph follows soon after. I lean my head back and try to just breathe. Something big is going on in Mexico, but I'm no closer to knowing what that is. At least now I know to watch Kearn. He may be the key. I get the feeling that none of us are going to be okay when this is all over.

Chapter 17

Jeremy

In the morning, I find Drew inspecting the boats that have already come in. To my surprise, he is walking with a shirtless, tattooed man. I've never met a freedom fighter in person, but I have imagined what they are like. Never did I picture them actually holding a conversation. They're supposed to be savages. At least that's what children in the colonies are led to believe. They are the stuff of childhood nightmares.

Drew grins stupidly as I walk up.

"Dispatch from Dawn," he explains.

Whenever he talks about Dawn, he acts like a lovesick girl. I've heard that he used to be just another rich ass in London. He fell for his girlfriend's sister so that should say it all. Drew would say that you can't help who you love. Gabby shrugs it off, but I know it hurt, not because she loved him, but because he didn't choose her.

"I'm Jeremy," I say, introducing myself to the large man. He takes my outstretched hand and squeezes it.

"Terk," he says.

"Dawn's on her way back to base," Drew says. "She says she found something in the Wastelands that could change everything."

Terk smiles at that. He knows what Dawn means.

"She wants me to return to base for a bit if I can get permission," Drew says.

"Okay," I reply. I don't know what else to say.

"What's your problem?" Drew snaps.

"Oh, I don't know, maybe it's the fact that there are bigger things going on than your girlfriend coming home," I snap back.

I don't know where this anger is coming from, but I can't stop it. After what I heard last night, I could never just leave.

"We hit a dead end in our search for answers, Jeremy. Banging our heads against a wall isn't going to bring us any closer to the truth," Drew replies.

"Neither will leaving," I retort. I then tell him everything I heard last night between Joseph Kearn and the Mexican, hoping that will change his mind.

"It doesn't sound like much to go on," he shrugs.

"But it's something!" I protest.

"Not really. You have two men talking about a project they were working on. It was probably a couple of smugglers. This is St. Louis after all. The only reason you think it's a big deal is because one of the men was Mexican. It's not enough."

"Would you be saying this if you weren't anxious to rush back to base? To Dawn?" I ask.

"Don't you dare," he growls. "I have worked endlessly, day in and day out to find answers. All it ever brings is more frustration. I have turned over every rock in this city. Don't you dare call me a quitter. You can stay or you can go. I don't really care what you do."

"I'm staying here and seeing it through," I say stubbornly.

"Just don't get yourself killed," he says.

Chapter 18

Gabby

"Got it!" I say as I push a stack of files off my lap so I can stand. "We know The Reverend is called by his real name in these files. Since most people only call him 'The Reverend', it makes it harder to connect him to anything."

"We've gone over this a million times Gabby," Adrian says as he leans back, exhausted. We've spent weeks now combing through every paper that Tia or Darren Cole ever touched.

"What did you say his name is again?" I ask.

"Joseph Kearn," he answers.

"Then I've got something, but it isn't much," I say, handing him the page I found. It is a parts requisition form for the weapons factory. Adrian's eyes go dark when he sees it.

"Why would The Reverend need all of this?" Adrian asks, not really expecting an answer.

"And why would he have them sent to St. Louis when he lived here?" I ask no one in particular.

"The parts would've come from Baton Rouge, right?" Lee asks, already knowing the answer.

He worked in the resources division of the Rebel base. Adrian nods anyway.

"Then he'd send them to St. Louis if he didn't want anyone to know who or what they were for," Lee states. "He probably paid off the inspector on arrival to keep the shipment off the books. He wouldn't be able to do that here."

"Do you think that's where he is now?" I ask the obvious.

"Maybe," Adrian says. His eyes never leave the page, but his expression goes from horrified to worse in a matter of seconds.

"What is it?" I ask.

"I need to go find someone," Adrian says, his reaction scaring me.

Ever since we started with the files, I've felt like there is something Adrian isn't telling us. He's holding back something important. Before I can press him, he hurries off, leaving Lee and I somewhat in the dark.

Chapter 19

Gabby

Lee and I waited in Adrian's office, but he never returned and by the time we left, it was dark. Lee insisted on walking me home. As we reach the steps, I remember the promise I made to get Allison the key card.

"I left something in Adrian's office," I tell Lee as I reenter the building.

"Do you want me to wait for you?" he asks.

"No, go ahead," I holler over my shoulder.

Since Adrian never came back, his office is still unlocked when I slip in. I know exactly where he keeps his master cards. The second desk drawer has a false bottom and everything Adrian has that's important is in there.

When I first got assigned here, I didn't trust Adrian so I watched everything he did. He'd be amazed at how much I know about him. Allison also needs the code that goes with this card. What I didn't tell her is that I memorized that the first time I saw Adrian enter it.

The key card is exactly where I expected it to be. Predictable. I slip it into my back pocket and put everything else back in place.

When I reach the street, I'm surprised to find Lee leaning against the building.

"You didn't find it?" he asks.

"What?" I ask.

"You went looking for something."

Oh crap, I don't have anything in my hands.

"It wasn't there," I lie.

I walk past him and he catches up and shrugs. Lee isn't someone who is going to pry. He's simple; easy to be around and easy to talk to. I like that about him, but I don't know how he'd react to the stolen key card in my pocket. We walk in comfortable silence until he leaves me at the front door of my building.

I climb the stairs and unlock my door. When I push it open, Allison gets to her feet.

"How did you get in here?" I ask, startled.

"Shh!" she commands. "Close the door."

I slam it shut and throw the stolen card to the floor at her feet. I'm pissed that she broke into my flat, especially when I risked a lot to get her what she needs.

"Do you have the pass code?" she asks, seemingly unaware that I'm angry she broke into my flat.

When I don't answer, she repeats, "The pass code? Come on Gabby, we need it tonight."

"7-2-0-7," I spit. "Now get out of my flat."

She leaves and I try to get a bit of rest, but my mind won't quiet as it processes everything that has been happening. There's a dangerous weapon with whereabouts unknown that may be in the hands of the Reverend, and a Rebel group going against the Rebels and the Texans. Then there's the fact that Lee might just be my only real friend right now, however that happened.

After hours of tossing and turning, the air inside my flat feels stale and everything seems so much smaller. I throw some clothes on as quickly as I can and practically run out of my building. When I reach the fresh air, I breathe deeply and steady myself. When my feet start moving, they take me in the same direction as every other sleepless night.

I feel the heat even before I turn the corner and see the burning building. The labs are engulfed in giant flames and I can't say that I'm too upset about it. This is what needed to happen. Everything bad that happened here can now be wiped away.

A huge crowd has gathered and I spot Adrian near the front, barking orders at a group of soldiers. He looks back and our eyes lock. His narrow as he pushes people aside to get to me. My smile fades when I see the look he gives me.

"What did you do?" he screams above the noise.

"This needed to happen, Adrian," I yell back. "It's a horrible place."

"You have no idea what you've done!" His face contorts in anger. "The labs were still open for a reason!"

"That's crap," I say as I purse my lips stubbornly and look him in the eye. He tries a different tactic.

"Do you realize how many people have been killed tonight?" he demands.

"They evacuated the building first. That's why I took your card," I say, but I suddenly grow unsure of the truth in my words.

"They needed to get in to barricade the doors from the inside. That is the ONLY reason they needed you," Adrian says.

"What?" I ask as I stumble backwards.

"They didn't want the sick to be released. They just wanted them gone," Adrian answers, as I turn away and run.

Adrian tries to grab my arm, but I'm too quick. The air gets hotter and hotter as I get closer. What did I do? These people are going to die. I choke as my lungs fill up with smoke.

Landon.

Are they already dead?

I throw my entire body into the door. The key pad has already been destroyed and the heavy door doesn't budge at all. I grab the metal handle and immediately pull my hand back; not quick enough. Pain sears across the skin of my open palm. It doesn't stop me. I propel myself forward once again to no avail.

"No!" I scream.

The first tear sizzles as it hits my cheek and my mouth and nose are filled with smoke. I feel an arm wrap around my stomach and pull me away from the burning building and the scorched bodies inside. He sets me down, but I can't stand. I sink to my knees as I sob and cough out the smoke. My hand throbs, but I deserve it. I deserve it all. I see Allison nearby and I find my voice.

"Lying bitch," I croak. "Murderer."

"They were sick Gabby. We couldn't risk them getting out," she says as she shrugs and walks away.

Her reasoning sounds exactly like Adrian's reasoning for keeping the labs open.

There are arms wrapped around me. Lee's. He lets me cry as long as I need to without saying a word. He's put it all together now. He knows about the card. He doesn't say a thing about it.

Chapter 20

Gabby

I wake up in the hospital and panic before I remember what happened. The sun is coming up and I want to get out of here. The only memory I have of this place is when Dawn was being kept in a coma by Dr. Darren Cole.

Lee is asleep in a nearby chair, with his head resting on my bed. I reach out and run my non burnt hand through his soft hair. He stirs slowly and eventually raises his head to look at me; his face serious.

"Are you okay?" he asks.

I just nod. My throat is raw and I'm loopy from the medications, but I'll be okay. For some reason though, I don't think he's asking about my health. Last night was horrible and I'm sure that when I'm off the drugs, I'll feel worse about it.

I smile at him and he shakes his head before returning the favor.

"Someone's on drugs," he laughs.

"Come here," I say as I pat the bed beside me.

He hesitates until I pull on his arm. As soon as he is next to me, I lean my head on his shoulder and feel his arm encircle me as I fall back to sleep.

When I wake up, the pain is no longer dulled by drugs and my stomach is feeling pretty manky. I look around trying to find Lee until I hear him talking to Adrian in the hall. I can't make out most of what they're saying.

"What did Adrian want?" I ask Lee when he comes back in.

Adrian must hate me now. I betrayed him. I, Gabby, who never trusts anyone, trusted the wrong people. I wouldn't blame him for hating me.

"He wanted to make sure you were okay," Lee says. He's lying. His eyes shift away from mine and focus on a spot on the floor.

"Just give me the damn truth," I say and Lee fidgets with the bottom of his shirt.

"All of your access is being revoked, as is your rank. Adrian is working on sending you back to base. He said he should let your father deal with you," Lee responds reluctantly.

I sink back into my bed.

"But there is so much more to do here! This is rubbish! What about the Reverend?" I ask.

"Adrian says he'll find someone else to help," Lee replies.

"That'll set him back too far," I say, but I'm arguing with the wrong person.

"Gabby, there was more in the labs than just the people that were sick," Lee explains tentatively.

"I knew it," I say quietly. "The experiments were still going on."

"If there was one person here you should have trusted, it was Adrian." Lee scratches the side of his face and looks away before bring his eyes back to me and continuing. "Adrian's aunt and uncle developed a biological weapon."

I inhale sharply and then finish his thought, "that's the weapon that Kearn has."

Lee nods and says, "they also developed an antidote, but Kearn took that too. They were close to replicating it. That's why the labs were still open."

I sit in shock for a moment before climbing out of bed and starting to put my clothes on, feeling worse by the second.

"I need to get out of here," I say.

"You haven't been cleared yet," Lee says, holding me back.

"Let go of me!" I yell as I make it out into the hall. "Just leave me alone."

I don't know where I'm going until I get there. Landon's flat. They still haven't cleaned it out after all this time. They will now that he's officially dead.

He's dead. Landon is gone and a lot more people are going to die.

I think Landon was my friend, for a short time at least. I didn't know him for very long, but he was one of the men who helped Dawn and I get out of Texas.

His apartment was tossed by the police right before the attacks on Texas and no one besides Adrian has been here since. He was Adrian's best mate. Go figure.

I trip over a box on the floor. "Bugger this!" I grunt as I fall to the ground.

The box falls as well and the carpet shifts slightly, revealing something shining on the ground. It's a door handle. There is a secret door in the floor. Oh, Landon, we could've been good mates.

I push some things aside and then pull on the small brass loop. The door opens up with the creaking and groaning of rust covered hinges. The space is dark and I can't see anything so I reach my hand down and feel around until I hit something hard and cold. I lift a bottle. Of course. I just found the man's stash. Landon distilled illegal hooch. I laugh as I count the number of bottles. This stuff is probably worth a lot now and by tomorrow the police will be here cleaning this place out. I take two bottles out and then do my best to hide the door.

I'm not ready to leave yet. I'm not ready to say goodbye or to admit to Landon that I couldn't save him. I promised him. My tears hit the glass bottle with a quiet sound as I sit down and unscrew the top. I take a long swig and do my best not to spit it out. I clamp my mouth shut and force myself to swallow. It burns my throat before settling like heat in my stomach. I raise the bottle to the sky.

"This is for you Landon. Your hooch might taste awful, but you were a good man." I say as I take another drink. "I'm so sorry I couldn't help you. I couldn't keep my promise."

After a few minutes and a few more swigs, I can barely stand. I use a table to pull myself up from my seat on the ground and stumble towards the door. By the time I reach it, I've forgotten all about the second bottle and head outside. This time, I know where I'm going. There are two people in this world right now that I trust. I have no idea where Dawn is at the moment, but I stumble straight for Lee's flat. My legs buckle and sway underneath me, but, finally, I get there. I knock four times and lean against the door frame to keep from falling over.

The door opens and Lee looks confused.

"Gabby," he says.

There is no "Where have you been?" or "I've been looking for you," even though I'm sure he has. He is just relieved. I'm seeing two Lee's at the moment so I'm glad when he takes my arm and guides me inside so that I can sit.

"Are you drunk?" he asks.

I don't respond. I'm too busy trying to stop the room from spinning all around me. I shoot out my arm to grab something, anything so that I don't fall out of my chair. I feel like a proper toss pot. I feel sick. I know Lee has a lot of questions right now, but he doesn't ask a single one. He helps me to his bed and I'm asleep within minutes.

It is dark when I open my eyes. The only light comes through the single window across the room. Lee is sitting near the window, looking out at the night.

"Hi," he says when he catches me watching him.

"How long have I been out?" I ask softly.

"A while," he replies.

My head feels clear except for the pain that throbs in my right temple. Nothing I don't deserve. Nothing compared to the pain I feel for what I have done. It all comes rushing back so quickly now that I'm not on pain killers or alcohol. I suddenly wish I'd brought more of Landon's stash with me.

Lee has removed my shoes and wrapped me in a blanket. As I look at him, I try to find the words to thank him, but the sound sticks in my throat.

"Come here," Lee says quietly.

My bare feet hit the cold floor and a stab of pain works its way up my arm from my tightly wrapped, burnt hand. I reach Lee and he holds me to see what he's looking at. An old woman is walking down the street carrying a single candle. She is followed by a trail of others with their candles raised high.

"See, Gabs, you aren't the only one who cares. They're mourning for everyone who died in the labs," Lee says.

I look at Lee and meet his eyes. When I first met him, I didn't like him one bit. I don't know how I thought that when he has such kind eyes. I run my fingertips through his hair and down his cheek. Then I surprise us both by leaning in and kissing him lightly. I lean back and look into his eyes once more. He stands up with his hands resting on my hips and pulls me to him.

All of our emotion of the last few days is poured into this moment. The anger. The hate. The guilt. Our kiss becomes hungry and desperate as the need deepens and I steer us towards the bed as I lift his shirt and run my hands across his warm skin.

"Gabby," he protests. "We shouldn't."

I look into his eyes and pull him back towards me. We can over think this tomorrow. Right now, this is what I need to forget about everything.

"Please, Lee," I whisper.

His protests end as he looks at me. He leans down once again, kisses me softly, and I'm lost.

Chapter 21

Dawn

"Hunter!" I scream as I try to fight an American woman twice my size. He can't help me because he has his hands full with a couple of the men from the Cincinnati Patrol. Every time I punch, a new pain races up my arm. It feels like I'm hitting a brick wall. I'm pushed to the ground as the woman pulls her knife. I look around frantically for something, anything to use as a weapon. My gun is lying out of reach so I grab a large stick.

I block her first attempt at a stab and on her second try the knife buries itself in the stick. I fling it as far as I can. Not missing a beat, my attacker runs to where her gun had been knocked free and aims it at me. I try to run, but a man's hands snake themselves around me from behind, holding me in place. I struggle, but it does no good.

"You're coming with us," he says.

I dig my nails into his arm until he loosens it for just a second. I duck down and away and practically collide with Ryan as he steps into the open.

"Hannah," he says, nodding. She lets out a long whistle and the men around her stop fighting.

"Ryan Smith," she begins. "Are you their prisoner?" She asks, motioning to where I now see Hunter pinned to the ground. He's alive. The rest of our group was not so lucky.

"No," Ryan states coldly. There is something in the stare he gives this woman that unsettles me. His hatred is so raw in this moment, so open and obvious.

"Then is it Ryan Smith, freedom fighter?" she asks mockingly. "After your father spent many years trying to keep the freedom fighters away from our borders."

"No, and don't you speak to me about my father," Ryan snaps.

"You're right," she says. "He is of the past. My father is in charge now and he'll reward me greatly when he sees who I've captured."

She grins and makes a move to grab him. He steps out of her reach, diving to the ground. He grabs my gun, aims, and fires in one quick motion. Hannah doubles over, surprise and pain etched on her features. Her cohorts frozen at what they've just witnessed.

"That's why you were never as good as me, Hannah," Ryan says. "I was always too quick for you and your sad excuse for a family."

Ryan aims at the other Americans who have started to back away.

"Just go home," he says. "We have not trespassed on your borders and our mission does not concern you."

They release Hunter and disappear quickly back into the woods, out of sight. After waiting to make sure they are gone, I move next to Ryan to see if he'll talk to me now.

"You said 'your borders'," I state.

"They haven't been mine since the day those people killed my father," she says angrily, as he helps Hunter to his feet.

"Hunter, you have a knife in your leg," I say as soon as I see it.

Hunter looks down as if this is the first time he's noticing it. To my horror, he grabs the handle and pulls it free. Ryan rushes over with some cloth to stop the bleeding. Once it is all wrapped tightly, Hunter wants to get moving immediately. I do too, if only to get far away from all these bodies, but he has got to be in pain.

"Let's go," he urges.

"Don't you think you should rest for a bit?" Ryan asks. Hunter looks at the both of us as if he is confused by our concern.

"A rest would be good," I agree.

"It was only a knife," he says, shrugging.

"Doesn't it hurt?" I ask.

"Yes," he says gruffly, ending the conversation as he leads the way once again. We're close to base now, only a couple days away.

"Why do you think the Americans were all the way down here?" I ask Ryan.

"Hannah would've wanted to find me to end our line." He pauses. "There are a lot of families in Cincinnati that would follow me over her father if I came back. A few of her men were from the smaller families. That's why I knew they would leave if I told them to. I'm never going back though, so Hannah got herself killed for nothing."

He shakes his head, continuing, "You know, we were friends as kids. I know Hannah, she wouldn't have quit until I was in the ground. For years, the power battle in Cincinnati has been turning friends and neighbors into enemies."

Ryan grows quiet. I spent most of my time in Cincinnati in the clinic so I didn't see much of anything else. I did see a lot of Ryan's day to day life there. He was a different person before he was forced to flee. He was happy and cheeky. He loved horses and building things. He was training to be a medic. Now he is a soldier who is forced to kill old friends. After all the amazing things we saw in the Wastelands, the only thing he'll ever think about is that we had to leave his sister behind. He could've stayed too. He even could've been a medic and lived a simple, safe life.

He chose this war. He realized that winning is the only way to ensure a future we can all enjoy. It gutted him to leave Emily behind, but there was no other choice.

We're moving once again, though slowly this time. I took quite a beating. Every step brings pain to my chest as my ribs scream in protest. My knee throbs, leaving me limping along in pain. My hands are cut up and sore from punching and clawing at that woman. I guess I got the better end of the deal though because, well, she's dead.

Hunter, on the other hand, doesn't limp at all. If I hadn't seen it, I wouldn't even know that he had been stabbed.

We manage to avoid trouble for the next few days, until we finally see the windmills and shack that signal that we're now standing over the Rebel base.

"How do we get in without an officer?" Ryan asks.

I shrug, thinking it over. This was an off book mission so there is no code to give the shack operator. We have no officer identification codes either.

"I don't know if this will work, but I've got an idea," I say, entering the shack.

I've never been in here before. I've only seen officers go inside and the ramp always opens up as they come back out. There isn't much in here. It's a bit dodgy, with a roof that looks as if it could collapse at any time and walls that feel like they are closing in. I close my eyes and breathe deeply. Damn it. I wipe the sweat from my face. I'd have thought I'd be over my claustrophobia by now, but I'm not, so I step back outside for some air.

"You okay?" Ryan asks. I nod and head back in.

The key is expediency. I find the key pad near the floor and start typing in random numbers. The operator is bound to take notice. That's when I see it. The cord connected to the keypad. I follow it with my eyes and the end looks like it's been cut. What do I do now? I take a closer look at the keypad itself. It's elevated from the floor, almost like there is something underneath it. I feel around the edges to confirm my suspicions and then pry it free. There is a large red button underneath. Without thinking, I press it.

"Code," a woman's voice demands.

"Yeah, hi," I start. "I don't have a code, but I need to get in."

"You need a code," the voice states.

"You should go get my father, General Nolan. See, I'm Dawn Nolan and I'm returning to base," I reply.

She doesn't say another word so I'm not really sure what's happening. I leave the shack.

"Did it work?" Ryan asks.

"I don't know," I respond honestly.

We wait for a while before the ramp finally opens up. My father isn't the man who comes to greet us, though. No, this man is someone with a much sweeter smile and a warmer welcome.

Drew stops right in front of me. I can reach out and touch him, but I don't. It seems like I've been away from him ever since we made it to Floridaland. We've only had moments. I'm hoping this isn't one of those moments. They usually end with one of us leaving on some assignment.

"I've missed you," I whisper, very aware of both Ryan and Hunter's presence.

"I've missed you too," he responds as he finally closes the space between us and kisses me.

Chapter 22

Dawn

Daddy spins mommy across the living room and my big sister Gabby and I giggle as we watch from the couch. Today is our favorite day. Our family is lucky enough to have a radio. It's because Daddy works for the government. Every night there are boring things on the radio that we have to listen to. Daddy calls it propaganda, but I don't know what that means. Fridays are different. Every Friday the government allows two hours of music on the radio. Once a month they play Jazz. That is the best.

Daddy walks to the couch and lifts me up as I laugh.

"Dawny knows how to dance," he says.

"No I don't!" I say, giggling as he sets me down.

"Just as I taught you," Daddy says. I step onto his feet and we start to move.

"I wanna dance too!" Gabby yells. Mommy grabs her hand and twirls her as the music speeds up. Their smiles and laughter rival mine and daddy's. We don't stop dancing until the last song is cut off abruptly. There is no "goodnight." No "See you next week". It's just over and we are all back to the boredom for another week.

I was young when I lost my parents. That's the term I use to describe it now. Neither of them died. They weren't taken from me. My father didn't just leave. They were lost to me.

Most of the memories I have of that time come from the stories Gabby has told me. She remembers a lot more than I do. Friday night dancing is something that I actually remember. I can tell the difference between what I've been told and what I've experienced because of the emotions they bring forth.

I have a hard time reconciling the mother and father in that memory with the two people before me now. I remember them as loving and fun and happy. These Rebel leaders are cold and I know little else about them.

My father, the general, is sitting across the long table flipping through the document that I brought back from the Wastelands. He didn't seem surprised when I told them about the town and about Riley. Miranda, my mother, was shocked. She paces behind the General's chair as he reads.

"Well," she says, "are you going to fill me in on what's going on?"

"Yeah, DAD," I say, using that word like a weapon, but it doesn't seem to faze him. "I'd like to know too."

"It's complicated," he responds, rubbing his temples.

"Why don't you start with the reason you had Riley build an entire part of town that nobody lives in," I suggest.

"Who is this Riley?" Miranda interjects.

"He's ex-British military," the General says.

"Bollocks," I argue. "He doesn't even look like a soldier and he has an American accent."

"Dawn," he says tiredly, "do you really think most of those people would follow him if they knew he was British?"

"I guess not," I concede.

"Miranda, there are some things you need to hear. Sit down." She does as she's told.

"For a decade at least, the crops in this part of the country have been in steep decline," he explains.

"How much longer can the land support us?" Miranda asks.

"With severe rations, a few years. We don't want to let it get to that. You should see these fields in the Wastelands! We should probably stop calling it that when we need to convince people that it is a good place," he smiles for only a second and then continues. "There is also the matter of England. The evacuations are starting soon. The land and the weather have become too volatile. Eventually, we will have ships of people that we need to house, feed, and protect."

"What is in that file Riley sent?" I ask, suddenly regretting that I didn't read it before.

"He details the crop yield for the past five years and the methods they are using. He also gives the number of people in the population and he has calculated the number of people that the town can support. That's what I've been waiting for. It's really amazing," he answers.

"Dawn, you're dismissed," Miranda says. She wants to have a word with the General in private.

"No, Miranda. Dawn still has to make her report," he says.

She glares at him.

"Later," she says.

He sighs and says, "fine. Dawn, you can go."

As I walk away, I still can't believe that woman used to be my mother.

Chapter 23

Dawn

"How'd it go?" Drew asks as soon as I set foot in the hall. He's been waiting for me, but I can't even begin to process and understand everything, let alone explain it to him. I grab his hand, needing something solid to hold on to. I don't know when he became that person for me, but I no longer worry about our relationship. I don't feel the jealousy or insecurity that I used to feel. I don't wonder why he chose me. That question used to be on a constant loop through my head, but it doesn't seem so important anymore. I believe that he loves me and that is enough.

It's the other people in my life that I worry about now. I can't decide if my parents are trustworthy and I don't want to spend enough time around them to find out. My father was responsible for much of what happened in Floridaland. He knew what was going on in those slave camps. Hell, he was in charge of the soldiers that did awful things to the slaves.

A rumor has circulated around Rebel base that my mother, Miranda, blew up a tube station that was packed with civilians. That's why she was sent here. I don't know if being assigned to the colonies was for her own safety or if it was a reward. Am I part of a group that rewards mass murder?

Then there is the one member of my family that I've counted on my whole life. Gabby. My sister killed someone right in front of me on our way to base and she didn't see what was so wrong about that. It just drove her deep into the Rebel mentality. Killing is okay when it serves the Rebel purpose. I didn't ask where Gabby was assigned. I knew she wouldn't be at base doing nothing.

I realize I haven't answered Drew's question and he's looking at me expectantly.

"Can we not talk about this right now?" I ask. "I just want to shower and get some sleep."

"Fine Dawn. Just, fine," he says as he shakes his head and leaves me outside the showers. I don't have the energy to talk right now.

I wake to a shift in my bed as someone sits on the end of it. Opening my eyes, I'm relieved to see Matty. He has a huge grin on his face and I answer it with one of my own. This is different from the kid I knew before. That kid had just watched his father die in front of him. Matty was the son of farmers who were unlucky enough to be forced into action by Texan soldiers. They were looking for me and my sister. Gabby shot his father without a second thought.

"I heard you went to the Wastelands," he says. "Were they horrible?"

Pretty much everyone that grows up in the colonies knows the stories of what lay beyond the charred outer rim of the Wastelands. They grow up terrified of the freedom fighters, who steal from their farms and ambush their people.

What isn't told in the stories is that the heart of the Wastelands beats with the pulse of a thriving people. That has been kept secret. Riley and his people have put in a lot of effort to remain hidden behind the protection of their fierce warriors.

"You want to see something cool?" I ask the young boy.

He nods, excited. I take his hand and lead him down the hall to the clinic. They're keeping Hunter isolated while they make sure he hasn't brought us some disease. I was so narked when I heard about it, but Hunter doesn't seem to mind.

There is a large window looking into Hunter's room and Matty stops as soon as he sees where we're going. His face tells it all. He's terrified.

"Do you want to stay out here?" I ask him.

He shakes his head and grips my hand tightly. The doctor stops me as I get to the door. I expect to be turned back but instead, he opens the door for us.

"His results are clean," the doctor tells me. "You can take him out of here."

The clinic staff wants him gone because his presence is making them nervous. They remember the ambushes that have killed so many Rebel soldiers. I remember those too. I was almost killed in one. I don't understand a lot of things about these people, but I know we need them on our side. We need to move on from the past. That is why I befriended Hunter.

"Hey," I say as I enter the room. "Matty, this is Hunter."

Matty shrinks back as Hunter stands and walks towards him. To my surprise, he crouches down so that he is eye to eye with the scared boy.

"Hello, Matty," Hunter says as he extends a hand. Matty hesitates before taking it and Hunter stands up straight.

"Doc says you can go," I tell him. "We'll take you somewhere that you can shower and then get a nosh." I look him up and down. "If the General wants you to stay here, you're going to need to wear more clothes."

His lips curve up slightly. I have learned how to act with this big man and he isn't as intimidating as he tries to be. The clinic seems full today and I stop when I recognize one of the patients.

"Lucas," I say as I round the corner of his bed.

"He's sedated," a voice behind me says.

I turn and Officer Grace Mills walks past me and sinks into a chair by the bed.

"What's wrong with him?" I ask, very aware that I have not seen Grace or Lucas in quite a while.

"He's sick," she says quietly, glancing at Hunter behind me.

I sense that now isn't the time to catch up so we leave without any real answers. I can't get Lucas out of my head, but there isn't anything I can do.

Hunter comes out of the bathroom wearing the clothes I found for him and I can't help but laugh. The cotton pants only reach halfway down his calves and the shirt is tight across his chest. Even Matty, who is still afraid of this man, is laughing hysterically. Hunter's face is stony and he says nothing as we enter the mess and sit down to eat. The other soldiers avoid our table like the plague, but Matty doesn't seem to notice as he witters on and on about everything that has happened since I left. All of it is through a little boy's eyes so I figure I'll get more details from Drew later.

Matty tells me that people have been coming and going quickly. Gabby hasn't been back since I left. Lee and Jeremy have been gone as well. I wonder what they're doing right now. Matty has learned that there are two prisoners at base, but he doesn't know who they are. I do. Tia Cole and Jonathan Clarke. The Texan "prophet" and the Rebel leader who some are saying was never right in the head. He just had everyone fooled.

I'm relieved that Jeremy is on assignment. When I left, he was in critical condition in the clinic. Jonathan Clarke had beaten him senseless before throwing us into a cell for days. Along with a few others, Jeremy and I captured Tia Cole. I don't know if we did any good though because the Rebels still managed to destroy Baton Rouge and kill a lot of people.

I realize I've zoned out when I hear Matty say, "and there's this Mexican boy here that they're training me with."

"Training you?" I interrupt.

"Yeah, it's so cool. I'm gonna be a soldier!" he exclaims.

I shoot to my feet so quickly that I almost knock our table over. Hunter gets up to follow me, but I wave him away. I wind through the tables at a run and collide with Drew as he enters the room.

"Hey Dawn," he says as he grabs my arm. "I want to talk to you."

"Not now," I say.

"Are you ever going to trust me enough to tell me what's going on?" he asks.

"Not now!" I yell again as I pick up the pace and head straight for my father's office.

His aide tries to stop me, but I push past her and barge through the door. The General looks up from a meeting with a few of his officers. His expression goes from annoyed to curious as soon as he sees me.

"We'll pick this up later," he tells the other men in the room. They leave swiftly.

"You're training them?" I growl as soon as we're alone.

"Who?" he asks tiredly. "Tell me Dawn, what is it you have a problem with now?"

"You're training kids to fight!" I yell.

"What is it that you think we should do with them?" he asks, not waiting for an answer. "Dammit, Dawn, we're in the middle of a war. There are two Texan cities that we're trying to stabilize and refugees from a third city to deal with. There is a cease fire with Mexico that hangs by a thread. The troops in Floridaland are splintered and the awful slave camps are still operational. There are people to feed with dwindling crops. In the midst of all of this, there is a timer. The English evacuations start soon and there are things that need to be done before that happens. We need every able body we can get our hands on. They need to be trained to protect themselves and to fight for the real prize:

an end to all of this. I don't have time for your indignant, naive, self-imposed missions."

I leave without another word. He's right, but I picture little Matty holding a gun and get chills. All of the people in command must have heard every word and now they watch me as I leave. I don't know if I've ever felt more useless than I do right now. I don't belong in a war. I don't know where I do belong, but it's not here. I get to my bunk and crawl into bed without speaking to anyone and start to cry. I can't stop the tears and my pillow is soaked in no time. My chest heaves as I breathe heavily.

I don't know how long I've been laying here when Drew squeezes in next to me and snakes an arm underneath my head. I curl into him as he strokes my hair and am asleep in no time.

Chapter 24

Dawn

"Morning," I say as Drew sits at the foot of the bed pulling on his boots.

"Are you going to tell me why you were so upset last night?" he asks.

"Thanks for being there," I respond instead of answering his question.

"Right," he says as he gets up. He's angry.

"Drew, stop," I say, reaching for his hand. He lets me take it and intertwine my fingers with his.

If there is one person I should be trusting, it's Drew. How can you love someone without first trusting them? I pull him back down to sit on the bed.

"I'm pretty naive, Drew," I say as he starts to protest, but I put a finger to his lips. "No, just listen. I'm not someone who can make the hard decisions. Half the time I don't even know what the right thing is. I knew that when I left without a word to help Ryan find his sister it would hurt you and it would hurt Gabby."

"We were only hurt because you didn't ask us to come," he says before pausing. "You didn't ask me to come."

"I was defying orders to do an off book mission," I say.

"You don't think Gabby and I would've left the Rebels to come with you?" he asks, his voice full of unspoken emotion.

"At the time, I thought I was doing the right thing. But really, our mission accomplished nothing," I answer, finally deciding to open up.

I tell him about the Wastelands and everything else that has happened since I left. He then fills me in on his assignment in St. Louis and his search for answers with Jeremy. Much like me, he feels like everything he did was for nothing because it didn't help anything.

"What about Lucas?" I ask finally. "What happened to him?"

"He was in St. Louis with me, trying to find out more information about what is happening in Mexico," Drew explains. "He should have stayed here. He was injured pretty bad in the attacks and never quite healed. Then he got sick. The symptoms didn't start until he was on his way back here. By the time I arrived, he was already pretty bad and living in the clinic. He just kept getting worse and worse and never got better."

"I want to see him." I say as I leave my bunk to head for the clinic. Drew follows me.

Officer Mills is in the exact same place as yesterday. She looks up, but doesn't say anything. As part of her patrol when we went to Cincinnati, I could see that there was something between Officer Mills and Lucas, but it was forbidden because he was her subordinate. Now I see it clearly. She loves him, deeply. I place my hand on her shoulder as I look at the sleeping Lucas. In this bed, he looks smaller, shrunken. We have been here for no longer than ten minutes when an alarm sounds overhead.

A doctor and two nurses rush over and push us back so that they can roll Lucas' bed to the isolation room.

"What's going on?" Officer Mills yells after them. She runs behind them, but they don't let her follow. My father's voice comes over the loudspeaker.

"We have received test results that a patient in the clinic is carrying Tuberculosis. There has been an outbreak in St. Louis and he came from there," my father says. "Until further notice, the clinic is under quarantine. No one is to enter or exit the clinic. Those inside, will be provided with food and other necessities. Don't be alarmed. We have this under control."

As the news sinks in, people begin to panic. I sit down on a couch in the waiting area and try to calm my nerves. Hopefully, they haven't shut down the labs in Vicksburg yet. That's where the Texans create medicines. They'll be able to help us.

Chapter 25

Gabby

It's still dark when I crawl out of bed and feel around on the floor for my clothes. I stop when I hear Lee turn over and listen for him to wake, but then start moving again when I realize he's still asleep. I don't know how any of this happened last night. We weren't in our right minds. Yes, that's what it was. I was upset over what happened at the labs and Lee was there for me. It was exactly the distraction I needed, but now I have to deal with the consequences of helping Allison.

I pull on my shoes and slip out, thankful that Lee is such a heavy sleeper. I can imagine how that conversation might go. I'd talk too much and he'd just be Lee, all silent and brooding like. It's the story of our lives. I take off running as soon as I hit the street. I have always used my runs to clear my head, but even that might not work today.

I stop when I get to the ruins of what use to be the lab building. Adrian already has people cleaning up the area. They've removed what was left of the bodies and cleaned up some of the scorched debris. I watch from a distance and, after a while, I use all of my will power to turn away and head for my flat. I walk past weeping Texans and a makeshift flower memorial. Minutes later, I'm home.

I shower and then do the only thing that will keep me from thinking about what I did. I go back to sleep.

I wake to someone knocking on my door. Assuming it's Lee, I don't answer. Last night happened and I can't change that, but I don't want to make it some big deal that we have to talk about. I roll over and try to sleep some more.

The next time I wake, someone is pounding on the door. It's not the polite knocking like before. This person just won't go away.

"Leave me alone!" I yell.

"Open this damn door!" Adrian sounds angry.

He hates me after what I did and I deserve it. My bare feet hit the cold floor and I open the door.

"What do you want?" I snap.

If there is anyone with enough anger to match Adrian's, it's me.

"You didn't answer the door for Lee earlier," he states.

"I didn't want to talk to him," I say, turning to let Adrian follow me into the room and shut the door.

"You don't really have that choice. He had come to get you because I needed to talk to you both and you've been MIA," Adrian replies.

"I thought we weren't speaking," I snap. I can't always control the words that come out of my mouth. They tend to just slip out when I'm angry.

"We don't have that choice either. Don't you get it?" He steps towards me. "We aren't playing here. I'm trying to run a city and appease you Rebels. Your actions have consequences Gabby."

"You sound like my father," I say. "You can leave now."

"Maybe I should send you back to him," he says. My jaw drops and I try to protest, but he cuts me off, "Yet another choice we do not have. I can't trust anyone else with the information about the Reverend. You and Lee are it."

"Me and Lee ..." I start.

"Are going to St. Louis," Adrian finishes. "I think the Reverend is there."

"I can do it by myself," I argue.

"There is no way I trust you enough for that. You betrayed me, Lee didn't. He leads this mission. You leave in one hour," Adrian pulls out a small jar and a syringe with a needle on one end.

"What's that?" I ask hesitantly.

"There has been a major outbreak of Tuberculosis in St. Louis." he answers as he jams the needle into my arm without warning.

I clench my teeth and try to fight him until he hands me the bottle of medicine.

"This is one of the last bottles of the vaccine. It is for people that you choose to help you in St. Louis. There is no more, you got that?"

As he leaves the room, he looks back at me one more time, saying, "Imagine how many people are going to die now that our vaccine supplies were lost when the labs caught fire. And that's the least of it. Now that the antidote is gone, we need to get to that biological weapon as soon as possible."

Adrian knew that his words would gut me. That's why he said them. One more dig before I leave. Once he's gone, I breathe deeply, trying to get rid of those thoughts before heading for the docks. I need to focus on my new assignment. If there's one thing I do well, it's going into soldier mode. Nothing can touch me when I focus solely on the task at hand.

The quickest way to St. Louis is by the river. I round the corner and see Lee in front of one of the boats. He's waiting for me. As soon as I see his face, I start to doubt that soldier mode is going to work this time. I'm far enough that he hasn't seen me yet as the events of last night play through my mind. I have never felt that close to someone. By morning, though, that feeling was gone and I was alone again. I'm always alone.

I take one step forward and then the next until I'm right in front of him. He doesn't take his eyes off me, so I shift mine away.

"Let's go," I say as I walk past him and board our ship.

He falls in line behind me and places a hand on my back to steady me as I step on board. He still has yet to say a single word to me as we settle in below deck. The captain is a middle aged man who seems nice enough. He introduces himself and then disappears to get us moving.

"How are you?" Lee finally asks.

"Lee," I respond, "let's not do this whole morning after thing."

"I meant, how are you after everything with the labs?" he says. "You we pretty upset."

Now I feel like an idiot. I know that he actually cares because he is a guy that never talks just to fill the silence. Why does he have to be so nice?

"I'm sorry," I say.

Lee doesn't respond so I keep going, "More people are going to die because of me. If we don't find Kearn ..."

I don't finish my thought, but we both know how it ends. Lee always makes me feel like I can say anything. He isn't going to lie to me and tell me that's not true just to make me feel better, but he's not going to judge me either. Instead, he reaches across the table to grab my hand. Normally that would be okay, but not after last night. I pull my hand free of his fingers.

"Lee, don't," I say quietly.

"Dammit, Gabby!" he yells.

I've never heard him raise his voice before so I'm startled.

"Do you really think it all just means nothing?" he asks.

I don't have to ask what he means by "it all".

"I can't," I whisper as I head for the stairs that will take me above deck to escape from this emotionally charged room.

"You don't own the monopoly on being damaged," he says before I reach the door. "The difference is that I know it doesn't mean I'm worthless."

I escape to the deck and welcome the fresh air. How can everything be so messed up? I finally had a true friend. Lee and I trusted each other. We could talk to each other about anything. I had to go and ruin it, didn't I? I ruined it for one night of stupid comfort.

Everything I touch turns to rubbish and I'm sick of being that person.

Chapter 26

Gabby

Dangerous days turn into dark nights on the river, but it's the quiet treatment I can't stand much longer. It shouldn't bother me because this is nothing new from Lee. He's usually the strong and silent type, but this seems more pointed. He's deliberately not speaking, which is why I'm so relieved when the captain comes into the room. He's been keeping his distance from us because he's a Texan through and through. He obeyed Adrian's orders to get us to St. Louis, but he doesn't like it. To him, we're just the Rebels that attacked his city. We killed people, some of which he might have known. We killed his "prophet".

"We're here," he says gruffly.

I look out the small window and all I see is the dark water.

"Then why haven't we docked?" I ask.

"St. Louis is under quarantine," he says as if I was stupid to even ask.

I know about the outbreak, but that doesn't explain why we're still this far out.

"We're okay"' I say. "We can't catch it. We've had the meds."

I want to bang my head against the wall as soon as the words are out. The captain and his men haven't had the meds. His eyes narrow angrily. Now we're the Rebel invaders who are getting special treatment. A faction of the Rebels blew up the labs and every medication inside. Now our lives are being valued over Texan lives.

"The port has been sealed," the captain says through gritted teeth. "Even if I wanted to risk the lives of the people on this ship, I can't. No one is allowed in or out of the city."

"We need to get inside," I protest.

"Come!" the captain commands suddenly.

We follow him. He brings us to the back of the boat and bends down. He hands us each a paddle and gestures to a small wooden dinghy.

"Now, get off my boat," he says harshly as he turns and leaves us without another word.

I look to Lee and he just shrugs and jumps down into the tiny boat. I take quite a bit more time. I can't swim, so being so close to the water makes me jittery. The only time I've ever been in a boat this small was when we were fleeing the Texan soldiers that had boarded Captain Collins' ship. Lee wasn't with me then. It was Allison, Drew, and Dawn. I didn't like it then either.

Lee gives me a hand to steady myself. I take it and stare at him as my heartbeat slows and I get my nerves under control. He has that effect on me. I breathe deeply and take my seat as the boat rocks slowly. Lee pushes us off from the larger ship and soon we can't even see it in the darkness. I hope he knows what he's doing because I can't see the docks and have no clue how far we are from them.

I don't speak for fear that if I open my mouth, I'll hurl. We row and row and row. It seems never ending.

"Lee," I say when my stomach finally stops doing flips.

"Yeah?" he asks quietly.

"Do you think there are animals underneath us?" My voice is just as quiet.

"Of course there are."

As he answers, I bring my free arm in closer to my side in case anything decides to jump up. Lee starts to laugh. Usually I can't even get a smile out of him and now he's laughing at me?

"Forget about it," I snap.

"Gabby," he says my name as he stops laughing, "You shoot guns and go into war and you're scared of the water?"

"I guess it doesn't make a lot of sense, does it?" I ask.

I still feel stupid, but there is no way I'm letting him know that.

"Who's there?" a voice comes out of the darkness as the docks come into view.

"We've been sent here from the capitol," Lee answers.

"The city is sealed," the man calls back. "You can't dock here."

We reach the docks and Lee raises his arm to grab hold of a metal ring.

"Didn't you hear what I said?" the man asks.

"I heard you soldier," Lee responds.

We can now see the man clearly. He is young, probably close to my age, and he wears a Rebel soldier's uniform. Lee tells me to grab the dock above us as he hauls himself out of the boat. He throws a rope down and I tie it to the end of the dinghy.

The young Rebel doesn't know what to do as Lee helps me onto the dock.

"There's an outbreak," he stammers in one last attempt to get us to leave.

I almost feel bad for him. He's been assigned to the night patrol of the docks during the quarantine. With no one coming in or going out, it's a fluff task. He didn't expect to see anyone tonight.

"We'll be fine," I tell him. "Official business."

I don't tell him that we can't catch the disease that he may die from. No one in this city is safe except for us. I keep being told that it isn't my fault, but I can't help feeling like it is. I did not blow up the labs myself, but I helped those that did. I never thought I'd feel this bad about the labs being gone. We leave the soldier with our boat and start walking towards the government sector of town. We need to report to the city mayor.

"You can't just leave a dinghy in a boat slip!" the soldier yells. "What am I supposed to do with it?"

I give him a little wave without turning around. It'll give him something to do tonight.

Chapter 27

The General

I stare at the list and my hand begins to shake.

"General?" my aide, Evelyn, says. "Are you okay?"

I'm standing in front of her desk when I tear my eyes from the page and hand it to her.

"These are the deaths today," I say, trying to infuse steel into my voice. "Take them out of the records."

I head back in to my office to do something, but I just stare at the wall, my mind churning.

The clinic is still under quarantine, but the disease has not been contained there. TB is working its way through my ranks, the ones that are here anyway. Luckily, most of the troops are deployed to the Texan cities or the Mexican border. Unfortunately, that also means that they are cut off from command. No messengers can get in or out. The outbreak in St. Louis began before ours, but we're in the dark as to how it's progressing. The medicine from Vicksburg's labs has yet to arrive, but my experts tell me it may not work even if it does. It's a new strain of the disease and by the time a new medicine can be created, our forces could be decimated.

Not everyone dies once they're infected. Miranda falls into this category. Some people are immune to it all together. Nevertheless, I sign the order. All training and non-essential assignments have been suspended to avoid large groups of people getting together.

I get to my feet and head toward the locked down clinic as I have twice a day for the past week. My daughter is in there. I don't let her see me because she can't know I've been checking up on her. Her symptoms started yesterday and this strain progresses quickly. My little girl is lying in a hospital bed. They don't have the personnel to take care of the sick anymore, but Dawn's friend Drew is there for her. He has proven to be immune.

I watch as Dawn gets violently ill and the sweat pours off her face. My soldiers think that I don't care about anything, but the sight of my daughter dying is almost too much to handle. For all my power and authority, I feel helpless. I watch Dawn's face and memorize every feature. She'd be amazed at how much she looks like Miranda did at that age. I close my eyes and tears well up beneath my eyelids.

When I open my eyes, I see Drew shaking Dawn. He's yelling something at her. I can't take this anymore. I burst into the room and rush to Dawn's bed. One of the few doctors that's still alive tells me that I shouldn't be here, but I'm the commander so I'll do as I please.

"Dawn, stay with me!" Drew yells.

"What happened?" I ask as I hurry towards him.

"Her pulse weakened as she closed her eyes," he answers, terrified. "The doc says she needs to sleep, but what if she never wakes up?" His eyes turn glassy.

I squeeze Dawn's hand and then lead Drew over to a couch.

"Rest is the only thing that can help her right now," I say much more calmly than I feel.

I lean back to get comfortable. Now that I'm in here, I can't leave, but it's okay, because this is where I need to be.

"Drew," I say as I take in the dark circles underneath his eyes, and his nervous hands, "When was the last time you slept?"

"I don't know," he answers as his leg bounces and his voice sputters. "A few days ago maybe?"

"Stand down, for both your sakes." I say, not meaning for that to be an order. That's just how it came out. "You need sleep," I say, softening my words, and he finally leans his head back.

Officer Grace Mills is sitting across the room. She nods to me as I step toward Dawn. She was close with a man in her patrol that was on the list of deaths a few days ago. Lucas Dillon was the first to die. He may have brought TB here. I give her a hopeful look before leaving to find Hunter, the freedom fighter. His immune system burned through the disease in under a day.

As I watch my people around the clinic, grief hangs heavy in the air. They've watched too many people die and they look to me, their leader, to provide them a sense of hope. How am I supposed to give them something that I'm lacking at the moment?

I find Hunter standing near a group of soldiers who quickly, but weakly, come to attention. I no longer remember what I wanted to say to the freedom fighter, so I stand silently by him instead.

Suddenly, a doctor rushes up to me. He delivers a bombshell when he says that our Rebel base serves as a kind of incubator for the disease because we use recycled air and live in close quarters.

"We must evacuate or this will just happen again," he says.

Turning, I say brusquely, "You heard him, Hunter, time to get out of this hole in the ground. We'll begin preparations as soon as we can get out of the clinic."

I just hope it's not too late for my girl.

Chapter 28

Jeremy

I open my palm and see blood. I only started coughing blood today, but I've been sick for much longer than that. I sit near the side of the road and can't stop hacking. I'm so damn tired. My muscles ache and I feel like I'm about to pass out. Am I the next one to die?

I crawl into an alley on my hands and knees to wretch. I wipe my mouth on the inside of my shirt and stand. On unsteady feet, I stumble toward the government sector. There is no way I can make it to the Rebel barracks tonight. Another coughing fit forces me back to the ground and I pass out.

"Jeremy?" a female voice says my name, but I can't raise my head enough to see who's out here in the dark.

I recognize her voice, but my mind is cloudy. I feel a cool hand on my forehead.

"Lee, he's burning up," she says.

Lee is here? Gabby. The girl must be Gabby. Or am I hallucinating? I try to swat her hand away and tell her not to get too close. I don't want her to get sick. My words come out all jumbled as Gabby and Lee swing my arms over their shoulders and start to carry me.

We enter a room and they lay me on the bed. I see Gabby pulling something out of her bag and a moment later she sticks a needle into my arm. That's the last thing I remember, until the sun, and a beautiful voice, wakes me.

"Jeremy," she coos. "We need you to wake up."

I open my eyes and see Gabby sitting next to me on the bed. She smiles at me.

"How do you feel?" she asks.

I take a minute to fully wake before responding. My fever is gone and the sweats with it. My head no longer feels like it was cracked open and sewn back together. My cough is still painful, but better. My whole body aches as I sit up.

"I feel better than dead," I say.

"Drink this," Gabby says, handing me a cup of water.

"Where am I?" I ask.

Lee is by the window with his back to us, but he turns when I start asking questions.

"The government sector," Lee says with a shrug.

"We went to the mayor," Gabby explains. "We told him we were here to help with the outbreak, which isn't a complete lie. He was so relieved that someone had been sent to help that he assigned us a flat right in the government sector. All we had to do was give him a shot of this." She finishes, holding up a small bottle that is now empty.

"That's what you gave me?" I ask.

"Yeah," she answers, nodding. "It's a good thing we found you. We had just arrived."

"Getting tired of saving my life, Lee?" I ask, laughing and coughing all at once.

He saved me when British soldiers shot me in the woods on the night they captured Gabby and took her to the Texan capitol. Lee gives me a tight smile, which fades, as my body is taken over by a coughing fit, yet again.

"How long have I been out?" I ask when I can speak again.

"Two days," Gabby answers. "We wanted to let you sleep off the rest of the illness, but we couldn't wait any longer."

Her hand has been resting on mine. Lee moves from where he has been scowling at Gabby.

"Let me help you up," he says when he sees me struggling.

My legs are still weak so I fall back onto the bed, irritated.

"Slowly," Lee cautions.

"You just need some more rest," Gabby says.

I want to protest, but I know she's right which only makes me angry. I wasn't expecting to see her in St. Louis.

"What are you doing here anyway?" I snap, regretting it instantly.

Gabby flinches away from me. It is harsher than she deserves, but I feel like crap. I still haven't forgiven her for everything that she said before the assault on Texas. She used my little sister Claire's name like a weapon against me. I may never get over that one. Lee moves between us.

"The mayor told us that you've been dealing with the refugees," he states and I nod.

"We're looking for a man named Joseph Kearn," Gabby says.

I look at her sharply before asking, "Really? Joseph Kearn?"

"You know him?" Lee asks.

Instead of answering him, I ask, "Why are you looking for him?"

"He is also called the Reverend," Gabby answers. "He was in cahoots with Tia and Darren Cole when they were in power in Vicksburg. He disappeared a while ago and we've been trying to find him." She pauses and her face grows even more serious, "Jeremy, this man is dangerous. The Coles developed a biological agent that can be weaponized. Joseph Kearn has it and the antidote."

I knew there was something important about the meeting I witnessed between Kearn and the Mexican man, but Drew didn't believe me and I haven't been able to find anything new since he left.

"He's here," I say. "Or, at least he was a few weeks ago. That's when I lost his trail."

I tell them about the rooftop meeting that I saw between Kearn and the Mexican.

"Los Condenados, are you sure that's what he called it?" Lee demands.

"Yeah. You know what it means?" I ask.

I never paid much attention to the name since I don't speak Spanish. Lee runs a hand through his hair before focusing intensely on Gabby.

"It means 'The Damned'," he says.

A cold shiver runs through my aching bones, as I repeat the name in a whisper,

"The Damned." A weapon in the hands of our enemy? Gabby tries to hide it, but her face gives away her fear. Her hand subconsciously slides back into mine as she struggles with the new information. She holds her eyes shut and sighs.

After a minute, she finally looks at Lee and me and says, "the three of us must find Kearn."

Chapter 29

Dawn

My eyes are unfocused, so Officer Mills is a blur as she comes to check on me. Lucas is dead and I can't completely wrap my foggy head around that yet. He spent his last days in the bed right beside mine. I don't know how Grace can sit here and not fall to pieces when she sees the empty bed. She loved Lucas deeply despite it being against the rules for officers to fraternize with their soldiers. He and Grace saved my life and then became my friends. He was a good person.

I wipe the tears from my eyes and grab Grace's hand as she passes by.

"The world needed more men like him, Grace," I say.

The doctors say that I'm on the right side of the disease now. My body has beaten it and now I just need to get stronger. They say the disease has run its course through the compound and the quarantine will be lifted soon. In other words, everyone who will get sick already has. Drew and Grace were spared, as was my father. My mother overcame the illness and they say I probably inherited the antibodies from her. At least I got something good from her.

The illness was brought here from St. Louis and could've spread elsewhere. I have no idea if Gabby, Lee, and Jeremy are alright.

I can see that my father is quarantined in the next room over. That's weird, right? I don't remember him being here, but I've been pretty out of it for a while now. He and Hunter have been pouring over maps and plans, but I just can't seem to care at the moment. What I do want to know is how many in the compound are dead. I've heard rumors that it hit us pretty hard, and not just here in the clinic. Everyone here is sick of death, and they're blaming Texas for it.

My eyes finally focus just in time to see Drew bringing me a bit to eat, but I have coughed so much in the past few days that my throat is raw and it even hurts to chew. Hell, it hurts to talk, and that's killing me too.

"I took a look at what the General and Hunter have been doing over there," Drew says. "We're leaving the compound."

I smile at the thought. I hate being underground. Fresh air sounds amazing right about now.

"Where would we…" I stop myself as I answer my own question, "The Wastelands, of course!"

Drew doesn't get a chance to respond because the PA system overhead switches on and Miranda's voice calls out to us.

"The quarantine is over," she says. "If you're still recovering, stay in the clinic. Otherwise, it's best to return to your bunks."

She doesn't mention the people that have died; she doesn't even acknowledge what we've just been through. Our ranks are thinned and our morale is down, and my mother is still a piece of work. Grace helps me sit up, but a nurse walks up and tells me that I can't leave yet. I get narked when Drew agrees with her.

"I don't want to be here any longer," I protest.

The nurse shakes her head. I lock my eyes onto Drew's.

"I can't stay here. I'm getting better and I'm no longer contagious," I argue as he frowns, but he doesn't move to help me. "Lucas died in that bed!" I point for emphasis. "And someone died in this bed before it became mine. I can't be here."

Drew doesn't budge, but to my surprise, my father intercedes.

"I'll help her to her bunk," he says in that no nonsense, don't contradict me, kind of way.

"Yes, sir…" the nurse stammers.

Drew brings a wheelchair over to my bedside and once I'm situated in its seat, my father insists on pushing me. He doesn't say much as we wind through the halls, but he does something peculiar when he drops me off at my bunk.

I stand to face him and thank him. For just a second, I get the feeling he's going to hug me. He seems to hesitate before deciding against it and instead, he puts a hand on my shoulder and squeezes quickly before marching off without a word.

"I'm sorry I didn't support you back there," Drew says.

I barely hear him because I'm too focused on my father's disappearing figure and our almost family moment.

"What?" I ask absently.

"In the clinic," he clarifies as he turns to leave.

"Oh, already forgotten," I rasp.

I'm not mad. I'm so tired of getting mad at people and don't want to do it anymore. I crawl into bed and the sleep is a relief.

Chapter 30

Dawn

I wake up hurting and starving, so I make my way to the mess hall slowly.

"Hello, this is the General speaking," my father's voice booms overhead. "I have sad news to report this morning. We have lost roughly one third of our soldiers who were located here at base. They were brave men and women who gave their lives for our cause. We're receiving reports that Vicksburg was untouched by the virus. St. Louis is still sealed, so we're getting no word from there."

He pauses to let everything sink in, before ending the announcement abruptly saying, "there is a mandatory meeting tonight. Be in the carpark at sundown. That is all."

People around the mess hall look as confused as I feel.

"Why do you think we're meeting in the car park?" I ask no one in particular.

"It's probably for some kind of training," someone answers, and I look to see who it is. Shay sits down across from me. I didn't even know she was at base.

I haven't seen Shay since before the attacks on Texas. I used to avoid her because she's outspoken and rude. Now, her presence is a comfort, because she reminds me of Gabby.

"Hey, Shay," Drew says.

He obviously knew she was here.

"Hi," she responds before turning her attention to me. "I heard you got sick, Dawn. Me too. We're pretty bad ass for beating it," she says raising her hand as if she expects me to give her a high five.

"Do you realize how many people died?" I ask, well aware that I'm being a proper bitch. "We were lucky, that's it."

"Geez, sorry," Shay says.

For a moment, I see a glimpse of the Shay that I met at the caves while I was on my way to Floridaland. She's changed, but then again, so have the rest of us.

"Let's just talk about something else," I say with a sigh.

"Well," she begins, "I heard that command is preparing to bug-out."

Her eyes light up with excitement and I glance at Drew. I watch as she speculates on what could happen. This Shay is happy and open. She's even pretty nice. She isn't so combative anymore. I can see why everyone likes her so much, but, right now, her excitement is too much. After scarfing down two bowls of grain, I lay my head on the table and zone out to the sound of the chatter.

I didn't even realize I'd fallen asleep until Drew puts his arm around me to wake me up. "Hey Dawn," he whispers into my ear.

"Yeah," I murmur, sitting up straight and looking around.

"Everyone is reporting to the carpark," Drew says.

"We should go," I say standing, but immediately fall back into my chair, light-headed.

"You should lie down," Drew says. "I'm sure you could be excused from the meeting."

"No. I want to go," I protest as I stand again and, holding onto Drew, and manage to stay on my feet this time.

The carpark is packed by the time we get there and no one seems to know what's going on. I lean on Drew for support as we wind through the crowd to the front. The ramp opens and all of us ascend outside.

"We're meeting outside?" I whisper to Drew, not really expecting him to have any answers.

He just shrugs. The only time this many Rebels have been outside the compound together was right before the assault on Texas. What's happening now?

For the first time in weeks, I feel the crunch of grass beneath my feet. I stop and look up at the sky, the big beautiful sky, before being swept forward in the crowd. Across the field, my father is standing with a string of large fires blazing behind him. A fetid smoke wafts over and all around us, as we all come to the same conclusion at the exact same moment. The smell of death is one that every soldier knows and can never forget.

The crowd murmurs until the General cuts it off in a booming voice when he says, "Tonight, we honor the dead. In the coming weeks, we embark on a journey to save the living."

Chapter 31

The General

"Tonight we mourn friends and even family," I begin. "They were Rebels for our cause, all of them, and although they were taken down by this tragic pestilence, they did not die in vain. All of them have helped us come out of the wilderness, to find a place for our people and all those who seek safety from tyranny and the ravages of a collapsing world," I pause for a moment before going on.

"Many escaped British slave camps. They bravely battled the Texans, bent on dominating and destroying. They stood up against the violence of the remnant Americans and invading Mexicans," I continue. "No, we can't bury them as they deserve. We can't risk more disease, but we can honor them like the warriors of old – sending their spirits into the air and their ashes into the soil they fought for. Breathe in, my comrades and remember this night, for tomorrow we march towards the future they gave their lives to bring forth."

"The last fire is going, sir," Allison says, walking up behind me. She has returned from Vicksburg today with two men in tow. Jack and Clay were Rebels stationed with her in the capitol. Along with some others, they've been helping me with this today.

"Thank you, Allison," I motion her past me. The moon is hidden by clouds now and the sky is dark.

A slow moving line is making its way from fire to fire with muttered prayers and sobs. Others sit on the ground and weep. I see Dawn kneeling next to a shaking Officer Mills and reaching out her hand. Grace takes it and then ends up draped over Dawn as she cries for Lucas. I turn away and remind myself that this was a good idea. As hard as it is to watch, people need to feel all of this now. They'll eventually be asked to push the sadness aside, but not tonight.

After a short time, I step forward once again. Now comes the harder part.

"I'm here to tell you about your future and mine," I say. "The rumors are true. England is dying."

I pause to let that sink in before continuing, "Even as our forces retake the government, we can do nothing to save the land."

A gasp ripples through the crowd.

"We aren't here to battle England, but to save her. Our future isn't in a war that we can never win or in a dying land that can no longer sustain us. Our hope is here in this new world." I take a deep breath before I keep speaking. "For the past few years a secret faction of fellow fighters has been carving a place for our people out of the wilderness. Eventually, we will go there to receive our people as they come to us. That is our future."

I still haven't told them where that nation is to be, but the word "Wastelands" is better left unsaid for now.

"Within a few weeks' time, we will be leaving this base behind. There is one last mission for the Rebels. Be prepared, we head for Texas."

Chapter 32

Gabby

The Damned. That is still all we know about the weapon. The name of a place in Mexico. They call it Los Condenados. What do we do with that? We haven't found the Reverend and we're beginning to think he already skipped town. I'd be out of here myself if I had a choice, but the outbreak has devastated St. Louis and every ranker, including us, has been tasked with removing the bodies.

None of the Texans will touch the dead for fear of catching what killed their loved ones. They hide as we enter their homes. When I became a soldier, this isn't what I thought I'd be doing. I wanted to be on the front lines. Instead, I'm sweaty and tired, holding onto the feet of a grotty corpse. We've been told to show compassion for the families of these poor souls. I ignore them instead. I just want to get this over with.

I nod to Lee and we swing the rigid body up into the back of the truck and head inside to collect another member of this family that died. It's a kid; a young girl. I run from the house and hurl.

I wipe my mouth on my sleeve as I see Lee walk out carrying the girl. Her long hair spills over his arm as he hoists her into the truck. He pats the side of the truck to let the driver know it's full and the truck heads off to the burning site, but the smell of death still lingers in the air and on my clothes.

Lee walks toward me and I stand up straight, trying to even my breathing.

"You okay?" he asks. It isn't said in the soft, caring way that Lee used to use his words. He is still angry with me.

"I'll live," I answer, knowing it's the wrong thing to say as soon as it leaves my lips. Lee scowls at me before taking off toward the flat we've been assigned.

They only had one to give us so I'm heading in the same direction. Before following him, I curse the fact that I can't seem to get away from Lee. We share a bathroom and a bedroom. He's been sleeping on the floor, but he's still always there.

No matter how much I scrub, I don't feel clean. The smell has seeped into my skin. I consider burning my clothes, but we're doing the same thing tomorrow so I just heap them in the corner.

"You going to the mess?" Lee asks.

"No," I respond curtly. I can't eat anything after today.

"Well, I am," he says as he pulls on his boots.

"I'm going to check on Jeremy," I say suddenly.

Jeremy is still recovering a bit so his assignment has been postponed. I think he's going to be with us tomorrow.

"Of course you are," Lee says, sighing as he leaves.

I don't have the patience for Lee's moodiness tonight. I wait a few minutes before I leave so that I don't have to walk with him.

Jeremy lives in the army barracks. That's where most of the Rebel soldiers live. Lee and I are only staying in the government sector because we were sent by Adrian. The Cole surname still scares the mayor of St. Louis.

I'm walking by the entrance to the Mexican sector of town when I see some-one suspiciously dart across the street. It's getting dark so my eyes could be playing tricks on me. I rest my hand on my holster and follow him into the Mexican neighborhood. I continue to follow him into a dark alley, but then I lose him.

This is really daft, I think and then I hear a whoosh from behind me. Before I know it, an arm is around my neck and my arm is twisted behind my back. I scream for help as if there could be help for a British girl in Mexican territory. He tightens his choke hold.

"Why are you following me?" he asks, growling, his accent thick.

I kick my leg out behind me, but he doesn't even flinch.

"I'm going to uncover your mouth," he says. "Don't scream."

He removes his hand and spins me around to face him. His right hand grips my shoulder tightly while the left opens my holster and removes my gun. I try to knee him in the groin, but he catches my leg and twists me to the ground. His knee digs into my back.

"Why are you following me?" he repeats.

I struggle against him, but he is too strong. I try to reposition myself so that I can grab my knife from its sheath on my leg, but he sees what I'm doing and takes it, throwing the blade aside.

"You won't be needing this," he says.

"Get off me you stupid git! Who are you?" I ask harshly.

"I ask the questions. Who are you working for?"

"No one," I answer. "I just saw you run across the road and I was curious."

"Curious?!" he practically yells before calming his voice. He doesn't want us to be heard. "Curiosity is a dangerous trait, even for a Rebel soldier." He unexpectedly gets off of me and pulls me to my feet.

"Luckily, we're on the same side this time." He lets go of my hand and I think he half expects me to run.

When I stay, he motions me to follow him.

"Come," he says. I may be a proper nutter for doing so, but I follow him.

We stop at a nearby house. The windows are boarded up so that no one can see inside and a man and a woman sit in rocking chairs on the front porch with assault rifles cradled in their laps. My new friend hasn't given me my gun or my knife back so I feel naked as we step into a room full of armed Mexican soldiers. They eye me suspiciously and I stay close to the man in front of me. I don't even know his name. What am I doing here?

I'm led up a staircase and into an empty room. The man I've been following shuts the door behind us and turns to me.

"I want you to know," he begins, "that if you weren't a Rebel, you'd be dead."

I look at him in stunned silence as he continues, "As it happens, we lost our contact with the Rebels. Miguel, my uncle, died from the outbreak. He was trading information with a Rebel contact. Now it's up to me."

"Who are you?" I ask again, but before he gets a chance to answer, the door bursts open.

"Rafael!" a woman yells as she stomps into the room flanked by two tall men, their rifles at the ready. "Have you lost your mind?"

"No, I haven't," he answers defensively. "While all of you were happy staying here and doing nothing, I've been out trying to find Miguel's Rebel contact, Drew."

"Drew was in contact with you?" I interject.

"Do you know how we can contact Drew?" Rafael asks.

He wants to talk to the Rebel that he already knows.

"He isn't in St. Louis anymore," I answer.

"See, we need a new contact," Rafael states. "We can't afford to stop searching now."

"I am well aware of the urgency of this situation," the woman responds. "That doesn't mean we're going to start bringing Rebel soldiers here. What would happen if any of the other cartels saw you? Did you ever think of that?"

Rafael's face falls as he realizes the danger he's placed these people in.

"There is a reason that Miguel was in charge of the contact and you were just his compadre. Get rid of this girl discreetly and then we can talk about what a waste of a son you are," she says before she turns and leaves without another word.

"That was your mother?" I ask, stunned.

"Yeah," he answers, inhaling deeply before he continues. "Come," he says as he opens the only window in the room.

"I'm not leaving before I have answers," I say stubbornly.

"My name is Raf," he says. "You've heard the name Joseph Kearn, I know you have. I also know that you've been looking for him. You are Gabby Nolan," he says before pausing and my head is spinning. What does Joseph Kearn have to do with a house full of armed cartel men and women?

"We need to find him," he finishes after a minute.

Chapter 33

Gabby

"Mexico is powerful, or at least it could be. Do you ever wonder how Texas can hold the Mexicans back?" Raf asks.

We leave his cartel's house through the window and he takes me to the place where his uncle met with Drew a few times. The basement is easy to get into and no one can see us there.

"Do you know anything about Mexico?" he asks.

"Not really," I admit. "I always just thought there weren't many people there. Texas is powerful."

"It would take no time at all for the Mexicans to defeat the Texans at the border," he explains. "Yet that is a war that has been going on for decades. Why? Because Mexico is on the brink of a civil war. There are cartels that control different parts of Mexico. Only three of those cartels are fighting at the border because none of the others butt up against Texas. Most are focused on protecting their borders from the other cartels. There are alliances constantly being made and broken."

"What a bloody mess," I say, leaning against the wall.

"My mother leads the Carlita Cartel," he states proudly.

"Then why isn't she in Mexico?" I ask, skeptical of everything he's telling me. It's a lot to process.

"She is only in St. Louis for a few weeks to check on the status of the search for Kearn. She doesn't trust people enough to send messengers when it's really important," he answers before asking a question of his own, "What do you know about a weapon that was developed in Vicksburg?"

"It's biological," I tell him. He nods slowly before I continue, because he already knew that. "We've been trying to find Kearn before he gets into Mexico."

"We think he's already there," Raf says, his voice is no more than a growl and his face grows even darker as he continues talking. "He's being financed by the Moreno Cartel," he stops talking and his eyes look dangerous. I can see that there is no love lost between the two largest Mexican forces.

"Why do they want it?" I ask lowly.

"We don't know their plans. The Morenos are...dangerous," Raf answers.

He and I have no more information for each other. He didn't get anything new from me, but he says they'll need Rebel help in this. I leave before Raf and book it toward the flat, the night seeming more ominous than before. After everything his mother said, I don't know if I'll be hearing from Raf again. After hitting dead end after dead end, I really hope I do. This could be the break the Rebels so desperately needed.

I forget all about visiting Jeremy, I need to talk to Lee. I don't care if he is still mad at me. He'll talk to me. He's the only person that won't yell at me for going into the Mexican sector alone. He understands me.

When I round the corner, Lee is sitting on the steps of our building, but he stands when he sees me. His look scares me.

"Do you realize how long you've been gone?" he asks, trying his best not to shout.

"Lee," I begin but he cuts me off.

"You're unbelievable, Gabby," he says, swaying just enough for me to realize he's been drinking.

I try again to say something but he puts up his hand to stop me. There is no way I can tell him everything that just happened when he is like this.

"How was Jeremy?" he asks, not giving me enough time to answer before he starts talking again. "You know, Gabby, I think I have you figured out. You like to be in control. You like for people to be weak so that they need you."

"Lee, I don't..." I stammer, reaching out, but he slaps my hand away and cuts me off.

"Let me talk," he snaps. "This is important." He pauses and I stare at him in the dark, waiting. "You raised your sister. In London, you two were close, right?" I nod and he keeps going. "Dawn was weak. She couldn't take care of herself. Heck, when I met her, she still couldn't defend herself. She was needy and she needed you more than anyone." He throws his arms in the air. "Well, guess what, she still loves you, but she doesn't need you anymore and you know it. And you know what? You just can't get over the fact that you don't have to take care of her anymore," he pauses again and I almost believe he's done.

At least he can't see the tears that have begun to pool in my eyes.

"Then there's Jeremy," he says, his voice getting louder.

I take a step backwards to distance myself further from the oncoming words.

"You fell for Jeremy while you were both slaves. He's told me the story. His sister died and you were there for him. He says he wouldn't be here without you. He needed you to be there for him; to comfort him so he didn't get himself killed. He was hurting. Well, when he got his cause, he didn't need you anymore, but he still wanted you. What did you do? You pushed him away and ruined everything. He didn't need you so you didn't want him." Lee's voice slurs more as each word leaves his mouth.

I sit on the steps and put my head in my hands. Every word feels like a dagger. Lee has put the knife in me and now he's just twisting it. It's cruel. I never had Lee pegged for cruel. He tries to kneel in front of me, but he falls backward. He is drunker than I thought and doesn't even realize how much he's hurting me.

"Don't cry, Gabby," he says, as his voice softens, but the alcohol gives it a mocking edge. "That's not what I wanted."

"Then what do you want from me?" I yell.

"Isn't it obvious?" he asks quietly. "I want you."

I look at him incredulously. After everything he just said to me?

"I want you, Gabby. Do you hear me? I don't need you. You can't fix me. You can't take care of me. You got that? You can't fix me and I don't want you to try," he says, taking one of my hands into his, but I pull it free and wipe my face.

"I love you," he whispers.

"I'm sorry," I whisper in response, and in the silence between us, I slip away.

Chapter 34

Dawn

"Sir," I say, saluting as I enter command.

Things are getting back to normal at the base. Everyone is amped for relocation, but that process is slow and irritating. We want to be on the move, but it feels like we're just waiting. Training has resumed even though we won't be fighting much these days. Everything is much less crowded than it was before the outbreak. It's an eerie feeling.

Today I've been summoned to command. I haven't seen my father since the night at the fires. Our relationship, if you want to call it that, has been odd lately. It started with him yelling at me when I was narked about Matty being trained as a soldier. Then I got sick. He wasn't in the clinic when the quarantine started, but Drew told me he risked becoming infected himself to check on me. Then there was the odd thing with the wheelchair. I swear he was going to hug me. Most of my life, all I've wanted was parents. Now, they're both here and I don't know what I want from them.

"Have a seat Dawn," my father says, "What I'm going to tell you is classified." I nod and he continues, "Tia Cole died during the outbreak."

"What?!" I say, a little too loudly.

"Do you understand why that can't get out?" he asks, unsure if he can trust me.

I stare at him blankly because I have no idea what he wants me to say.

"Very few people knew we had her. If word got out in Vicksburg that we had been holding their prophet, they would riot. They believed her to be dead which is why they followed Adrian. All of our work would come undone," he explains, pausing to take a sip of coffee.

"But she's dead now," I clarify.

"Yes, unfortunately," he replies.

My face must show my confusion because he explains, "She died before we were able to get much information out of her. That is why you're here."

"I don't understand," I say.

"We did get something," he pauses. "Texas developed a biological weapon. That's why we're not heading for the Wastelands yet," I nod, unsure why he is telling me this. He doesn't seem so sure either.

"Is there something you need me to do?" I ask, feeling uncomfortable under his stare.

"Adrian sent Gabby and Lee to track down the man suspected of having the weapon," he answers.

"So they survived the disease?" I ask, suddenly relieved.

"They did," my father responds before asking, "And how are you feeling?"

The way he's looking at me suddenly clicks. He didn't summon me here to update me on Gabby or give me information that is classified. This is him checking up on me after I was sick.

"I'm fine," I say, smiling.

"Good," he says, breaking eye contact and pretending to go through some papers on his desk.

"You're free to go," he says quietly. I give him one last long look before getting to my feet and leaving.

I'm distracted when I run into Allison outside. She seems happy to see me.

"Hey Dawn," she says cheerfully.

"Hi," I say briskly. I don't want to be rude, but I'm on a mission.

"I saw Gabby when I was in the capitol," she says, catching my attention, so I turn toward her. My father only gave me a shred of information about Gabby.

"How is she?" I ask.

I haven't had news about my sister in so long. I try not to think about it, but I miss her. This is the longest we've ever been apart.

"She seemed good," Allison says. "She helped me out with something big, and then she was sent to St. Louis with Lee right before I returned here."

St. Louis was hit hard by the outbreak, but my father says Gabby is alive so I'll have to trust that.

I miss you, sis.

Chapter 35

Jeremy

Gabby won't tell me what is going on with her. I try not to care, but that isn't me. There is no trust left between us and I'm stuck just watching her brood.

"Is she going to be okay?" I ask Lee as we watch Gabby practice her shooting. Everything about her lately seems destructive.

"She hates herself right now," Lee says sadly.

If I didn't already know that Lee had feelings for Gabby, his eyes would give him away. He talked to me about it a few days ago because, for once, the big American just needed to talk. It's strange, I thought I'd be jealous of Lee and Gabby, but I kind of just feel bad for the guy. Gabby isn't an easy person to love, but at least they have each other.

I'm drifting alone. I have no family; no one that I really love. I don't really have a reason to keep fighting. I was born and raised in a Floridaland slave camp. My mother died there. My sister died there. I have nothing left. Sometimes I tell myself that I'm fighting for the people that still have families, but that's horseshit. I'm just here because I have nowhere else to go.

"We should go tell her that we've been summoned back to base," I say.

Lee nods but doesn't move, so I walk across the field toward Gabby.

"What is it?" she snaps as she reloads her rifle.

"The General has recalled about half the troops in St. Louis. We have to go with them. Officer Lincoln is expecting us at the docks," I answer.

Gabby looks at me and then turns and starts firing again, never missing her target. After emptying her clips, she loops the gun's strap over her shoulder and walks past me.

"Good," she says. "I'm over this place."

She doesn't stop when she reaches Lee. She expects us to follow her, and we do. That's how she likes it.

We're due at the boat in an hour, so Gabby heads straight for the flat she's been staying in. I break off from her to walk in the direction of the barracks, and Lee opts to come with me. Neither of us speaks until we're almost there.

"The Capitol really did a number on her, didn't it?" I ask.

Lee looks away before he answers.

"Things happened there that I don't think she'll ever get over," he says. "She won't let anyone be there for her or help her."

"I know," I say, realizing how pathetic the two of us are.

I may not love her, and I may resent the hell out of her, but I'd still follow Gabby into a burning building. Lee would follow her in and then use his body as a shield against a shower of bullets to get her out safely.

I grab my few belongings and we make it to the boat with time to spare. I'm ready to be done with this city. The things I've seen here, the illness I experienced here, I'm done with all of it.

I find Gabby leaning against the rail on deck as we shove off. She doesn't look up as I stand next to her.

"What?" she snaps.

"You anxious to get back to Dawn?" I ask.

When I say her sister's name, there is a flicker of apprehension that quickly morphs back into the cold expression she wears most of the time these days. Most people wouldn't catch that, but I know this girl. Gabby feels like she's screwed up so many things and she's afraid that includes her relationship with her sister.

"We don't even know she's there," Gabby says quickly.

"I guess we'll find out soon enough."

Chapter 36

Dawn

"Dawn, I want you to meet my friend," Matty says as he pulls me down the hall.

"Alright, Matty, I'm coming!" I say as I laugh at his eagerness.

To my surprise, we stop outside the shooting range. That's right, they're training the kids. I push the image of Matty aiming a rifle out of my mind as we enter the room. Only one person is in here at the moment so we stand at the back wall, waiting for him to finish. When he sets his gun down, he turns to us.

"Dawn this is Antonio," Matty says.

I stare at the willowy boy in front of me with his dark hair and even darker eyes. He doesn't smile at me.

"I've heard a lot about you," I say finally. "I'm a friend of Matty and Drew."

Drew saved Antonio and another boy in St. Louis.

"Where are you from Antonio?" I ask.

I know he's Mexican, but I want to know how he ended up here. The kid just shrugs.

"He's a Moreno," Matty blurts out, proud that he has the answer I want.

I catch the sharp look Antonio gives his friend, but then his shoulders sag and he walks across the room to put his gun in the locker. He then leaves us without a word.

"How much do you know about Antonio?" I ask Matty.

"His mom still lives in Mexico," he answers.

I glance at Matty and see that he's just excited that he's helping me. Young boys can't be expected to keep secrets and I'm glad for that.

"Come on kid," I say as I tousle his hair and lead him to the mess, hoping he has more information. Food is the way to a young man's heart.

Chapter 37

Dawn

There's yelling coming from my father's office and it's not him. I turn the corner just in time to hear the row end as Allison storms by me. I want to know what that was all about, but the general would get narked at me for even asking.

I step into his office and take a seat without being invited. His back is turned to me, but I can see he is still shaken from whatever Allison was shouting about.

"Dawn," he says when he finally greets me, his anger at Allison slowly disappearing from his eyes.

"Did you know that we have a Mexican kid here?" I ask.

"Yes," he responds, because of course he knew.

"Does the name Moreno mean anything to you?"

"What?" He snaps, suddenly alert. "Where did you hear that?"

"Apparently the kid is a Moreno," I state.

His face looks stricken as he covers his mouth with his hand.

"What's a Moreno?" I ask after a stunned silence.

"The Moreno's are a cartel in Mexico," he says, slumping back in his chair. "There's a rumor that they are trying to acquire the weapon from Kearn."

"Shite," I say as I lean back as well, not knowing what else to say.

"Are you sure of this information?" my father asks, his gaze not leaving my face.

"He told one of the other kids," I say. "What is he doing with the Rebels?"

"Captain Collins raised him since he was young," he responds. "He thought he was an orphan. I want to know why he was north of the border in the first place. We're going to have to go in to Los Condenados sooner rather than later."

"Where's that?" I ask urgently.

"It's where the Moreno great house is," he answers.

"Oh," I say, because it's the only response I can formulate as he reaches for a map and unrolls it.

He scratches the week old beard that he just hasn't bothered to shave and hovers over the desk before pointing to a region on the map.

"That's Los Condenados," he informs me.

"I wonder, has the kid changed his name?" he muses.

"Why would he do that?" I ask, confused.

"There is a story about a child taken from the Morenos years ago. He was named for his uncle Juan, who now leads the cartel. His mother was a Moreno. The boy is the oldest heir to Juan, but many say that it was for his own safety that he was brought to the colonies," he explains.

As my father speaks, his eyes light up conspiratorially.

"No one in the colonies knows exactly why he'd be brought north, but the Morenos are dangerous so we can guess," he says.

I leave my father to his planning and my head is still reeling when I run into Allison lurking outside his office.

"Hey," I say, trying not to let my suspicions get the best of me. She could be doing something completely innocent. I stare at her until she speaks.

"What's up Dawn?" she asks, trying to be subtle. "Why were you in the General's office?"

"I can't tell you that," I say as I sidestep her to try to get away. She's acting weird.

"I know you can't tell me everything, but come on, we're friends, right? Or, at least I thought we were," she says.

I have to stifle my own laughter. Friends? I haven't seen this woman since before I went to Cincinnati, and, even then, she was never a friend. I'm saved by Ryan as he hurries toward me.

"I have to go," I tell Allison.

She looks frustrated and I suddenly get a bad feeling about her. Ryan takes my arm and guides me away from the situation.

"Dawn, I need to talk to you," he says, the tone in his voice making me forget about Allison immediately.

"Is everything okay?" I ask.

"No, not really," he answers, looking away as he scratches at his arm furiously.

He's seems nervous. We haven't really talked since returning from the Wastelands.

"What's wrong?" I ask.

Sensing a sadness, I reach out and squeeze his arm to let him know I'm here for him.

"I have to go back to Cincinnati," he blurts out.

"What?" I ask.

That isn't what I was expecting him to say.

"Ryan, your parents are..." I stammer.

"Dead. Yeah, I got that," he snaps. "The rest of my family is still fighting though. I can't just do nothing."

The Americans in Cincinnati are divided into their "families". That doesn't always mean they're related, but they're loyal. Ryan's family, the Smith family, is the largest and had control of the town. The other big families always resented the dealings that the Smiths had with foreigners. Things reached a head when my patrol showed up asking for aid. Eventually, Chief Smith had to smuggle me out along with Ryan and Emily. He was killed shortly after that and the Smith family lost the chiefdom, but is still fighting to protect the smaller families from being wiped out.

"I know you can't," I say quietly as my eyes fill up with tears. "But you also can't go alone."

"I have to," he says, hanging his head. "Things would only get worse if any foreigners got involved."

That's me. I'm the foreigner he's telling not to come. It breaks my heart to see Ryan like this. When I first met him, he was pretending to be my doctor in the Cincinnati clinic after I'd been shot. This is the boy who loved horses and fishing. War has made all of us into the people that we would never have wanted to be.

I stare at my best friend and think of everything we have been through together; everything we have done for each other. Ryan is family to me. Who knows what is going to happen to him in Cincinnati? There's a very real chance that I'll never see him again.

"So, this is goodbye?" I ask, as tears stream down my face and Ryan pulls me to him in a strong hug.

"No," he says. "I'll see you again. I promise."

In this war, promises mean nothing and we both know that. We stand like that for a few moments, both understanding that as soon as we break apart, he has to go. I love this man. This feels like it did when I lost Sam. It feels like losing a brother. Ryan isn't dead, but he's going to walk straight into the fire. He'll be the biggest target in their civil war.

Ryan finally releases me and steps back. We don't say anything else as he backs away, still facing me. He reaches the end of the hall and gives me a smile and a wave before disappearing around the corner.

For a moment, I let the sadness settle on me then shake it off. We all have to do what we have to do in this damned world.

Chapter 38

Gabby

Lee looks much more peaceful when he sleeps, even with he's snoring. Life hasn't been easy for us. Lee has seen some terrible things. Heck, he's done some terrible things. As I've gotten to know him, I've realized that every one of those things stays with him. He never forgets or forgives himself. He says that I'm the same way, and maybe I am. Lee knows me better than anyone else right now. He understands me because we're alike. If we were together, we would only add to each other's pain. The hurtful things he said to me in St. Louis are a perfect example of that. He was trying to tell me he wanted to be with me and ended up throwing my failings in my face. They were all true and that just makes it worse.

I hate hurting him. I've never cared for someone like this before, but the pain would only be worse later on when I buggered it all up big time. I look down at him and brush the hair out of his face. It was a silly impulse and I bring my hand back quickly so that I don't wake him. His lips curve into a smile, but his eyes stay shut.

I'm on watch right now and enjoying the quiet. Moments of peace are hard to come by these days. The other soldier assigned to watch has fallen asleep, but I don't mind the solitude.

The trees block my view of the sky above our shoreline camp, but the chilly night breeze feels good.

I was relieved to get off that boat. It smelled funky and we were all living on top of each other. We'll be back at Rebel base by noon tomorrow.

I hear the snap of a twig and see movement in time to duck as someone tries to grab me. I yell and Lee is up in a second. He knocks the guy out, but stops as a rifle is aimed high on his chest. The rest of the camp is roused at gunpoint.

Someone is shouting, "Tie them up!"

I realize the orders aren't for us. Over half of our Rebel group are waving their guns around. Lee grabs my arm and pulls me behind him. I reach for my gun before realizing I left it in my rucksack on the ground.

"Everybody move!" someone screams.

"What is the meaning of this?" Officer Lincoln barks as he steps out of his tent.

He doesn't get an answer, but he does get a knee to the gut. As he doubles over, he is pushed to the ground and his hands and feet are tied. Jeremy has been knocked out and bound. I try to run, but am caught and thrown into a tree. My head snaps, hitting the large trunk and sending me sprawling at its base, only to have a gun barrel greet my face. It takes three men to get Lee tied up.

"What is going on?" Linc tries again for answers.

"A changing of the guard," a woman answers with a laugh. "You all are in for a rude awakening. We'll teach you what happens when you follow Nolan over Jonathan Clarke."

Chapter 39

Dawn

I watch from my hiding place as Clay and Jack lead a group of Rebel soldiers toward command. It's only been a few days since I overheard Allison screaming at my father and I've been keeping an eye on her and her friends ever since.

They enter command, guns drawn, and begin marching people out with their hands tied behind their backs. My father is last, bound and bloodied. I duck back around the corner to avoid being seen. They're headed towards the cells where Jonathan Clarke is being kept, or "was" being kept I'm guessing. There are many soldiers who were fiercely loyal to him. He's behind this, I just know it. I need to find Drew.

Earlier, Drew said that he was heading to the firing range so that's where I look first. The halls are eerily empty until I pass the weapons room. The room is packed with men and women arming themselves. This can't be good.

I step into the firing range and lock the door behind me. Shay sees me first and stops shooting. I don't come here much so she raises her eyebrows quizzically. Drew does a double take and they both remove their earplugs.

"There's something happening out there," I say, breathing hard.

Shay puts up a hand for me to stop talking. It annoys me at first until I see her go to the camera I'd failed to notice and pull on the cord at the back. It comes free.

"No one can hear us now," she states.

"I saw a group of soldiers arrest every person in command, including my father," I explain.

Drew comes to me and tries to hug me, but I push him away. Now isn't the time.

"Then I saw another group arming themselves next door. It must be Jonathan's people," I continue.

"Did you recognize anyone?" Drew asks.

"Yeah," I pause. "Allison, Jack, and Clay are involved."

"Shite…" Drew mutters, mussing his hair.

Shay has already busted the glass doors of the weapons locker that holds everything for the gun range and she starts handing things to us. By the time she is finished, I have multiple guns and a sack full of ammo. I don't like it, but I have no choice.

Drew uses his fingers to count to three. I open the door and he looks around the corner with his gun drawn.

"Clear," he whispers.

I follow him out and Shay brings up the rear. We don't see another living soul, so we leg it toward the living quarters. There have to be soldiers there who aren't a part of all of this. As we get closer, we hear the unmistakable sound of gunfire. Three soldiers have another one pinned down in one of the bunk rooms.

"Who's on our side?" I whisper.

"It's gotta be the one that's pinned down," Shay answers. "I'll bet these people out number us."

"Okay, then I have an idea," I say. "I know how we can get in behind the shooters."

"You sure you know what you're doing?" Shay asks suspiciously.

"Just shut up and follow me," I respond.

We slip inside the boiler room and I hurry to the opposite end of the room and point to the door.

"They're in the hallway here," I say.

"Great," Shay moves to open the door, but I stop her.

"Aim for their legs. I don't want to kill them," I say.

She looks at me like I'm crazy and then asks, "Do you think they'd ever hesitate to kill us?"

"We're not them," I answer.

I slowly open the door, hoping that the rusty hinges won't give us away. We'll only have a few shots before they're aware that we're here. Shay starts shooting as soon as she steps into the hall. Drew and I follow suit. Shay kills the first man before he even knows what hit him. Drew drops the second one by taking out his knee, and we jump back into the boiler room as the third one turns on us. Our handguns are no match for his rifle. One last bullet sounds on the other side of the door and then silence. We stay put because we don't know who took that last shot. I almost jump out of my own skin when someone knocks on the door.

"Dawn?" a woman's voice asks.

I open the door and Officer Grace Mills is standing there, terrified. She throws her arms around me.

"You just saved my life," she says.

She releases me and I step back.

"Is there anyone back there?" Drew asks, pointing to the room Officer Mills was guarding.

"There are some, but they're not armed because only officers carry weapons while at base," she answers. "There were a few more officers back there, but they're dead now."

She hangs her head and Drew puts his arm around her to guide her down the hall. Shay and I stand on either side of them, ready for anything. We pass the two soldiers we killed and the third that is writhing in agony on the ground. There is nothing we can do for him right now. He chose his side and now we need to save ours.

We pick up a few dazed but loyal soldiers and give them weapons. To my dismay, Matty, Henry, and Antonio appear and want to help. I'd rather they stayed safe, but everyone agrees that we need the numbers.

"So, what's the plan, Dawn?" Grace asks.

Isn't she supposed to be the officer? Everyone is looking to me to figure this out and I feel my pulse quicken. I'm not the leader type. Drew squeezes my hand to reassure me and also to tell me I need to do this. I calm down enough to speak.

"Jonathan has probably been released by now," I begin. "My father," I stop myself. "General Nolan has probably taken his place in the cells along with most of the officers. These people are being led by a woman named Allison. Most of you don't know her. I obviously don't either, because I wouldn't have expected this from her. She's smart though. We need to be careful here."

Chapter 40

Gabby

"We got word from Allison," I overhear one of our captors say and start listening intently as soon as he says her name.

"And?" someone asks.

"Things are underway and moving quickly. We just need to keep them here," the first person replies.

"What's underway?" I yell. "What has Allison done now?"

One of the traitors walks towards me and spits on the ground at my feet.

"You're going to get your answers soon enough," he says. "You just won't like what they are."

I struggle against my ropes because I want to hurt this man. No, I want to kill him. He walks back to the others. I recognize a few of the faces, but I wasn't in St. Louis long enough to get to know them. Jeremy is another matter. Some of these people were his friends. He lived with them.

"Gabby, calm down," Jeremy says.

"Didn't you hear them?" I whisper urgently. "Allison is behind all of this."

Both Jeremy and Lee look confused.

"She's the one who got Dawn, Drew, and I out of Texas," I explain.

They don't get it. They think I'm hurt because she was a friend.

"She's the traitor who blew up the labs," I say angrily.

Now they get it, or at least Lee does. He knows that I don't want to save her because she's my friend. I want to stop her because she never really was.

"So, what do you think is going on at base?" Jeremy asks. "Do you think Allison is taking control?"

"Who do they have locked up there that still has a loyal following among the Rebels?" I ask. It's obvious to me what's going on and I watch it come to them.

"You think Jonathan Clarke is behind this?" Jeremy asks, sounding surprised, even though he shouldn't be.

We all have seen what Jonathan's followers will do for him. On our way to Texas, they burned farms and destroyed villages. Here in the colonies, burning farms is about the worst thing you can do when food is in short supply. It is unforgivable. Even Miranda was upset by the stupidity.

"No talking," one of our captors, a woman this time, barks before rejoining the others.

There are four of them. The rest left to join their counterparts at base. There are eight of us: Me, Lee, Jeremy, Linc, and four others that Jeremy seems to know. I lean back so that my head is close to Lee's.

"We need to get to base. Something big is happening there," I whisper. He nods, but that isn't enough for me, so I explain further, "Lee, Dawn might be there. We need a plan."

They took our weapons so none of us have knives to cut through this rope. Think Gabby. How do I get to Dawn? I notice a slight movement from Jeremy. His hands are working on something. They relax suddenly and the rope falls from his wrists. He puts a finger to his lips to tell me to keep quiet as he tosses a sharp rock my way. It lands behind me, near my hands.

I run my hands along it, cutting my finger as I feel the sharpened edge. I begin to saw at my rope. It takes me a while, but as soon as my hands and feet are free I give the rock to Lee.

"Now what?" I ask Jeremy.

He seems to be the one with the plan. One of our captors glances back and I make sure my arms stay behind my back.

"We need to get to our guns," Jeremy says.

They've taken all our weapons and piled them up. They're unguarded. Why guard them when your prisoners are tied up?

"Hey!" one of the soldiers yells. "That one isn't tied up!"

He points to Jeremy and I look at him frantically as all four soldiers close in on him. He is grabbed by the hair and yanked to his feet. Jeremy stumbles as they push him forward with the nose of a gun, pressing it into his back. Once he is where everyone can see him, he is pushed to his knees.

"You can't beat us," the armed soldier says. "Watch what happens when you try."

He releases the safety on his gun and Jeremy closes his eyes, but before he gets a chance to pull the trigger, I jump to my feet and start running, hoping they'll come after me. I pass the weapons pile, grab a rifle, and run like hell, hoping to draw our captors away from Jeremy. Someone shoots at me from behind, but I dodge through the woods as the bullets splinter the trees around me.

I don't stop running as I aim my gun behind me and fire rapidly, hoping to hit someone. But they're still coming on fast.

I turn, take aim, and fire. The closest one goes down screaming. Two more keep coming until the space behind me erupts in shooting, taking down my final pursuers. I close my eyes, expecting to be next.

"Gabby?" someone asks.

I recognize the thick accent immediately.

"Raf?" I ask in response.

I open my eyes as he grins.

"What are you doing here?" I demand.

"It's a good thing I'm here," he grins. "You're welcome."

"I had it handled," I snap. "But you might as well help me. There's one more."

I take off running back to the group, hoping Jeremy is still okay. We reach the others and the final captor lies dead on the ground at Jeremy's feet.

As soon as he sees me, Lee rushes over and pulls me into his arms. I let him, as my body sags against his. You never get used to almost dying. I feel him tense up as he sees Raf behind me. I never told him about our meeting in St. Louis. That was the night Lee basically confessed his love for me and I walked away.

"This is Raf," I tell Lee as he releases me.

I turn my attention to Raf and say, "You haven't told me why you're here."

"I was following you," he says.

"How?" Jeremy interrupts. "You can't follow someone on the water."

"We have boats too," Raf responds, sounding irritated. "Gabby, can I talk to you alone?"

"Fat chance," Jeremy says.

Lee uses his body to say pretty much the same thing. He towers over Raf, and I have to squeeze between them. I place a hand on Lee's chest to tell him to back off.

"You can talk to me on the way to the Rebel base," I say. "There's something big going on there."

"How do you know this guy, Gabby?" Lee asks as he pulls me away.

"Not now, Lee," I say as I break free and find Linc. He's the only officer here.

"We need to get moving," Linc says.

"We will, I just don't know how we get into base once we get there. The ramp operator is probably compromised and we don't want anyone to know we're there," I say.

"I can get us in," he promises. "Let's go."

He's one of the few officers I trust so I follow him. Raf stays close to me as we move quickly. It's not far from the river to base, but we have to be careful. Allison could've more patrols out here.

"We couldn't afford to lose another Rebel contact," Raf says. "We need you to go into Mexico."

"I can't think about this right now," I say. My only care at the moment is stopping whatever is happening at base.

"If another cartel was caught on Moreno land, it'd spark a civil war," he continues, not listening to me. "We need the Rebels."

"Rafael," I snap, "Not now!"

He finally shuts up and allows me to concentrate on getting into base. We stop before we reach the clearing and Linc searches for something at the base of a large rock.

"What are we doing here?" I ask him.

"The base stretches out here. We're above it as we speak," he says as he gets to his knees and begins to dig.

A few of his men help him until they reveal a rusted metal door with a long chain on top. Linc lifts the chain and we all grab on and begin to pull. At first, nothing seems to be happening, but we keep pulling with all of our strength. Finally, the door begins to open, revealing some kind of empty box.

"Here we go," Linc says.

Chapter 41

Dawn

There are traitors patrolling every hallway. We're stuck. We were able to get this far without having to split up, but we need to find others that are trapped. There have got to be more Rebel soldiers that aren't involved in this. There have to be. We've found a few, both alive and dead. These traitors seem to have no problem killing the people who were their friends and allies.

"We're near the Rebel Tech labs," I say. "We should hide out in there for a bit."

"How do you know where the labs are?" Grace asks. "Soldiers aren't supposed to go there."

"Does it really matter right now?" I ask.

"Not really," she says. "So, how do we get there?"

"When we leave this room, we need to go left and get down that hallway without being seen. There is a door marked **CLASSIFIED** at the end. That's the records room," I explain. "Go inside and wait for me."

"Where are you going?" Grace asks, worried.

"Drew and I are going to make sure you all can get there," I say as I look to Drew and he nods.

"Be careful," Grace says.

I open the door and look around the corner. "It's clear," I say as Drew and I slip out to the right. "You'll know when to go."

We leg it to the generator room. The labs use most of the energy, so I know it's near here. I've never actually seen it, but I remember hearing the dull hum that I'm hearing now. It gets louder until we reach a door marked **GENERATORS**. Easy enough. I turn the knob, but the door is locked.

"We need to get in there," I say urgently.

"None of these doors are very strong. They're old and falling apart," Drew says as he looks up and down before suddenly throwing his body into the door.

I hear wood splinter, but the door stays shut. He repeats it three times before the door finally bursts open. We hurry inside.

The massive machine takes up most of the small room. "My God," Drew says before turning to me. "You're the one with the plan. What now?"

My head is spinning and I can't seem to form the words.

"Dawn!" Drew has to yell to be heard. "What's the plan?"

I snap back to reality.

"It's a generator," I yell above the noise. "And not a very advanced one. There has to be a gas tank here somewhere."

I search the machine until I find the small tank. It's almost empty, but it will do. I show Drew.

"Like I said, this thing is pretty old school," I say.

"How do we ignite it?" he asks.

"We don't have matches so there's only one way," I say.

When I stop speaking, he looks at me like I'm nuts.

"It'll be okay," I assure him. "There isn't much gas in there anyway."

The two of us back into the hall and are immediately spotted. Two traitors run towards us as I aim my gun at the gas tank and pull the trigger.

The explosion throws us into the wall and the generator room erupts into flames. The fire alarm screeches for just a second before it cuts off. The hall lights go dark and we can only see each other by the light of the flames. We've just cut power to the entire base. I take off running, but am tripped by one of the soldiers as he gets to his feet. I kick my foot into his groin. The force sends him into the wall and I scramble to my feet as I knee him in the gut. He doubles over and I hit him over the head with my rifle. He falls to the ground.

"Drew!" I yell.

"I'm here Dawn," Drew says, taking my hand as we start to run.

I can't see him, but at least I can feel him. I run my free hand along the wall to count the doors as we move.

"It's here!" I yell and pull him through a door to our right.

"Grace!" I yell once we're inside.

"We're here," she responds as I try to catch my breath.

In the darkness, I can't see their faces, but I can feel their fear.

"Follow me," I say, leading them into the labs, relieved to see that there are dim lights near the ground. Leave it to the techs to have backups.

We weren't the only ones who have come here to hide out. There are people everywhere. I look toward the familiar desk and see a messy haired boy crumpled on the floor.

"Connor," I whisper as I rush towards him, my whole body protesting as I lower myself to the ground.

"Hi Dawn," he says weakly.

"Are you hurt?" I ask.

"I think so," he says, his words ragged as they pass his lips and he struggles to breathe.

"Stay with me Connor," I yell as his eyelids droop closed.

That's when I notice the blood. He is covered in it. I search him for the source and find a bullet wound in his leg. He's lost too much.

"Get me something to tie on his leg," I say.

Drew takes off his belt and hands it to me. Connor doesn't move as I tie it as tight as I can. He is beyond feeling pain. I put my hand under Connor's chin and lift his head to look at me. "Do not die on me, Connor. Do you hear me? Keep your eyes open. You do not die today."

Chapter 42

Gabby

Our way into Rebel base is a crank lift. Linc says it was built a long time ago in case of emergencies; in case anyone needed to make a quick exit. It's only been used a handful of times.

"Where in the compound does it come out?" Jeremy asks.

"Near the tech labs," Linc answers. "Only three at a time can fit. When you get to the bottom, slip through the nearest door and wait for the rest of us." Linc motions us forward, saying, "Lee, Jeremy, and Gabby go first. Take the lift, assess the situation and report back in 20 minutes."

We climb in and the lift starts to move. It drops suddenly and I grab onto Lee.

"Shite," I say, squeezing his arm as he works the crank.

Steady now, we prepare for what could be waiting for us. I grab the wall when the entire thing begins to shake as something explodes below. A wave of hot air rushes up towards us, making it hard to breathe. I cover my mouth when the smoke follows, but there's no going back.

We reach the bottom with a loud thump. As soon as we're off, they begin to pull it up again. A fire rages nearby, providing the only light in a dark and smoldering hall. I trip and fall over a body lying in a pool of blood. Lee pulls me to my feet.

"What the hell happened here?" I ask.

Suddenly the lab doors open and we're staring at two men with rifles.

"We've got some traitors here!" one of them yells.

Thinking quickly, I lower my weapon.

"That's rubbish. We are not traitors!" I practically scream. "Don't you dare call me a traitor. I'm General Nolan's daughter and you will let me in."

I rarely drop my father's name, but I need these guards to stand down.

"Gabby?" I hear her voice call and push my way past the guns.

"Dawn!" I yell.

She stands and runs towards me, the look on her face a mixture of relief and disbelief. I hug her tightly and feel her shake as she tries not to cry.

"What are you doing here?" she asks with a watery voice.

Lee steps forward. "Allison's people were keeping us hostage at the river," he explains.

"We knew something big was going down," Jeremy chimes in when he finally joins us.

"Did you send a signal up to Linc?" I ask him.

He nods and a few minutes pass before Raf and Linc come barreling in, guns pointed.

"We're okay," I yell to Linc. His serious gaze scans the room slowly before he relaxes and lowers his gun. "What's the situation like," I ask my sister.

"There are a lot of them Gabs," she says. "Allison and Jonathan Clarke are trying to take the base."

"Do we know where they're basing their operations?" Linc asks.

"The officer's wing," Officer Mills answers.

"Are most of the officers compromised then?" he asks matter-of-factly.

"No," she answers. "There aren't many officers stationed at base right now. The few there were are either dead or imprisoned. Most of the traitors are low level soldiers. We have some injured here that we need to help before doing anything else."

Linc follows her to survey the room and check on the injured.

"Where have you been?" Dawn asks me. I put an arm around her, not wanting to let go.

"Texas," I finally answer her.

She looks at me, expecting more. I'll tell her about it later.

"I'm glad you're okay," I say.

"Was the explosion you guys?" Lee asks.

"Yea," Drew answers. "We needed a diversion."

"When did you get back to base?" I ask Dawn quietly.

"A while ago," she answers. "I have so much to tell you about what we found out in the Wastelands."

"We'll have time," I assure her.

She looks at me with wide-eyed fear and I squeeze her tighter against my side. I allow myself one more moment of my reunion with my sister before we have to figure out a way out of this mess.

Chapter 43

The General

The lights are off, but I know Miranda is sitting next to me in our cell because she won't shut the hell up.

"We need to get out of here," she keeps saying.

"Don't you think I know that?" I snap.

"Well, what are you doing about it?" she retorts.

We heard an explosion and then the power went off. That probably means someone blew the generator. I doubt Allison would've done it. She wants the compound and everything in it. She wouldn't destroy its power source. There must be people still fighting for our side. Thank God.

Allison has never spent much time at the base so she knows nothing about it. That is to our advantage. By now, Jonathan Clarke is probably running the show. I always knew there were quite a few soldiers that were loyal to him, but I could never prove it. The officers and rankers still loyal to me continue to arrive unarmed, unfortunately. But outside we can hear the sounds of resistance.

Who is leading it? I wonder. Dawn is still out there and she knows this compound better than anyone. She's smart. She'll be able to figure everything out if she makes it to the control room.

I welcomed Allison to the compound with open arms not so long ago. I never thought she'd go this far. We fought about the relocation. We fought about an end to the fighting. I assumed that was as far as her disobedience went. As much as she detested the Coles, Allison bought in to all that shite about the Mexicans. If she had her way, the Rebels would march into Mexico and wipe them out. Only, she knows nothing about Mexico. We would be the ones losing everything. We aren't strong enough.

"Miranda, we need to focus on the future," I whisper. "The first boat from England could arrive within months. Those are the people we should be protecting when we get out of this."

"Do you really think these Rebels, who have never set foot in England, are going to risk their lives for an invasion force?" she asks. "To them, they are just another group of foreigners. To them, they are just the slavers in Floridaland. That is why they are fighting back now."

The door opens and Jonathan Clarke enters, his face ghoulishly illuminated by a flashlight. I can make out Allison standing behind him. It's obvious who is in charge now. Soldiers press themselves into the walls as Jonathan steps up to me.

"Get on your feet, General," he commands.

I do as he says, not once taking my eyes from his. He grabs me by the shirt and steers me out the door. I'm taken to my office; which Jonathan has now claimed as his own. There are candles around the room, giving me a glimpse of the people that have betrayed me. I knew some of the soldiers were still loyal to Jonathan and kept a close eye on them, but it obviously wasn't enough.

I'm shoved into a chair. Jonathan swings his leg over the corner of my desk and sits down.

"How the tables have turned, my old friend," he says, his eyes wild.

"You were once my savior, Nolan. You took me from your slave camp and sent me here. I used to revere you," he says with a laugh. "And then, my trusted friend became my jailor."

"People always seem to die around you, Jonathan," I growl.

"Shut up!" he yells. "I did not say you could speak. You care nothing for your soldiers. You only care for power."

"That is not true!" I yell back and he slaps me across the face with his gun.

"You were my interrogator once. Now, you will give me answers," he says.

He stands and starts to pace as I feel warm blood trickle down the side of my face.

Jonathan stops moving and leans in close to me.

"Where are your people hiding?" he asks with a growl.

Before I get the chance to answer, he punches me. I do my best to hide the pain as my lip splits and I taste the metallic flavor of blood as it fills my mouth.

"That was for the lie you were about to tell me. You see, I think you know where they are and you were about to tell me that you don't. Don't lie to me, General," he spits out my rank like it's a curse.

"I don't know," I say.

Jonathan hits me in the ribs and I bend forward, trying to breathe while choking out the blood. Jonathan grabs my hair and lifts my head to look at him.

"Fine. Let's go for what I really want to know," he says before he lets go and I use all my strength to hold my head up. I have been around enough people like him to know that their pleasure is in seeing your weakness.

"Where are the English refugees coming ashore?" he asks.

"They're your people," I wheeze. "Why do you want to stop them?"

"I'm the one asking questions," he snaps, but then he goes on a mad rant, answering my question.

"This is our land," he says, his voice getting louder as he speaks. "In England, we lived in hiding, constantly fearing for our lives. And when we were no longer good enough for even their slums, we were sent to work as slaves."

He licks his lips and snarls at me.

"The government has been overthrown," I say, trying to reason with a mad man. "These are the refugees."

"It is our land!" he screams. "Our food. Our resources. They can't take it away from us!"

He jumps to his feet and kicks the chair out from under me. Still tied to the chair, I crash to the floor and lay in agony as Jonathan kicks me again and again. When he finally stops, I can barely move.

"You see that?" Jonathan asks as he bends down to look in my eyes. "The great General is dying."

He turns to his men, saying, "take him back to the cell and do try to keep him alive, for now."

Two soldiers untie me and drag me to my feet. I hang like a limp noodle between them and they return me to my cell.

Chapter 44

Dawn

I'm surrounded by cooks and clerks, not soldiers. These people shouldn't be here. Then again, neither should I. I was so relieved when Gabby came and took charge. She's over in the corner, making plans with the few officers that are with us.

I'm sitting on the ground with Connor's head in my lap. His breathing is labored. Connor is going to die here and the rest of us may not be far behind. I hold his hand in mine.

"How's he doing?" Jeremy asks as he takes a seat next to us and runs a hand through Connor's hair.

I look up into Jeremy's eyes. Only Jeremy would understand what it feels like to lose Connor. He is good in a place where no one is good anymore. He is kind. He is braver than most of us. He put his arse on the line to sabotage many of the bombs that would've destroyed the Texan capitol. He is like the awkward little brother that you can't help but love.

"He's not going to make it, Jeremy," I say as I look at him, knowing he feels the same way I do.

The evil in this world keeps winning and sometimes it seems like the good people are buggered before they even begin to fight. It's all rubbish. As if confirming that thought, Connor suddenly breathes deeply before his body just goes limp. I feel for a pulse, but I know it's no use. He lost too much blood. I look at Jeremy and the sight of the tears on his cheeks guts me and I can't hold mine in any longer. I'm full on bawling when Gabby walks towards us.

"We need to get out of here," she says. "It's only a matter of time before they find us. We're going to start evacuating people using the crank lift. Captain Collins says his boat isn't far."

"We're just leaving?" I ask.

"Those who aren't soldiers are leaving. The rest of us have a job to do," she says as she reaches down to help me up.

I gently place Connor's head on the ground and grab her hand before she says, "Dawn, I want you to go with them."

"Not gonna happen," I state matter-of-factly as I walk past her toward the officers and other soldiers.

Gabby doesn't try to stop me. She knows I won't just leave.

Officer Lincoln is in charge of the evacuations and as soon as they leave, we split up into three groups, each with a job to do. Officer Mills leads my group towards the control rooms. She carries a flashlight we found in the lab so we can find our way. Our group is the smallest. Lee and I are the only soldiers who might be able to figure out the controls. Officer Mills and a soldier named Kris are our backup.

"Won't the control room be messed up without power?" I ask as we round the corner.

"The control room is protected," Lee explains. "It runs off its own power source. If it didn't, we wouldn't have oxygen down here."

"It's probably being guarded," Officer Mills tells us.

We cut through one of the training rooms and open the door on the other side, slamming it shut just as two soldiers spot us and come running. Kris opens the door only enough stick the nose of his rifle through the opening and fire. We hear screaming on the other side as he fires again. When there is no more noise, he opens the door and we step out into the hall. The two traitors have been shot in the head. I'm glad I'm on the same side as Kris with a shot like that, especially since I'm just now realizing I don't have my gun. I try not to panic, but that only makes it worse.

Officer Mills turns the light off so that we can't be seen. We have to use our hands to feel along the walls for the right door.

"Hey!" someone yells as we're caught suddenly in a flashlight beam. A door to our left opens and more people begin piling out. Without even thinking, Lee and I run at two of them before they can even draw their guns. Lee drops his guy to the floor while I claw at the eyes of mine. He finally throws me off of him just in time for me to see Kris hit the floor.

The man lifts his gun from its holster and trains it on me. He hesitates. I don't know why he does, but it gives me enough time to reach for my knife and plunge it into his foot. He screams as a bullet ricochets by my ear, and his gun clatters to the floor. I reach for it without thinking and lean back, taking point blank aim. I pull the trigger and the man falls at my feet. When the fight is over and Officer Mills turns on her flashlight, I see that his face is twisted into a mix of pain and surprise. It is a face I know. Clay.

Still on the ground, I scramble toward the far wall to get away from him.

"Dawn!" Officer Mills is yelling.

I can barely hear her above the rest of the noise in my head. I feel myself lifted and placed into a chair in the control room.

"Dawn," Lee says, shaking me.

I look at him and reality comes rushing back. Officer Mills stands guard while Lee and I stare at the controls in front of us.

"Oh wow," I whisper.

"What is it?" Lee asks.

Lee is a soldier, but he worked on supply which means he understands more about this place than most. That is why he came with me. I stare at the lights in front of us.

"Every room in the place can be controlled from here," I answer.

"What does that mean?" he asks.

I look up at the screens overhead. They are connected to the security cameras and I can switch between every room. There are soldiers everywhere. I switch to the command offices and inhale sharply when I see Jonathan Clarke and Allison. Most of the rooms are dark so I can't make out who is in them, but my father's office is well lit.

"It means," I begin. "That we can make people go where we want them to go."

I find the chart that tells me the number for each room. The Command offices are 1, 2, and 3. There is a knob marked **O2**.

"Let's see what we can do," I say as I push the buttons for 1, 2, and 3 while turning the **O2** knob.

On screen, we see people beginning to struggle as the oxygen leaves the room. Jonathan Clarke clutches at his throat as he follows his people out into the hall. That will teach him to stay out of my father's office.

There's no time to pat ourselves on the back as Lee switches between views of the halls. He's looking for Gabby's group. We find them in the middle of a fight. Gabby is losing. Lee turns the sprinklers on and Gabby is able to use her attackers' surprise to twist out of his grasp. Lee smiles like I've never seen him smile before.

I look back at the screen that shows the control room hallway.

"Incoming!" I yell as I see two of Jonathan's men running down the hall.

"Finish up!" Officer Mills yells. "I'll hold them off."

She slams the door, closing us inside the room. We don't have much time. I press the number 8 for the prison cells and then the button that says **Doors**. On the screen, we can just barely see the doors swing open in the dark. *Okay, one more thing.*

"Where are the ramp controls?" I scream as we hear gun fire on the other side of the door.

Lee and I scour the entire control board and find nothing.

"I don't see them," Lee yells frantically.

We need to get out there and help Officer Mills, but not before we do this. I start to feel hopelessness creep in until my knee hits something underneath the control desk.

"Of course," I say, getting to my knees. "They wouldn't make it obvious."

I shine the light under the desk and see a small wheel. I begin to turn it and before long, it's turning on its own. I hit one last button and jump to my feet.

"Time to go! We need to get out of here," Lee says, both of us not wanting to face what's in the hall.

It has grown eerily quiet. I open the door slowly and a man's body falls into the room. I scream and jump back. Lee helps me through the door, but I stop in my tracks. There is another dead traitor and next to him, Officer Grace Mills, my friend. She saved my life once and has done it again.

I crouch down to look into her vacant eyes.

"You're with Lucas now," I whisper as I close her eyes and straighten up.

There will be time to mourn when this is all over.

"Let's go," I say.

Chapter 45

Jeremy

"Hurry up!" I yell as we run down the hall.

We don't have far to go. The fire needs to start near the labs. Once it reaches the labs, with all of the explosives and extra gasoline stores in there, the whole place will go up in flames. I look back down the hall as I wave my group into the open training room.

I follow them in at the last minute before a squad of traitors step into the hall. I watch from my hiding place as they enter the labs. They're looking for us. Dammit. We barely made it out.

I look around the training room... it's perfect. There are so many things in here that can feed the flames. Mats, ropes, and wooden targets.

I point to Drew and motion for him start pouring the gas around the perimeter of the room. He nods, but doesn't move. I crawl across the floor to see what his problem is.

"If we start this too soon, they might not make it out," he whispers urgently. "We need to give them time."

"You're letting your feelings interfere with the mission," I say, grabbing him by the shirt collar and pulling him close.

"Pour the gasoline," I growl, releasing him and shoving him into the wall.

He glares at me, but when I reach for the can to do it myself, he grabs it and starts to pour.

I run a hand through my sweaty hair as my squad douses the room. This plan is crazy. It's risky and relies on guesses rather than facts. The underground base has to be getting oxygen from somewhere. Officer Mills thinks the control room is the key, but if she's wrong, we're all screwed. We might still be screwed even if she's right.

I pace back and forth and shine my flashlight along the walls so that we can all see. A soldier brings me a rag. I walk to the other side of the room and dip it in the gasoline. Then I wait. *Please, Dawn, give us time to get out before you flood this place with oxygen and turn it into an inferno.*

A door bursts open across the room and traitors begin piling in. It's now or never. I light the rag and throw it into the pooling gasoline. The gas vapors explode into a fireball as we dive for the exit. We run down the hall to the chorus of screaming traitors behind us.

Chapter 46

Gabby

We took out the guards, but it cost us. We lost two soldiers. There are probably more guards coming and we have no idea where Jonathan and Allison are.

"Turn off your lights," I whisper urgently to the rest of my crew.

Lights go off one by one until we're in complete darkness waiting for Dawn and Lee to open the doors. I press myself against the wall and crouch down. I run through every scenario that could've happened to my sister. I worry about Dawn every second of every day. I can't help it.

I suggested Lee go with her. No one actually believed that he'd be able to figure out the controls, that was all Dawn. I wanted Lee to be with her because he is the only person I trust to protect my sister when I can't. She has to be okay. Lee wouldn't let anything happen to her.

I hear something on my left. The doors to the cells are beginning to open.

"Shay!" I whisper urgently to her crouched figure across the hall.

"Yeah?" she responds.

"Take your squad into the second cell. Get as many people out as you can and head for the ramp."

"Sure thing," she says as I take my soldiers in the opposite direction, further into the cell block.

I turn my light on before stepping through the doorway and see some familiar faces staring back at me. They're frightened.

"Soldiers, follow us towards the ramp," I order.

They completely snap to and make their way past me at the door.

"Is anybody hurt?" I ask.

"Gabby," Miranda says in a small, pained voice.

I shine my light on her and rush over. The General is slumped against the wall covered in his own blood. I think he's dead until he coughs weakly.

"We need to get him out of here," I say, putting one of his arms over my shoulder, but Miranda doesn't move.

"Miranda!" I yell, but she stills doesn't move.

"Mom, please," I stammer.

The words stick in my throat, but seem to snap her out of it and she helps me get the General to his feet. We leave a smear of blood behind us as we carry him down the hall.

"Stay with us, dammit," I say to him.

We slow down as his weight becomes too much.

"I need to stop," Miranda says.

"Don't you dare," I say, gritting my teeth as I strain to keep going.

There are explosions behind us. Soldiers rush by and one stops to help. When we finally reach the car park, it's full of flames. Miranda is near the point of collapse when another soldier steps up to help out.

As we cross the car park toward the ramp, a voice screams at us from behind. "Stop!"

I turn my head and see Jonathan catch up with us. We keep moving.

"I will shoot!" he yells.

Miranda wheels around and a shot rings out. Her knees hit the concrete first and then she falls to her side. It happens so suddenly. *My mother is dead.*

A loud cry rises up from my father and he lurches towards Miranda, taking me with him. We tumble to the ground and I'm pinned beneath him. Jonathan stands over us.

"You ruined everything!" he yells, pointing his gun at my head. "If I'm going down, you're going down with me!"

Suddenly, Allison runs up to Jonathan and pulls on his arm.

"Come on!" she yells desperately. "We need to go!"

Then, as if in slow motion, Jonathan takes a blade from his belt and plunges it into her stomach. There is shock and betrayal on her face as she stumbles backward, falling to the ground as blood pours from her body. Then Jonathan turns toward me once again. As he glares down at me, he doesn't see a large man walking up behind him. He doesn't look at anyone but me until he feels the rope around his throat. He struggles, but it's too late. His eyes bulge and his mouth opens, but nothing comes out. A moment later, he stops struggling and his body goes limp as he drops to the floor.

The weight of the General is lifted from me and then, just before I pass out, I see the face of the man as he bends down to take hold of me.

Lee.

Chapter 47

Dawn

Smoke is rushing up from below. Lee and I made it to the ramp in no time, but there's no sign of Gabby or the others.

"Do you think something went wrong?" I ask Lee.

"They're running out of time," he says, just as worried as I am. I've never seen Lee so scared before.

"The oxygen that we released is pouring into every room now, feeding the fires. It'll be hard for them to escape the fires once they're going," he says.

"Any word?" Officer Lincoln, asks as he walks up to us.

"Not yet," I say before turning when we hear screaming.

It isn't our people. Terrified traitors are running up the ramp.

"I'll take care of this," Officer Lincoln says as he goes to round them up.

Lee and I follow his lead. The traitors drop to the ground with their hands in the air, blubbering about a fire. Jeremy and Drew aren't far behind. Choking, they come running up the ramp.

"We lost three," Drew says, heaving and hacking.

"We lost Kris and Grace," I respond.

He looks away so that I don't see his pain. We all loved Officer Grace Mills.

The smoke coming up the ramp thickens as it billows around us. Officers and Rebel soldiers and traitors alike are running out. By this point, everyone has realized that the base is a total loss. I search the faces. *Gabby, where are you?*

"She'd better not have pulled some idiotic hero shit," Lee says as he frantically searches for her.

We can no longer see down the ramp. I find Shay all but collapsed on the ground, coughing and trying to breathe.

"Have you seen Gabby?" I ask her.

She nods, unable to speak through her coughing. She points towards the ramp and Lee takes off running.

"Lee!" I scream after him.

He won't be able to find her alone in all that smoke. I try to follow him, but Drew holds me back.

"Let me go!" I kick and claw at his arm.

"You'll get yourself killed," he yells back.

I turn to face him, tears in my eyes.

"Drew, she's my sister," I say.

At that, he loosens his grip for just a second and I take off.

"Dawn!" I hear him yell as he runs after me.

Down into the smoke and heat, among all the bodies, I go…running bodies, collapsed bodies, and dead bodies. I look around in a panic and then see Jonathan across the ramp. He is clawing at his neck and when he falls to the ground, I see Lee standing over him. Drew has caught up and we rush over. Gabby is trapped under a body and our mother is lying dead next to her. Drew rolls the man off of her and I gasp in recognition as he lifts my father. Lee bends down and lifts Gabby into his arms.

I follow them, but stumble in the dense smoke and confusion. Someone grabs my foot and trips me. It's Allison and she has a knife sticking out of her stomach. I get to my feet. No time to think. I drag her by her shirt as the ramp starts to collapse, drowning out the screams of those who didn't make it. We leave a trail of blood and it takes all of my strength, but I keep going as the ground becomes unbearably hot.

"You aren't dying here," I say, clenching my jaw as I strain. "You saved me once. This is payback."

After going a few more feet, I realize her twitching has stopped and her eyes are vacant.

"No!" I scream.

Drew has run back to help me and he tries to pull me away from the dead traitor.

"She's gone," he says as I fight to drag her anyway.

Allison was good once. We all were.

Drew's grip around me tightens as he whispers into my ear, "your sister needs you."

I stop fighting and let him lead me away from Allison and above ground. Out in the open, Gabby is lying down, but her eyes are open. She's okay. Lee is kneeling by her side with tears running down his face. I've never seen him cry. He reaches toward her and strokes her hair, only stopping when I come running up beside him.

"Gabby," I whisper, flooded with relief as her eyes focus on me.

"Hey Dawny," she says as she tries to smile, but ends up coughing instead.

Lee helps her sit up to keep whatever she is coughing up from going back down. She falls back, but Lee and I catch her.

"The world is spinning," she says faintly.

We keep her upright because we don't want her passing out on us.

"It isn't safe here. We need to get going," Jeremy interrupts. "Captain Collins says his boat has dropped anchor near here."

We lift Gabby to her feet. She tries to help us, but she's too weak.

"Whoa!" she grunts, grabbing on to us. "It feels like someone is spinning my head."

She is too weak to walk so Lee lifts her gently into his arms.

As we follow the group toward the river, I look back one more time and watch the flames near the ramp before focusing ahead, unsure of what comes next for a fractured Rebel force without a home.

Chapter 48

Gabby

I open my eyes and have no clue where I am until I feel the rocking. *I hate boats.* I look around and see three boys watching me. Matty realizes I'm awake and comes closer.

"Antonio, Henry, she's awake!" he says excitedly. "I'll go find Dawn!"

He runs off while the other two stay staring.

"Dawn told us to stay here until you woke up," Captain Collin's son, Henry, explains. "You're in the Captain's quarters."

That's why I don't recognize this place. I've been on this ship enough by now to recognize every other part.

Dawn comes rushing in with the Captain on her heels. She sits on the bed and looks at me for a moment before asking, "How do you feel?"

"I think I'm okay," I say, feeling a lot better than I did.

"We're on a boat," she explains as if I wouldn't be able to tell.

"In my quarters," the Captain intercedes roughly, obviously none too happy about the situation.

"How long have I been out?" I ask.

"You've been in and out for a few days," Dawn explains. "Do you remember what happened?"

"Of course I do," I snap. "I'm not some dumb prat."

"I've missed you sis," she says, laughing, and then adds, "we're heading to Vicksburg."

"Why the hell are we going there?" I say as I sit up a little too fast and fall back.

"Dad says that the Capitol is the best place to plan our next move," she says. "Dad?" I say. "How is the General?"

It all comes rushing in…the images of dragging my father through the burning compound and my mother dying right beside me.

"He'll be okay," Dawn answers. "He's worse off than you, but he pushed the Captain to give you his quarters so you didn't have to be below deck with everyone else."

I nod and she takes my hand and says, "you got him out."

"Miranda…" I stammer, my voice thickening.

"She's dead," Dawn says quietly.

"I know," I say, looking away. "I saw it."

The look on Miranda's face as she was shot. Her body falling to the ground. That's something I'll never forget. The tears blur my vision and I suddenly need to get out of this bed. *I need air.*

"Move," I suddenly snap at Dawn, yanking my hand from hers.

She steps back and I scramble out of bed and toward the door. Dawn knows me well enough not to stop me, but she does follow closely.

I run out of the room and don't stop until I'm at the side of the boat, gripping the rail. The fresh air allows me to breathe more easily.

Dawn gives me a minute before joining me at the rail.

"What happened down there?" she asks. "To our…" She stops herself. "To mom."

"Jonathan happened. He shot her." I say, looking away. "She died in front of me."

As Dawn's hand reaches for my shoulder, we're suddenly interrupted.

"Now that she's gotten some of her strength back, can I have my damn room?" Captain Collins asks loudly. "A captain needs to get away from you crazy folks."

Without looking, I spin away from both of them and head below deck. I need to see the General. His bunk has been curtained off to give him the privacy to heal. One of the medics tells me I can go talk to him, but my feet won't move. Someone pulls back the curtain to change his bandages and I see him. He still looks pretty bad, but he is awake.

Between all the people rushing about, the General looks up and our eyes meet. I wasn't sure if he'd remember everything that happened, but it is clear now that he does. Our connection is cut off when the curtain closes once again.

Chapter 49

Dawn

My sister stares into the distance with vacant eyes and I can't seem to reach her. My father is fighting for his life, my mother is dead, and I have turned into a mass murderer. So many people died because of what we did in that control room. I'm tired of the fighting; tired of the killing and I haven't a clue when or if this will all be over. I just want to sleep in. I want to read. I want to just hang out with my boyfriend and my sister. I want to fish with Ryan, if he's even still alive. I want this all to end.

I'm staring into the dark water when Lee joins me.

"Dawn," he says, greeting me.

"Hi Lee," I say quietly.

"You okay?" he asks.

"Do you believe in Heaven, Lee?" He doesn't answer right away so I look at him.

"I don't know," he says honestly.

"Your family at the caves did," I say.

"I want to believe in it all," he says, his voice low. "I want to believe in something better than this, but I guess it's kind of messed up to believe only when you need to."

"I don't think it is," I reply softly. "Drew believes in it without question. I guess I'm jealous of that."

"Me too. Sam never had any doubts and I was always envious," he says.

"If Heaven is somewhere out there, that's where Sam is," I say, smiling slightly.

"Knowing my brother, he's probably hunting with the same people that shot him in those woods," he says with a laugh.

"If they can stand his constant yakking," I say as I laugh too, and it feels good.

"They won't mind," he answers, "because it's Sam."

"Yeah," I say as I sit down and lean back. Lee does the same. "He's up there worrying about me and laughing at you for falling in love with Gabby." I elbow him and he looks surprised. "You need a god to help you with that one. I don't know if Gabby can love anyone the way you want her to. She doesn't even love herself," I say.

"Yeah, I know," he says, sighing.

He's silent for a minute before saying, "if there is a Heaven, we're probably going to see Sam real soon. I don't see us all getting out of this. The way things have been going..."

"I know," I say, cutting him off.

My heart can't take much more of this loss.

Lee reaches out to me and then quietly leaves me to my thoughts as I watch the thousand stars winking in and out of the nighttime sky.

Chapter 50

The General

"General Nolan," Adrian Cole says, greeting me at the docks.

I lean on one of my soldiers as we walk off the ship.

"Have your soldiers follow mine to the barracks," he says.

I'm relieved to see Adrian's cart pull up. Most of my strength was left back at the burning base.

"We've fixed up a nice room for you and an office in the government building," Adrian informs me as we make our way to his office.

"Are you briefed on what has happened?" I ask.

"Yes sir, the outbreak and the uprising at base are tragic events. We were lucky that Vicksburg was untouched by the disease," he answers.

"Lucky is an understatement," I say. "Should we wait for your advisers?"

"No," he says. "I don't trust a single one of them. We'll proceed without their assistance."

"Okay," I say.

Smart kid, not trusting those that were around when his aunt was running things.

Our cart passes signs everywhere of people just trying to survive. The streets are crowded with people and I've only seen one soldier policing the crowds. Tia Cole's curfew is a thing of the past. It's hard not to notice some of the burned-out buildings that were destroyed during the Rebel attack. It shames me to see the distrust in the eyes of the Texan citizens. Before, this city always felt like a prison. Now, there are parts of the wall that have yet to be rebuilt and disorder everywhere I look.

"Now, tell me why the labs were unavailable to create a vaccine," I say. "We had no medicinal help from your city."

"We've had our own bits of uprising here," he explains. "I believe you know Allison and the trouble she brings."

"Damn that woman!" I curse. "The Rebel cause is almost dead because of her."

"So, what do you need from us?" Adrian asks calmly.

"No one knows this yet, but I'm sending a mission into Moreno controlled Mexico," I respond.

"Are you mad?" Adrian asks angrily. "With all due respect, sir, that's a suicide mission and you damn well know it."

"Mr. Cole, I have been told that you are aware that Joseph Kearn and your late aunt and uncle created a biological weapon right here in this city. Kearn must be stopped. A lot of lives are at risk here. You know that England is coming. The people are fleeing a dying land. We think that Kearn can unleash death and destruction on all of them. We know how the Morenos feel about the English. They won't want ships of them landing in Floridaland or anywhere else."

"I know you're right, General," he says, "I just can't wrap my head around sending people into that part of Mexico. If they are caught, it's game over."

"Mr. Cole," I say, trying to keep my anger at bay, "you don't think they'll stop at the English, do you? They'll come for Texas too."

"How sure are you that Kearn is with the Morenos?" he asks.

"He's there."

Chapter 51

Gabby

I never thought I'd be back here. So much has happened in this city. I walk by the government building where I once perched on the roof as a sniper ordered to take out civilians. My feet take me to the familiar spot where I watched the labs, and everyone inside, burn.

I'm surprised to find that I'm not the only one here in the middle of the night. Adrian sees me walk up beside him, but doesn't move. The last time I was in Vicksburg, I learned that Adrian spends quite a few sleepless nights here. He sees the labs as his greatest failure. His citizens, including his best friend Landon, died here.

"Hi," I say tentatively, not sure how much he still hates me.

It's been a while, but stealing his key card to help destroy the labs and kill the people inside isn't exactly something you get over.

"Hi Gabby," he responds quietly. "I knew you'd be here tonight."

"How?" I ask.

"Do you really think the General's daughter isn't being watched?" he asks.

I want to be mad, but I'm just relieved he isn't avoiding me. After a drawn out silence, I can't take it anymore.

"I'm sorry, okay?" I say.

"Sorry for what?" he snaps, turning toward me.

"What do you want to hear? How much I regret my part in that night? How Landon is never far from my thoughts?" I pause. "Do you want me to tell you that it haunts me? Because it does and I deserve it. I deserve all of it ... "

"Gabby, you were one of the only people I trusted. You and Lee. Your betrayal left me on my own with no one to trust," he says, grabbing my shoulders and twisting me to face the scorched building. "All of this, well, this was going to happen with or without you. We're all caught up in something we can't really control."

Maybe I misjudged him. I know what his family did to him, and how much he has sacrificed. The General trusted him. Lee trusted him. And I betrayed him by stealing his key card to help Allison set the lab building on fire.

"We were friends, weren't we?" I ask.

"Yes, we were," he says sadly before walking away.

I don't move as I listen to his footsteps echo through the empty streets. I stay there, staring at the ruins. I can't get over everything that's happened, but I can try to live with it. I can try not to let the dead cloud every thought. When I see my sister coming toward me, sunrise at her back, it all becomes a bit easier. She doesn't know everything that happened here. She doesn't look at me like I'm wounded. She just smiles and it reminds me of happier times. In London, things were never easy for us, but we had each other. I've missed that.

I loop my arm through hers as we head to get some food. Two spots in the mess have been saved for us. Shay is there. So are Lee and Jeremy and Drew. These are our people. I sit across from Lee and his eyes immediately tell me that he's been remembering things too. This city is where things changed between us. He was there for me when I needed it. I love Lee. I've known that for a while. In another life we could've even been happy together, but we're at war and we might not both come out of this alive.

Before I get a chance to eat much, a Texan soldier arrives at our table to tell us that the General would like to see me and Dawn immediately.

The soldier leads us to the government building and up the stairs to a large office.

"Come on in," the General says. "Take a seat wherever you like."

He is writing something at his desk and doesn't look up as we sink into a plush leather couch. The silence is deafening.

"Stop fidgeting," Dawn whispers as she grabs my hand to still it.

Finally, the General stops what he is doing and focuses on us.

"Good morning soldiers," he says.

I almost laugh at the formality.

"Good morning, dad," Dawn retorts.

A smile cuts across his face.

"Why are we here?" I ask.

Dawn pinches me as she always does when she thinks I'm being rude or insubordinate. The General doesn't seem to mind.

"You are here because our work isn't finished," he begins. "You're both familiar with the name Joseph Kearn?"

"He's the one who built the biological weapon with Adrian's aunt and uncle and took it to Mexico," I answer.

"He is doing so with the help of the Moreno cartel. They control a large portion of Mexico along the coast. There is a small town there named Los Condenados," he explains.

"That's where we think Kearn is now, right?" I ask.

"Yes," the General continues. "Moreno controlled territory is dangerous. They don't appreciate outsiders on their land."

"That's putting it lightly," Adrian says as he enters the room. "Really? You're sending them?"

"Listen Adrian," I say angrily, getting to my feet.

"Sit down, Gabby," he demands, cutting me off. "You have no idea what's going on."

"Sending us where?" Dawn asks.

That's the question that I probably should have asked as well.

"I hadn't gotten to that yet," the General says. "But, yes, Adrian, you may come in and join us," he says in a way that tells me he's irritated.

That's never good.

Adrian perches on the arm of the couch with his arms crossed over his chest and his face stern.

"You want us to go into Moreno territory," I say when it finally comes to me. "You're sending us to Mexico."

"Why us?" Dawn asks.

"Because," the General says, tilting his head to the side, "you're the only people I can trust."

Chapter 52

Dawn

"General, you have more experienced soldiers that you could send," Adrian says. "Gabby and Dawn aren't even officers. They're too young and too weak."

"That's rubbish!" Gabby argues. "I am not weak!"

"Gabby this isn't the time for stupid heroics," Adrian says, refusing to wilt under Gabby's glare. "This is the time for logic and extensive planning. This is what officers are trained for."

"You're wrong, Adrian," the General states. "None of those officers were able to do a thing about the traitors at the Rebel base. These girls saved us all, and it wasn't logic that they used. It was spontaneity, and out-of-the-box thinking. My officers are trained to do the opposite. You didn't see it, Adrian. These girls, my girls, they beat Jonathan Clarke."

And suddenly he sounds like a proud father. Gabby rolls her eyes. Her sarcasm is her favorite defense against actually feeling something, and I'd hit her if I wasn't so scared.

"So, let me get this straight," Gabby says, "you want us to get into the most heavily guarded territory on this side of the planet. What happens if we get caught?"

"You can't," my father answers.

I might be seeing things, but his eyes look sad. I don't for a second think he'll actually shed a tear, but he isn't okay with this. I don't see how we can do better than the officers. We're just a couple squaddies.

"Think about this, General," Adrian pleads, "It's too risky."

"I don't know what else to do, and I sure as hell don't know who to trust anymore," my father replies as he fidgets nervously. I can see his injuries are still taking a toll on him. Every movement comes with a wince of pain.

"This is our best option and I believe you can do it," he says directing his words to us, rather than Adrian. He musters all the strength he can to stand and come closer. "I have watched you girls pull off amazing things. Dawn, you broke Gabby out of a heavily secured slave camp. You met Americans along the way that trusted you when their culture tells them not to trust anyone. Then you were shot and, once again, gained the trust of people, this time in Cincinnati, when it took me years to prove myself to them. You amazed me again when you went to the Wastelands and came back to tell us about it. The way that people trust you, and genuinely like you, is your greatest asset."

He pauses and looks to Gabby. "Gabby you've been on Kearn's trail for a while now and haven't given up. You are resilient and, yes, brave to the point of stupidity sometimes. That's why I need you. That's why our people need you. That's why I have to send you when everything inside of me is telling me not to. Everything is at stake."

Even Gabby doesn't have a response to that. Suddenly, we're no longer sitting in front of the General. It's our father, the man who abandoned us to save us; a man who is giving his life and asking his flesh and blood to do the same.

"I'll do it," I say softly.

My father stares at me.

"I can't order you to do this," he says. "This kind of mission has to be volunteer only."

"I'm in too," Gabby states.

Adrian sighs and my father leans back in his chair. Part of him was hoping we would say no.

Chapter 53

Gabby

"Of course, I'm coming," Jeremy says when I ask him to join our team.

The General made me a commissioned officer so that I can lead this mission. Dawn wants to help, but she doesn't want to be in charge. We were also told we can decide who goes with us because we need to be able to trust them completely. There are very few people who fit the bill. Jeremy is one of those people. He has an excellent shot that will come in handy and, after everything we've been through together, I trust him completely.

A part of me doesn't want to ask the people that I care about. I want them all to stay here, safe. If I had a say, Dawn wouldn't be coming, but that isn't up to me.

"Thanks, Jeremy," I say. "There's one more thing, though."

"Yeah?" he asks.

"Are we good? Because I need people that have my back and I don't think you've forgiven me yet."

"It's not the forgiving that's hard, Gabby. I did that a while ago. It's the forgetting that's a bitch," he pauses. "With that said, I'll always have your back."

I nod and shake off the tears. We may not all come back from this and I can't imagine life without any of them.

"I wish I didn't have to ask you this," I admit.

"I would've come anyway," he says.

I place a hand on his shoulder before leaving to ask another one of my friends to risk their life. If we screw this up, it's a one-way mission for all of us.

I bump into Raf outside the barracks, which is good because I would've gone looking for him next. We haven't talked much since I learned he followed us from St. Louis. He didn't think the events at the base were his problem, so he evacuated with the techs. I've been avoiding him ever since.

"We're going to Mexico and you're coming with us," I say.

"Of course," he responds. "That's what I've been waiting for. The Carlita cartel wants in on this."

"Fine," I respond, walking past him quickly.

I go off to find Shay, leaving Lee for last. There is no question in my mind what he'll say. He's going to say yes to risking his life for me, yet again.

Chapter 54

Dawn

Things are moving quickly because we don't have much time to get this done. The weapon needs to be destroyed before England's relocation efforts are in full swing. The General isn't saying it, but we're talking months, not years.

There are people sitting around this room who won't be here when this is finished. My father has made that pretty clear to everyone. Yet, here they are, ready to go.

I grip Drew's hand tightly. When I told him about the mission, he was in before I even finished asking. Then I told him about the dangers and he just said that he's going if I am. I crawled into his bunk last night and he just held me. In a perfect world, he'd hold me every night. I don't know what this world is, but it is far from perfect, and I can barely imagine what normal is.

At the last minute, Gabby asked me to talk to Lee. She just couldn't do it. As he listened to me explain the risks, he was the same stoic guy that I met in the caves. He doesn't care about the risks. He said he wants to be there to keep me and Gabby safe. Gabby would get narked if she knew that Lee thinks he needs to protect her, but it comforts me.

No one says a word until my father walks in with Adrian and Officer Lincoln behind him.

"Has what we're asking you to do been explained to all of you?" the General asks.

I nod along with everyone else.

"Gabby, Dawn, Lee, Jeremy, Drew, Shay, and Rafael," he says the names for Adrian to write down. "I'm sending Officer Lincoln with you as well."

Gabby is about to object, but my father stops her.

"He isn't going to out rank you, Gabby," he says. "You will be leading this mission, but Linc has some skills that will come in handy down there."

He pulls out a map and rolls it open on the table in front of us. He then nods to Adrian and steps back.

"The border isn't far from here," Adrian begins. "The fighting is at a standstill with the Texan forces on our side and the Mexican forces on the other. That part of the border is occupied by troops from the Cillo cartel. The good news is that we currently have a treaty with them. That's why the fighting has stopped."

"I have some contacts with them," Lee offers. "I helped negotiate the treaty after the Rebels conquered Texas."

"Good," Adrian says. "You will need those contacts. As friendly as we act toward one another, they will still be reluctant to let you behind their battle lines to travel through their territory. I'll send a letter signed by both General Nolan and myself with you. They still don't trust us, but it may just be enough. Whatever you do, don't tell them the real reason you're there. We don't want them marching on the Morenos or you all will be caught in the middle of a war between two powerful cartels. Once you reach the southern border of Cillo land, Rafael will guide you from there."

"How are we getting to the border?" Gabby asks.

"Like I said, it's not far," Adrian answers. "We have a supply run to our troops tomorrow. You will go then."

"Each of you needs to head to the armory today," my father says. "Weapon up! You will use them. As for other supplies, we don't know how long you'll be gone, so we will make our best judgments about how much to send with you. This is it, people. Everything the Rebels have accomplished will mean nothing if you fail."

His hands are shaking as he speaks, and he deliberately looks away from me as he leaves the room. I hurry after him.

"Dad!" I yell after him, struggling with the term.

He stops in the middle of the hallway and turns around.

"Dawn, I ..." he stammers, unable to finish his sentence.

The great and powerful General Nolan would never show his emotions. He'd be cold and cut off. The General isn't the man standing in front of me now. For the first time that I can remember, I'm looking at my father; a father who has no choice but to send his daughters into danger, a father who believes that there is a good chance one or both of his kids won't be returning, a father who is scared.

"We're going to get this done," I say.

"I know you are," he responds.

"And we're coming back," I state matter-of-factly.

He smiles at that. We both know that there are no sure things, but it feels good to say it.

"I have something for you," he says, reaching out and handing me a folded letter.

I look at it, confused.

"Read this when you leave on your mission," he says.

"Okay," I say with a nod and there's a long, uncomfortable pause.

"Well, I should head to the armory," I say, pointing behind me.

When I turn and start to leave, I barely take two steps before my father calls to me.

"Dawn?" he says tentatively.

"Yeah?" I respond, not turning to face him.

"I love you," he answers, his voice breaking.

I smile, still facing away from him. I start walking again, and the words slip out of my mouth before I can stop them,

"Love you too, Dad."

Chapter 55

Gabby

"We need to be armed at all times, but we can't go marching into Mexico like some damned army," I tell the group as we head into the armory. "We have to operate under the assumption that no one in Mexico is our friend, not even our supposed allies. No one will trust us, so let's return the disfavor. We will receive help from certain cartels, but they'll want us off their land as quickly as possible."

No one argues with anything I'm saying. *That's a first.*

My father put me in charge, because he knows I'm more likely to run toward a burning building than away from it. He also trusts that I don't have a problem doing some of the things we might need to. *How like him I have become.*

"Lee, I need you to go to the kitchen to see about some provisions. Drew, go with him. Jeremy, you and Shay head for the clinic, I want basic medical supplies. Dawn, find Adrian for some other supplies; flashlights, matches, whatever you think we'll need," I say. "Also, get him to finish that letter he's writing to help us at the border. Linc, Raf pull the maps. By the time we leave, I want to know every inch of the landscape across the border."

They all look at me, a bit amazed, and scatter when I snap, "Well, what are you waiting for?"

I take a holster and wrap it around my waist, sliding two hand guns into it before strapping on a sheathed blade. *I'm ready.*

Chapter 56

Dawn

Goodbyes are hard.

We try our best not to drag them out. I step in front of my father and look into his face. The tears that have been building up let loose when I see his glassy eyes. He wraps me in a strong hug like he never has before. For the minute or so that he holds me, I feel safe. I feel like he can make everything okay, because, well, he's my dad.

Gabby refuses to say goodbye to anyone, because she says we'll see them again as if that's a sure thing.

Drew helps me into the truck where we sit on top of the food crates that are being sent to the soldiers at the border. We shut the door and can no longer see the people we're leaving behind. Leaning back against the wall, I wipe the last remnants of tears from my eyes.

No one speaks. There's nothing to say.

Ryan once told me, "You can't be brave until you are first afraid. Courage is not the absence of fear but the will to overcome it."

It was something his father, Chief Smith, used to say that to him when he was a child in Cincinnati. Something like that sticks with you. We start moving and I pull a flashlight out of my pack and unfold my father's letter.

Dear Gabby and Dawn,

By the time you read this, you will be well on your way to Mexico.

I'm so proud of you and know you'll do your very best. Never forget that you're on a mission to save our people. I'd like to say "stay safe," but I gave up the delusion of safety years ago. None of us are safe. The world isn't a safe place, our people saw to that centuries ago when they let loose a series of changes that destroyed the global order and forever altered the landscape.

England is dying and its people need a new home. Your mission is an essential part of a larger plan to provide such a home for our people.

I can't begin to undo the pain and suffering my absence caused you for all these years, and I know that knowing that your mother and I tried to leave you in good hands doesn't change things. If there is any trust left, any love left, please believe that we did it for you. We did it to save you and to save our people.

As you begin your mission, you will no doubt suffer many risks. But, I know you will succeed. I've known it ever since I first discovered that you were in Floridaland. Both of you possess a strong will and believe in sacrificing your own safety for the cause, just like your mother. Yes, I know that this will sound strange and unbeliev-able, but she missed you every day of her life. That separation and the strain of the Rebellion, was too much for her. It broke her, and when she saw you again here in this land, the pain and guilt was too overwhelming. But she loved you, as do I.

I can't begin to explain all the circumstances that sent me to Floridaland. I hated the assignment, but it was the perfect cover under which to execute our greater plan – preparing for the migration of our people.

This is a broken land, as you know. "The States," as they used to call them, have suffered their own calamities. Hundreds of millions have died in the chaos that both nature and evil created over the past several hundred years, things I'm sure they never taught you in school.

But now, you, my daughters, have the opportunity to change the course of our history. You and our allies in Mexico and the Wastelands have the chance to shape the future.

What has kept me sane and focused through all that has happened, is the knowl-edge that you two were alive. Everything I have done, I have done for your future. I'm so proud of the women you have become, and I know our people can depend on more than just one Nolan from here on out.

Until we meet again, love always,
Dad

I turn off the flashlight as tears streak down my face, and I hug the letter to my chest. After a while, I nudge Gabby next to me and hand her the letter filled with my father's words.

"Read this," I whisper.

Chapter 57

Dawn

Adrian said the border isn't far, but, let's just say, the ride isn't easy or short. We feel every bump and rut in the unpaved road. After a while, we pull up to a Texan checkpoint and hear voices.

"Let me just check the back," someone says.

I tense up.

"It's okay, Dawn. We're legit this time, remember?" Drew whispers to me.

I relax. He's right. The back door opens and the light is blinding. I shield my eyes to try to see the soldier standing there. Texan soldiers still make me uneasy. They chased us all over the Texan lands and then killed Corey's parents for helping us. They made Matty join them to come after us. He's the only one that survived that mission. Their blind obedience reminds me of Jonathan's men and we all know how that turned out.

"What are y'all doin' back here?" the soldier asks us, smiling.

It isn't an accusation. Gabby hands him our credentials from Adrian and he grins again. "Y'all are goin' to the border?" he asks, and Gabby nods. "I'd kill for some of that action. Most of us 'round here are bored as hell."

"Can we get moving?" Gabby snaps, never one for politeness.

"You don't sound like no Texan," the soldier says as he leans in and looks around at all of us.

"And you don't sound like someone who wants to be arrested for insubordination," Gabby snaps again.

At that, he closes the door quickly and the truck lurches forward. We pass through the next checkpoint without a problem, and a few hours later we come to a stop. I climb down from the back of the truck, and, when my eyes adjust to the sunlight, I see that we're standing in the middle of a sea of Texan soldiers.

"Lee," a small man in uniform says as he rushes up to us.

"Travis," Lee says as he extends his hand and Travis takes it.

"What are you doing back around here?" Travis asks.

Lee pulls him aside for some privacy before quietly telling him, "we're heading toward Mexico."

"Why the hell would you want to do that!?" Travis asks incredulously. "I thought working on that treaty with those bastards would be enough of Mexico for you."

"I can't say any more," Lee replies.

"I get it, man," Travis says, stepping back. "You're all big and important now, on some secret mission."

Lee laughs and claps his friend on the back before motioning Gabby forward.

"Travis, this is Captain Nolan," he says. "She needs to see Briggs."

Travis eyes her up and down before taking her hand and kissing it. I have to hold back a giggle. This guy is even shorter than Gabby and he's just been told that she's an officer which is something I still can't get used to. Maybe it's our lack of uniforms that keeps him from taking us seriously. Gabby pulls her hand away abruptly.

"Travis!" Lee snaps.

"Alright, alright," he responds. "Follow me. I'll take you to see the damn Colonel."

The Colonel is a tall, thin man and he's in the middle of a card game when Travis brings us to him.

"What is it Travis?" he says irritably, not stopping his game.

"I have a Captain Nolan to see you, sir," Travis informs him.

"Captain Nolan," the colonel muses as he lays down another card. "Any relation to General Nolan, leader of those damn Rebels?"

"Sir," Lee beings, stepping forward. "We only need a minute."

"Lee," he says when he finally looks up from his game.

When he stands he is as tall as Lee, but so thin that he still seems small in comparison.

"Gentlemen, I'm sorry, but you will have to continue the game without me," he nods, handing his cards to one of the other players and leading us away.

"Lee, this better be good. I had two aces in that hand," he says before turning to Travis and saying, "I've got this from here."

"Yes, sir," Travis says, hurrying off.

"Sir," Gabby begins. "I am Captain Nolan."

She holds out her hand, but he doesn't take it.

"Let me be frank," the Colonel says. "I don't like the Rebels. I never have and I never will. I was a follower of Tia Cole, and you came in and destroyed everything that we knew. I had family die in that attack while I was down here, fighting those bastards across the border. Then y'all come in and decide that this war ain't worth fighting no more. Texans fight Mexicans. It's what we've always done. This peace ain't gonna last forever, and when the fighting breaks out again, my men are gonna be too fat and lazy to do anything about it because they've been sittin' around doin' nothin', all thanks to you godforsaken Rebels."

"Colonel!" Gabby snaps.

She grabs his arm and leans in to whisper something in his ear. Startled by her action, and then her words, he straightens up. Gabby hands him the letter from Adrian. He reads it quickly and then looks up at us.

"Well, why didn't you say so?" he says before yelling. "Travis!"

Travis runs up to receive his orders.

"Call up a cart from the pound," the Colonel says. "These folks have need of it."

Then, turning to Gabby, he says, "Good luck, Nolan, you're going to need a lot of it."

Chapter 58

Gabby

Word travels fast. I walk out of the Colonel's tent to wait for the cart, and immediately all eyes are on me, the female Rebel captain who just ordered their Colonel around. These Texan squaddies are a sad excuse for an army. All they do is sit around playing cards and drinking like a bunch of proper tosspots. They're all drunk by the time the sun goes down, but that doesn't stop the angry stares directed my way.

To them, my team and I are the Rebels who attacked their cities, which they only heard about after the fact down here on the border. To them, Adrian is Tia Cole's errand boy, who used to deliver dispatches to the border. They weren't in favor of the treaty with the Mexicans and they want to fight their war, but I really don't give a shite.

A young soldier stumbles toward me. I hear laughter and turn to see his friends watching from a distance.

"Hey pretty lady," he slurs. "You up for a good time?"

I stand and walk toward him. His eyes light up with the thought that his ridiculous advance may be working. I get real close to him and press my body into his. He smells like piss.

"I'm always up for a good time," I flirt, sure to be loud enough for his friends to hear.

"Do you like it rough?" he asks, and I roll my eyes, but he can't see that in the dark.

When he tries to smell my hair, I bring my knee up wicked fast, connecting with his crotch. I step back as he doubles over, holding his balls. Next, my fist connects with his eye socket and it feels good. He falls backward, and I deliver one final kick as he lies on the ground.

"I had a good time. Did you?" I ask sarcastically as I shrug and walk past his friends who are now howling with laughter.

"That was awesome," Dawn says when I sit back down.

Lee tries to look at my hand to make sure it's okay, but I pull it away.

"Just getting warmed up," I respond.

"Yeah," Drew chimes in, "Well, I for one can't wait to get to Mexico where everyone likes us."

His sarcasm lightens the mood a bit and we're still laughing when Travis pulls up ready to go. We climb into what he calls his cart. Really, it's just a car with no roof. There's a flagpole in the front where a white flag hangs with a light that illuminates it so the Mexicans can see that we're not a threat. When the treaty was signed, both sides pulled back to create a strip of land that serves as a buffer between the two armies that hate each other. We can see the lights of the Mexican camp as we drive across the expanse.

The cart is surrounded by soldiers, yelling in Spanish, as soon as we pull to a stop. Travis says something to them in Spanish, and then tells us to get out slowly and take our gear with us. As soon as we do, he gets back in the cart and heads back to the Texan camp. He said he didn't want to be here any longer than he had to.

"Raf," I say. "What are they saying?" For whatever reason, he stays quiet. It's almost as if he fears these people.

Then Lee steps forwards unexpectedly and says, "Elia Cillo."

"What are you doing?" I whisper harshly.

"Does anyone speak English?" he continues. "I need to see Elia Cillo."

"What is your business with Elia?" a man with dark features asks, stepping forward.

"Luis," Lee says, acknowledging the man with a nod.

"Lee," he responds coldly.

"How do you know these people?" I ask urgently as the two men stare at one another.

"I was down here for quite some time working on the treaty," Lee explains, not taking his eyes off the man in front of us. "Luis tried to convince his soon to be father-in-law not to sign it."

"I still think it was a mistake," Luis states as his eyes scan the rest of us. "What are you doing here Lee?"

"I'll be happy to explain that to Elia and her father," Lee snaps.

"You can't just come here and expect a meeting," Luis growls.

Lee is about to say something else, but I pull him back.

"We're here on a special mission. I have a letter for your leader's eyes only," I say.

"And who is this?" Luis asks, looking from Lee to me and then to my hand that is still resting on Lee's arm.

He steps closer.

"You're a pretty one, aren't you? For a Brit that is," he sneers.

"And you're a dumb one," I spit. "That fits with what I've heard about Mexicans."

"You must either be really brave, or really stupid to say that when you're standing in the middle of a Mexican army," he says, cocking his head to the side in amusement.

"Look," I start. "I'm Captain Nolan of the Rebels. Your boss is going to want to see me."

"Fine," he says, looking at me intensely. "But I'm not letting all of you in to see him."

"That's fine," I say. "I'll come by myself."

"No!" Lee and Dawn object in unison.

"You can come too, Lee," Luis says with a sigh. "Elia will be cross if she hears that you were here and didn't see her." He spits on the ground and uses his boot to rub it into the dirt before saying, "Vamanos."

The three of us wind our way through the camp in the dark until two heavily armed men stop us.

"You can't bring weapons in," Luis explains.

Unsure, I look to Lee and he nods. I huff as they take my gun and then begin to pat me down. They find every weapon. When I'm unarmed I feel vulnerable and I hate feeling vulnerable. That's why I'm already irritated when a woman walks out to greet us.

She's beautiful with dark hair and piercing dark eyes. Her movements are fluid as she walks toward us in a simple soldier's uniform.

"Elia," Lee greets her.

She grabs his shoulders and plants a kiss on each cheek.

"Uh, hi," I butt in, unable to stay quiet any longer.

I don't know who this chick thinks she is.

"Elia, this is Gabby," Lee tells her.

I ignore the fact that he didn't tell her my rank as I step in front of him and extend my hand. She takes it and pulls me toward her, kissing my cheeks as well.

"Buenos noches," she says. "Come."

She disappears into the tent and we follow her. Luis follows us in without an invitation.

"Elia and I worked together for weeks on the treaty," Lee explains in a hushed voice.

I picture them huddled together in a tent for weeks on end. *I don't like it.*

As if he can read my thoughts, Lee says, "we also worked with the rest of the Rebel team and the Mexican team. There were a lot of us there."

He gives my hand a squeeze before we take our seats.

In walks a man whose very appearance oozes authority. "Buenos noches," he says as he calmly shakes Lee's hand and pats him on the shoulder. "It's been a long time, my friend," he says before he turns to me and asks, in perfect English, "And who is this enchanting creature?"

"Gabby, this is my father, Martin Cillo," Elia introduces us. "Father, this is Rebel Gabby Nolan."

"What can I do for you, my dear?" the Mexican leader asks, cutting to the chase.

"We need safe passage through your lands," I say.

Sitting on the corner of his large desk, he lets my words sink in.

"Safe passage, you say," he restates what I said as he rubs his chin. "And why would I grant you such privilege?"

"For your people and for mine," I say, handing him Adrian's letter.

Chapter 59

Dawn

When Gabby and Lee return, I can see they are arguing.

"Gabby don't," Lee says dangerously. My sister doesn't take the warning.

"It just seems like you two are really close," she pauses. "You know, all those weeks she mentioned where you worked together."

"And her fiancé," Lee states. "We were friends. Like you and me apparently are. Friends. Besides, we don't have time for your jealousy CAPTAIN."

He emphasizes the last word to get his point across. She stares at him as her eyes regain their focus. Message received. She walks off. He stares after her and shakes his head.

"You guys okay?" I ask Lee.

"No," he answers before changing the subject. "We're staying here tonight," he says. "Come on."

We follow him to a tent that has been made up for us. I wish we didn't have to stay. This place makes me nervous. After everything I've heard about the Mexicans, I hate being surrounded by them. As wary as I must look, though, Rafael is downright jumpy.

"What's wrong, Raf?" I ask him.

"The Cillos aren't known for welcoming other cartel members," he says, his eyes shifting to the side as he quickly enters the tent.

I hadn't even considered that. From what I've been told, most of the cartels don't play well with others. They probably think Raf is a spy.

"Dawn," Jeremy grabs my arm and pulls me to where Drew is standing, away from the others.

"Do you know where Gabby went?" he asks.

"No, but I'm sure she'll be back soon," I answer.

"I don't like the looks we've been getting," Drew says, putting a protective hand on my back.

"Gabby can take care of herself," I say, suddenly defensive.

"We all know that," Jeremy agrees. "But no one should go off by themselves while we're here."

Before I get a chance to respond, Gabby appears, walking with Linc.

"See," I say. "She's not as reckless as you think she is."

Thankfully, the rest of the night is uneventful. No one bothers us and we eventually get a few hours of sleep.

"Lee," I hear someone say as I wake to the sounds of hushed voices and roll over to see who it is.

Elia has woken Lee.

"You need to get going," she says.

"It's still dark," he protests groggily.

"Yeah, but my father wants you gone before most of the troops wake up," she replies.

"Good idea," he finally agrees.

"You know where you're going?" she asks.

"We have a map and a guide," he answers.

"The Carlita man?" she asks, a hint of disgust in her tone.

"How else do you expect us to get through Carlita territory?" he asks. "They're even worse than you Cillos."

"I don't think we'll see each other again," she says suddenly.

"No," Lee responds sadly. "I don't think we will."

"Then good luck, mi amigo," she replies.

"Thank you," he says, and then she's gone.

Lee rouses the rest of us and we're out of the Mexican camp before the sun comes up. I feel like I can breathe much easier now, but I also know that I probably shouldn't feel that way. The easy part is over.

The sun finally makes an appearance as we reach the top of a hill. To the east, the sky is brilliant. The clouds are outlined in pinks and oranges as the light bends around them. To the south, the direction we're heading, the sky is still dark as heavy storm clouds rumble against each other.

"Shite," Gabby says. "This is just perfect."

We follow her down the hill and into a valley. If the weather is our only problem today, then I'll call it a success.

Chapter 60

Jeremy

It starts to rain about midday, but we keep going. Rafael says that we should be off Cillo land in two days. Even though we have permission to be here, we keep an eye out for trouble.

"They don't have the men for armed patrols," Linc says. "All their fighting men are at the borders."

"How do you know that?" I ask.

"I know how these things work," he says. "Trust me."

"That's asking a lot when you won't explain how you know," Drew says, backing me up.

"Shut it, guys," Gabby snaps.

I don't get why she isn't asking him to explain. The General said Gabby is the only person in charge on this mission. Then he sends Lincoln. He may not out rank Gabs, but that doesn't mean he isn't going to act like it. Gabby and I escaped the slave camps in Floridaland together and I trust her with my life. I barely know Officer Lincoln.

"Telling information without much explanation is something officers do," I say. "Lincoln can't treat us like subordinates anymore."

"He's never treated me like a subordinate," Gabby says, getting angry.

"You were one of his prized snipers," Drew says with a shrug. "We were told that we would be equals on this mission. That's all we want."

"That's enough!" Gabby snaps. "You guys quit this right now."

"Is that an order?" I ask indignantly.

"Yes," she growls. "It is."

"We're all on edge," Dawn says. "Let's just chill."

She takes Drew's hand and he immediately relaxes. I move to the back of the group and fall in step with Lee.

"You're surprisingly quiet back here," I say.

"I don't like that storm," he says pointing to the sky. It seems to be getting darker, if that's possible. The air has stilled and the clouds roll and crash into each other.

"Look!" Dawn yells as we crest over another hill.

In the distance there is a house. I squint and we move closer. It isn't just a house. It's a village.

"Why would there be a village so close to the border?" Gabby asks.

"They have to put the villages where the fertile land is," Dawn guesses. "They don't really get much of a choice in where they live."

"We aren't going to be welcome there," Lee warns.

"We don't really have much of a choice," Gabby says, making the decision as the wind begins to blow harder and the rain continues to pound. "We can't just stay out here in the open."

She takes off at a jog and we follow her. My overstuffed pack slams against my back with every step. As we get closer, the ground turns to mud.

"There's a barn," Dawn says, gesturing toward a small structure.

Having no other choice, we follow Dawn through a side door into the barn. Lee and I have our weapons drawn in case we aren't the only people in here. I walk the perimeter, but we're alone except for the horses. Dawn walks right up to the nearest one and runs her hand along its nose.

At least we have a roof over our heads. The wind and the rain can't reach us here, but every clap of thunder shakes the shoddy walls and makes me jump. It isn't an easy night for any of us.

Chapter 61

Gabby

The next few days were surprisingly uneventful. The storm gave way to the hot sun by the time we woke in the morning and the rest of the day was quiet and muggy. It seems Linc was right about all Cillo fighting men being mostly at the border because we haven't seen any. Leading is hard and lonely. I was warned that it would be tough- making the decisions and ordering my friends and even my sister around.

The hardest part has been keeping my distance from Lee. I can't sort out any of my feelings, so I just focus on the mission. I've only ever had feelings for two guys before. Drew, in London, was fun and dangerous. I was just having a good time. Jeremy was comfort in a harsh place. I wanted to be there for him after his sister died and it just turned into something more.

All of this walking has given me way too much time to contemplate how much I hurt the people I love. Lee was right. The sound of grass crunching underneath my feet snaps my focus back and I sigh. If we don't make it out of this mission, none of it will matter anyway.

"Stop!" someone yells in front of us and we're quickly surrounded by men on horses, their guns drawn.

We'd been walking through an overgrown pass and had our guard down. I swing my gun around and rest my finger on the trigger, but Raf pushes aside my barrel as he steps forward, yelling something in Spanish. The man in front replies and then orders his men to lower their weapons.

"We've reached Carlita territory," Raf says. "This is my brother, Carlos."

My gun is lowered, but I don't take my finger off the trigger.

"They've been sent to get us to the Moreno border," Raf assures me.

I want to object. We don't know the men looming before us. I glance to Jeremy on my left and then to Lee on my right.

"What if we decline the escort?" I ask Raf.

"We can get there much faster with them," he responds. "The Carlitas have as much to lose as the British do if this mission fails."

I nod and let out a long breath before responding.

"Okay," I say. "Let's go."

Raf's face relaxes as we're helped into saddles. Each of us is riding double. I hold onto the man in front of me as we take off at a gallop.

"You're the leader?" the man asks, having to yell over the wind that whips past us.

"Yes," I answer.

"We've been watching for you for days," he says.

I don't respond. I'm lost in the sound of hooves racing across the hard ground and the movement of the horse beneath me.

I crane my head to check on my sister. Dawn looks much more comfortable than I feel. She gives me a small wave and I send her a tight smile.

We cover more ground in a day than we would in a week on foot, only stopping to rest and water the horses. Raf and his brother Carlos know the land so we find water and cover easily.

By the time we stop for the night, the moon is high overhead and my body is stiff. I slide from the saddle and start setting up our camp. I just need to move. I'm staring into the fledgling flames of the beginnings of a cook fire when Dawn walks up beside me. She puts her arm around my shoulders, but doesn't say a word. As we get closer to Moreno territory, dread fills my heart. I'm not the only one. I see it in the eyes of every person on this mission. I lean my head on Dawn's shoulder until Shay interrupts us.

"Raf and Carlos want to talk to you," she says to me.

Dawn drops her arm and I go off to find Raf. They are sitting on the ground in deep discussion when I walk up. Raf offers me a bit of food and I take it as I sit across from him.

"How much do you know about the Mexican wars?" Carlos asks.

"With Texas?" I ask.

"No," Raf answers, "the cartel wars."

"Not much," I admit. "I didn't know much of anything about Mexico until a few months ago."

"Most of Mexico is controlled by four cartels," Carlos explains. "The Cillo cartel controls most of the border with Texas. The Perez cartel rules the south. The Moreno's control much of the eastern coastline and then there is us. The Carlitas have much of central and western Mexico."

"Is that why you're helping us?" I ask. "You want the eastern coast?"

"No," Raf answers. "We want the fighting to stop. We have lost a lot in this war. Our people starve as the Moreno troops burn our land."

"You're on a mission to destroy a weapon that could wipe out your people," Carlos lowers his voice to a deep growl. "Who do you think they've been testing it on?"

"We've lost entire villages," Raf says. "I've seen bodies upon bodies sprawled in the streets of farming villages and..."

He stops talking and I reach out to take his hand.

"What does the weapon do?" I ask, hoping to finally get some answers.

"It's a virus," Carlos says when Raf fails to answer me. "It spreads through contact. I've seen what it does to people and how fast it can move. They use missiles to..."

He looks away and shakes his head sadly, unable to finish.

"We will stop them," I state. "We won't fail."

Carlos looks into my eyes for a long moment and then nods before speaking.

"Our intel tells us that the weapon is no longer in Mexico," he says.

I drop my hand to my side at Carlos' words and curl my fingers into a fist.

"Then what are we doing here?" I demand.

"You will need to learn where they've sent it and hope they aren't preparing to use it before you get there," he answers.

"They won't use it until the first boats from England arrive," I respond, wishing I was as sure of that as my voice sounds.

"I wouldn't be so sure," Carlos says. "The Morenos purchased this weapon from Texas because they want Floridaland. That's where they'll start. I'm guessing that's where they're taking the weapon, but we can't be sure yet."

"This is a land grab?" I ask, disgusted. "They're willing to kill all of those people for a piece of the colonies?"

"It's not Floridaland itself that is so valuable, but what grows there," Raf explains. "Food is the new gold."

"How does Mya Moreno fit into all of this?" I ask, remembering that my father said to find her. "Who is she?"

"The sister of the Moreno leader, Juan," Raf says.

Why does my father trust her? What does his message to her mean? *The time is now.*

As if he can read my thoughts, Raf continues.

"Juan keeps her locked in that house, under guard. The story is that her father wanted to pass his power on to her, not Juan or their brother Marco. If you ask me, I think Juan killed his father so that he could never announce Mya as his successor. But that's only one theory," he explains.

I nod, choosing not to tell them about the General's message because I still don't understand it myself. "How long until we reach Moreno territory?" I ask.

"Two days at most," Carlos answers.

"Good. Because we're running out of time," I state.

"There's one more thing," Carlos says. "They'll know you're coming."

Chapter 62

Dawn

My arse hurts from this damned horse. The last time I was on a horse, Ryan, Emily, and I were fleeing the American town of Cincinnati. We rode so fast I didn't have time to think about my bum. Ryan and I needed to get to the Republic of Texas before Jonathan Clarke and the Rebels destroyed the whole damn place. The adrenaline overpowered any aches and pains I should have had.

It's our third day with our escort. We will reach the Moreno border tomorrow and part ways with them. Darkness creeps up on us fast and we stop to make camp. I walk up behind Gabby when she is in deep conversation with Carlos, Raf, and a Mexican woman named Ana. Gabs looks up at me and then calls the rest of the group over.

"Ana has experience with the Morenos," she says. "She was a part of their household as a Carlita spy." Gabby steps back, essentially giving Ana the floor.

"Mya Moreno is on the top floor," she begins, her accent thick. "That is where you need to go."

"She'll be able to tell you exactly where Juan has sent Joseph Kearns with the weapon," Carlos cuts in.

"How do we get her to trust us?" Drew asks.

"Dawn and I have that taken care of," Gabby nods toward me, but I stay silent.

My father didn't tell the others about his message for a reason. He trusts his daughters.

"Good," Ana says, not bothering to ask what Gabby meant.

"That's the easy part. First, you must get to Mya. There are old tunnels on the south side of the house. They are no longer in use and hard to navigate," she explains, going on to spell out every turn and twist.

"How is your climbing?" she asks no one in particular.

She glances around and no one responds so she continues with the plan, "I have a rope you can take, but you will need to climb up the garbage chute. It'll take you near the slave quarters."

We listen as the rest of the plan is laid out and then disperse to catch some sleep. By tomorrow afternoon, we will be on foot in an enemy land.

I wake to the sound of water hitting the flames of our cook fire. It sizzles and steams before dying completely.

The landscape has changed slightly from yesterday. The ground we ride across is dry, amplifying the echoes of our speeding horses. We stop twice before midday to rest the horses. I dip my hands into a stream and splash water onto my face. Ana kneels down next to me to take a drink and that's when it happens. There is a shot and then blood is running into the water. Ana falls forward and her splash hits my face. I jump to my feet and run back to the others.

"Find cover!" I scream.

It is only then that I realize my warning is too late. The battle has already begun and the ground is already stained red.

"Dawn! Get down!" Shay yells.

I duck and she takes out the man running behind me. I run toward her and we join the rest of the group. I shoot toward the trees where more men are appearing. I don't know if I hit anyone, but I don't stop firing.

My eyes dart from side to side until I see Gabby nearby. Our eyes meet in relief before we both jump back into the fight. There is a man on his knees in front of me with a large man standing over him. I run the few steps toward them, but he is able to fire before I slam my rifle into his knees. Both men sprawl on the ground. One unmoving and the other trying to stand. I don't give him a chance. One bullet is all it takes before he is as still as his victim beside him. Rafael. He's been shot a number of times. Nothing I can do.

A sharp pain radiates from my back, leaving me paralyzed for a few seconds. Blunt metal slams into my stomach and I double over before hitting the dirt. No one can help me. They are all in the middle of their own fights; All of them except Officer Lincoln. He jumps over a body on the ground and fires. Officer Lincoln never misses.

My chest rises and falls rapidly as I lay on the ground until Officer Lincoln pulls me to my feet as the fight winds down and I search the scared, tired faces. Our Carlita escort lost five men. We lost Rafael. Gabby's right sleeve is soaked with blood.

"It isn't mine," she says as she puts her arm around me.

I find Drew next. He has a large gash above his eye and a bullet grazed his arm, but he is otherwise unharmed.

"I'm okay," he says as he wheezes, still trying to catch his breath.

I don't smile or show my relief because, at that moment, I catch sight of Carlos. Rafael's body is cradled in his brother's lap and his tears leave trails through the blood on his face. Gabby puts a hand on the grieving man's shoulder and squeezes. She knew Raf more than any of us.

"We need to leave this place," Carlos finally says. "This ground is now cursed."

"This was an ambush," Jeremy says. "They knew we were coming and were waiting for us."

"And they won't be the only ones," Gabby says.

Carlos stands and two of his men hoist Raf's body onto the back of a horse.

"Leave the Moreno men to rot. We must return our men to be buried and honored," he tells them before he turns to Gabby and says, "This is where we part ways."

"I'm so sorry," she replies, her voice is soft. "Raf was a friend. Thank you for aiding us."

"Obtain the information and wait along the coast," Carlos says with a grunt. "We'll be there to help once again. I hope to see you there alive."

"Be safe," I say, mirroring his concern.

"Do not fail," Carlos says in farewell. "Please."

Chapter 63

Gabby

The first few days in Moreno territory went like this - we walked until our legs couldn't move any longer, and then pushed them further. We rationed our food and didn't get nearly as much sleep as we needed. I kept everyone going whether they wanted to or not. We lost the first member of our squad, and I'm not ready to lose another just because we weren't vigilant enough. We posted a watch at night and someone was always scanning behind us as we moved.

We haven't seen another Mexican patrol since the fight. None of us are in any shape to fight, but I'm itching for something to do other than walking. Lee and I went hunting during one stop yesterday, but the whole thing turned weird when Lee gave me that look. Most girls would melt under his stare.

"Not now. Not here," I told him.

As the sun goes down, we run across an open field, stopping to hide behind an outlying house. There aren't many people moving about so we venture further into the territory.

The houses are all dark, without even candles in the windows and the air is stagnant. We take cover in an alley upon hearing the sounds of a horse and a cart. They rumble by us.

"Hola," a soft, small voice says.

A young girl stands against the opposite wall. She holds up a lantern to see us better, and her face is contorted with fear. Jeremy bends down to talk to her, but her eyes don't show a bit of understanding. The kid is extremely thin. Her collar bone protrudes from under her torn clothing and I could probably wrap my hand all the way around one of her legs. As she presses herself flatter against the wall, Dawn pulls some food out of her pack and approaches the girl. She snatches it greedily and holds it as if it is precious and will be taken away from her at any moment. The girl looks from her food back to us before stepping out onto the street and motioning for us to follow. Dawn goes after her without looking back at me, so I have no choice but to follow.

She takes us to a cellar door down the street and knocks four times. I don't know what I expected, but it wasn't what I get. Two equally skinny boys open the door. Their faces are angry until they see the food clutched in our guide's tiny hands.

As I go down into the cellar, the smell of must and unwashed bodies assaults me. There are at least fifteen kids huddled together in the glow of the lanterns.

"Does anyone speak English?" I ask and am met with blank stares until an older girl speaks up.

"Yes," she says. "Do you have food?"

Dawn opens her pack and starts emptying it of food without even thinking or consulting me. I give her a disapproving look, but I don't tell her to stop. We can hunt and such to find food, but I doubt they can. The kids quickly eat what she gives them. After a few minutes of silence punctuated with smacking lips and greedy chewing, there is a knock at the door. The two boys from before open it and a few more children enter.

"What is this place?" I ask the older girl. "Where are your parents?"

"Gone," she answers. "The patrols take most of the men in our town. They don't come back. Only grown-ups are given food allowances," she pauses and looks away. "My ma died when the last disease came through. I'm not given food without her because I can't work the fields yet."

"How can they do that?" Drew asks. "You're kids! You shouldn't have to fend for yourselves."

"The Morenos don't care," she says, fidgeting and shifting uncomfortably as if she just did something wrong. What would Juan Moreno do if he heard this girl?

No one speaks after that. Like me, they're all probably plotting an end to every single member of the Moreno cartel.

Chapter 64

Gabby

I wake with my hand in Lee's. I don't remember how that happened, but I feel his gaze as I pull it away and then move across the cellar to sit with Dawn and Shay.

"I wish he'd stop looking at me like that," I blurt.

"He loves you. What's your problem?" Shay snaps.

"Excuse me?" I say, suddenly angry.

"You treat Lee like you're so much better than him and I think we're all a little sick of it," she answers.

"I do not," I spit.

"He's the one who's too good for you," she continues.

"You don't think I know that?" I clench my jaw to keep from yelling.

"I need some air," she says as she shoots to her feet and runs up the stairs, disappearing through the door.

Dawn and Lee call after her to stop, but she doesn't listen. I don't know what she's thinking anyway; going out there alone.

Why is she so narked all of a sudden?

I look around for an ally, but everyone, except for Lee, is staying out of it.

"We need to go after her before someone else finds her," he says as he moves toward the stairs.

"Let's split up and meet back here," Linc agrees quickly.

"Dawn, you come with me," Lee says, pointedly avoiding me before hurrying up the stairs.

Drew and I spend hours looking everywhere for her.

Where would she have gone?

We've pretty much given up when we head back to the cellar to see if anyone else has had any luck. I'm about to step out onto the street when Linc shows up and pulls us back.

"Stop," he whispers.

"What is it?" I ask, suddenly nervous.

The three of us peer around the corner to where a large group of men block the road. We can't hear what they are saying, but they part to reveal a man holding Shay by the throat. Her screams reach my ears, but I'm powerless to help her. "We can't take on that many men," Linc says.

We look on in horror as the man pulls out a long knife and drags it across Shay's neck. Blood pours out and she is thrown to the ground. Then, from around the corner, several more men arrive, shoving Dawn and Lee to the ground. I breathe in sharply and Linc strengthens his grip on my arm to keep me from charging.

"We need to help them," Drew whispers, his voice strained.

I'm clutching Linc's arm as my knees buckle and I almost fall forward. Dawn and Lee struggle as they are loaded onto horses, leaving Shay's body on the ground surrounded by onlookers who have come out to see the horror.

I try to push through the crowd to where Shay lays in a puddle of blood, but Linc holds me to him.

"She's already gone," he says.

For a moment, I'm frozen in shock and indecision. Whatever else happens, this has just become a rescue mission. I'm not leaving Mexico without Lee, and definitely not without my sister.

I turn toward Drew and look into his pained eyes.

"We'll get them back," I assure him.

Chapter 65

Dawn

I'm still shaking when someone grabs the back of my shirt and yanks me to my feet. They killed Shay. Her body hit the ground in a pool of her own blood. They slit her throat like it was butter. They didn't even blink.

The leader of the group stands in front of us, blood spattered and grimacing.

"Do I have your attention?" he asks.

Shay was killed for our benefit. When we found her, she had already been caught and was being guarded by two men. Lee shot the first one and knocked the second out. We tried to untie her, but we weren't fast enough. The rest of the patrol had heard the gun go off and came running.

"Are you going to kill us?" I ask quietly, my voice breaking on the word "kill".

"Why would I do that?" he responds as he wipes his knife on his pants and puts it away. He leans in close.

"I killed her for you," he says as he steps back and looks at Lee. "You killed one of my men so I killed one of yours. It was only fair."

He doesn't smile. Lee and I got her killed. If we hadn't...I try to push those thoughts away because the Mexican has said something else to me.

"We've been looking for you," he repeats.

Gabby was right. They knew we were coming. And now we're here on their terms.

He turns away to give orders. Our talk is over.

"You okay?" Lee whispers.

"No," I answer, the word shaking as it comes out of my mouth.

Our captor tightens the ties on our wrists before lifting me and handing me to someone on a horse.

"Where are we going?" I ask.

He doesn't respond. I try to wipe the tears from my face, but my hands are chained to the saddle.

"We'll get out of this," Lee says, but there is no belief behind his words; no conviction. They mean nothing.

Chapter 66

Gabby

"Hurry up!" I yell. "We need to move! Every second we waste here is another second they gain on us."

"Whoa, slow down, Gabby," Linc says calmly. "They're on horses. We'll never catch them."

"You want to give up on them?" I accuse.

"No one is saying that," Jeremy says, trying to take my hand, but I rip it away.

I don't want to be comforted. I want to be listened to; obeyed. "They'll probably take them to House Moreno and that's where we we're headed anyway."

"You're right," Linc says. "We should just keep going in that direction."

"Let's go," I say impatiently.

We avoid the street where Shay's body still lies, and slip out of town unnoticed. Having given away so much of our food, we fan out to look for more. Drew keeps to my right. He hasn't said a word since we saw Dawn being dragged away. I don't know what he's thinking, but I do know that he'll do anything to save my sister. I can count on him for that.

After a little while, Drew finds an injured deer in a ravine. He pulls out his knife and stabs it into the animal viciously.

"Why don't I take care of that?" Linc asks, removing Drew's dagger from his clenched fingers.

Drew runs a blood soaked hand through his hair and walks away. I follow him.

"Leave me alone Gabby," he barks.

"Yeah, that's not going to happen," I respond. "I'm scared for her too, you know."

"It isn't the same and you bloody well know it," he retorts.

His words sting.

"We both love her," I argue.

"I'm in love with her!" he yells before pausing to calm his breathing. "It's no longer your job to protect her and keep her safe. It's mine. If I lose Dawn..."

His voice trails off and his eyes search mine desperately.

"We keep losing her over and over again," he says when he finds his voice again.

"She always comes back to us," I say more to myself than to him. "We all knew the risks of this mission. We knew we might not all make it."

"How can you look me in the eye and try to rationalize everything that has happened?" he asks incredulously.

"I'm not, I just..." I give up trying to defend myself because I can't find the words to finish.

Even once the risks were explained, I always thought we could beat the odds. Me and Dawn. We've beaten them before.

"Aren't you worried about Lee too?" he asks though it sounds more like an accusation than a question.

"Of course I am!" I snap. "I care about him."

"You care about him?" Drew spits.

"What do you want to hear? Half the time, he pisses me off because of the things he says. Half the time, he pisses me off because of the things he doesn't say. He has gotten under my skin. You happy now?" I respond.

"Under your skin? Sounds like... love," he says quietly.

"Alright, I love him, dammit," I finally admit.

Drew steps back, wide eyed at my confession. We stare at each other for a long, uncomfortable moment, and then he starts picking up wood for a fire.

"Dinner, sleep, and then we go find both of them and kill the bastards who took them from us," I promise.

Chapter 67

Dawn

Lee and I are chained inside one of the tents for the night. We can hear laughter and chatter outside, but we can't understand any of it.

"What do you think they're going to do with us?" I ask.

He shrugs, but doesn't say anything, so I ask the next question weighing on my mind, "How can we get away?"

"Dawn," he says finally, "We have no weapons and we're outnumbered. We'll only get ourselves killed if we try anything now. And, if we can escape, we'll still be in Moreno territory. No one would help us here."

He's right. The people here are completely loyal to the cartel. The Morenos only have the power that fear gives them, but it is enough. Fear takes over the mind until you will do anything to keep it at bay. Fear made an entire town leave the orphaned children to fend for themselves. Fear made neighbors and family turn against each other. Fear devours humanity and hope.

I know Gabby and Drew will come for us, and it is enough to keep my own fear from consuming me.

The glow from the fire outside disappears as the men crash for the night. Lee is already asleep, but I can't get the image of Shay out of my head. I lay there for a while before the tent flap is pushed aside and a large man comes through. He stops and crouches down when he reaches me. I try to sit up, but my chains won't let me. I fall back and stare at his dark figure.

He reaches out and clamps a rough hand on my leg, holding me down.

"What are you doing?!" I scream. "Get off me!"

He clamps his free hand over my mouth and crushes me with his weight. As soon as he lets my legs go, I kick and thrash. He doesn't budge. Instead, he sticks a hand underneath my shirt.

"Dawn!" Lee yells, suddenly awake. He tries to get to me, but he can't. I hear the sounds of his chains crashing together in between my screams as the man on top of me tugs at my clothes. He has a grin on his face and continues to press into me. I hit him and try to bite him. He responds by grabbing my chin. He says something in Spanish, but his words are cut short by a single gunshot. The man goes limp and I try to push him off me as I feel his warm blood soaking into my clothes.

Standing in the doorway of our tent is the Mexican that leads this patrol. He still has the gun in his hand and I wait for him to aim it at me, but he doesn't. He slips it into its holster and then bends down to roll the man off me. As soon as I'm free, I scramble backward as far as my chains will let me. I pull my knees to my chest and hug them close. The leader orders two of his men to drag the body from the tent.

"No one is allowed to touch you," the Mexican says.

Out of my mind, I almost thank him, but then he says, "My brother needs you to arrive in one piece for questioning."

Questioning.

I shiver at the thought. I know what the Texans did to Drew for answers. Who the hell is this guy's brother?

When I'm alone with Lee again, he tries to get to me, but can't. Instead, he reaches toward me and I grab his hand, holding on for dear life. He doesn't say anything and I'm glad. Just holding his hand is enough to slow my heart and calm my shaking.

Neither of us sleep the rest of the night and by the time we're loaded up onto the horses again, the blood has dried in my hair and on my clothes, leaving me a crusty mess. I flinch when I'm lifted up, not wanting these men to touch me. None of them seem fazed by the rider-less horse. I'm staring at it when the patrol leader pulls his horse in beside me.

"They all know the rules," he says, almost as if he had read my mind. "They all know the consequences."

"What do you want from me?" I ask quietly, having lost the energy needed to fight with this man.

"Nothing," he responds. "But Juan Moreno will want answers."

"What answers does he want from me?" I ask, afraid I already know the answer.

"That isn't for me to discuss," he says, and his face remains serious. "But, I tell you this, when you meet him, it will be better for you if you just give him the answers he wants. Your death may even be quick."

"My death?" I stammer as all the air leaves my chest.

"Spies are executed. If you cooperate though, you may be spared other punishments," he explains.

"What's your name?" I ask.

We're his prisoners. Shay's blood is still on his clothes. I need to know who is doing this to us.

"My name is Marco Moreno. Juan Moreno is my brother," he answers with a grunt as he digs his heels into the sides of his horse and trots to the front of the group without looking back.

Chapter 68

Dawn

The Moreno house is huge, like an English estate. Dark stone walls give the place a dreary and foreboding feel. Along the outer walls stand heavily armed men. They wave us through the gate into a courtyard, our horses' hooves echoing off the cobblestones.

We stop abruptly and the guards drag me and Lee from our saddles. I stumble and fall to my knees. Someone grabs the back of my shirt and lifts me back up. They don't undo our chains.

The courtyard is busy with soldiers and attendants coming and going. They glare at us as they hurry by. Marco gives orders to the guards and they take the horses to the barn. I spin around when I hear a large metal front door open behind me. Three men in chains walk out carrying buckets of what smells like literal shite.

"They aren't Mexican," I whisper to Lee.

"No," he says. "They look like slaves."

My eyes follow their skinny frames until they disappear around the corner. I hear the rattle of chains as someone bumps into me from behind.

"Sorry," a small female voice says.

It's a child.

"Lee," I elbow him, "she's British."

The little girl gives us a weary look before turning away.

"Don't go," I say, reaching out, but she flinches away.

"I'm sorry miss," she says, looking at her feet. "But I must be getting my work did." She rushes off just as Marco returns to us with two guards.

"Take him," he says, pointing to Lee, who fights them as they grab his arms. There's nothing he can do.

Marco looks at me coldly before saying, "Let's go."

Marco grabs my chains and pulls me through the metal door. The inside of the house is even more extravagant and crowded than outside. Guards, slaves, and cooks all rush by and don't give me a second look.

"This way," Marco says, pushing me down a dark hall until we stop in front of a large set of ornately carved and gilded double doors obviously meant to impress. After a tap on one of the doors, they open and Marco yanks me through them.

I stumble in hard as I regain my footing and my eyes begin to adjust. There, at the end of the room, past the blood red walls with gold trim paneling, is a single ornate throne of a chair occupied by a beautiful, yet terrifying man. As Marco urges me forward, I can't take my eyes off the man in the chair or the guards behind him.

He looks like a dark prince sitting there in judgment. His curly black hair reaches his shoulders. He is clean shaven and dressed to be seen, but it's his eyes that I can't look away from. They are dark, almost black and they bore into me.

"Brother," Marco begins, "a present for you."

The Moreno leader smiles, but there is something very wrong in that smile. It twists his face into something that I no longer want to look at. If I didn't know it before, I do now. This is an evil man.

"Hello," he says, getting to his feet. "I am Juan."

He walks down the steps toward me and begins to circle me. He puts a hand under my chin to examine my face.

"She is one of the British spies that you had us looking for," Marco explains. "I sent the other one to the dungeon to await your questioning."

"Thank you, Marco," Juan says, not bothering to look at him. "You may go."

Marco glances at me one more time before hurrying from the room. Juan continues to examine me…every part of me. I'm frozen in fear until he finally steps back and reclaims his seat.

He says something to his guard in Spanish before turning back to me.

"I'll see you again soon," he says.

He'll see me again soon? Does that mean he's not going to kill me yet?

I'm pulled from the room and quickly led down a flight of stairs. The air gets colder with every step. A door opens and I'm shoved inside before it slams behind me.

"Are you okay Dawn?" Lee asks as I rush toward him and hug him as much as our chains will allow.

"This is a bad place Lee," I say.

"I know," he responds.

We've been in the cell for hours when the door swings open slowly with a groan. A man enters carrying a bucket. He has chains to match ours and a scar across his bare chest. The door closes and he surveys us before setting the bucket down.

"You need to clean yourselves before being taken to Juan Moreno," he says, his American accent evident.

"Why does he care?" I spit. "He's just going to torture us."

"You're British," the man states the obvious, cocking his head.

"Yea," I say. "That's why we're here. Apparently we're spies."

"You're not?" he asks.

I shrug in response.

"You're American," Lee states. "What are you doing in Mexico?"

"I could ask you the same thing," he answers. "I won't though. There is a guard waiting for me outside the door. They won't want me talking to you. Clean yourselves up. I'm Boone, by the way. I'll be back when they decide you can eat."

After he's gone, I take the rag from the bucket and scrub the blood and dirt from my skin. Lee does the same and then we wait.

I don't know how long we sit here. No food comes and we aren't taken for questioning. Boone doesn't return, either, and we have no idea what's happening out there.

My stomach growls, reminding me that we've missed yet another meal. I'm too weak to stand when the door finally opens and Juan Moreno walks in. I cower away from his piercing stare, but it isn't me he trains it on. He points to Lee, and the guards drag him from the room, leaving me alone in the damp darkness.

I curl up on the floor and sink into unconsciousness, only waking when Lee is brought back. Light floods into the room behind him, allowing me to see clearly. His jaw is swollen and his lip is split. Blood trickles from a gash near his hairline and his shirt is soaked through. As soon as we're enveloped in darkness once again, I crawl across the floor to Lee's huddled form, dragging the bucket with me.

"Lee, what did they do to you?" I whisper, dabbing a rag across his brow.

He flinches away from my touch when I try to clean his lip.

"They know why we're here," he says. "They know who we are."

"What did they ask you?" I ask him.

"I didn't tell them anything," he responds weakly.

Before I say anything else, Boone enters the room, carrying a small bowl and a plate. He sets it down in front of us and takes a seat.

"I have to stay here until you've finished eating," he explains, ignoring Lee's broken appearance.

The food is a bowl of tasteless mush and dry bread. Neither it nor the cup of water are nearly big enough to satisfy both of us.

"Are most of the slaves British or American?" I ask.

I suddenly want to know. My father ran Floridaland for years, which means he ran the slave trade. Was he selling his own people to the Mexicans?

"Both," Boone says. "Some were sold and others chose to come."

"Why would anyone choose this?" I ask.

"There are spies everywhere," he answers cryptically, putting a finger to his lips to quiet me, but I don't think he's talking about Mexican spies.

Does my father have allies here? What about Mya Moreno? Maybe there are people who are loyal to her.

Chapter 69

Dawn

Two days go by with no word before I'm roused from my sleep by someone manhandling me to my feet. The guards shove me down the hall and up the stairs. I do as they say.

We stop, and the door in front of us is opened, revealing a large table set with a sickening amount of food. Juan Moreno sits at one end.

"Ahhh, Ms. Nolan, have a seat," he says, not even looking up as he speaks.

I'm pushed into a chair opposite of him and an overflowing plate is placed in front of me. My stomach urges me to eat, but I hesitate.

"You know who I am," I state the obvious.

"Yes. Dawn Nolan. Daughter of the Rebel general. Rebel spy," he states in return.

"I am not a spy," I say quietly.

"You came here to gather information, did you not?" he asks, his accent giving his voice a purr that sets me on edge. "You were planning to steal that information. That makes you a spy."

He stands and walks around the table until he is behind me. He bends down so that his mouth is near my ear and whispers, "Eat, for I have many questions for you."

Unable to ignore my empty stomach any longer, I do what I'm told, barely chewing any of the food as it goes down.

Juan is still standing behind me when my plate is taken from me. He pulls my chair away from the table and turns me to look at him.

"When is the first British ship set to arrive?" he asks.

"I don't know," I answer, barely getting the words out before he backhands me.

"Do not lie!" he yells. "I will get answers, or I'll send you home to the General piece by piece."

"All I know is that it will be within the year," I lie.

Juan kicks the chair over and I go crashing to the floor. He reaches down and grabs a handful of my hair, forcing me to look into his distorted face. Tears trail down my bruised cheeks unchecked and he smiles.

"Let's try an easier question," he says. "Where are the ships landing? Is it near Floridaland?"

There is something behind his words. Why does he care about Floridaland?

"I don't know," I croak as his hands encircle my throat and he lifts me to my feet.

I squeeze my eyes shut to keep them from betraying the lie. Juan drops me as he walks back to the table and grabs a knife. He returns to me and presses the cold, flat edge onto my cheek and my breath catches in my throat.

"Please," I plead.

He turns the knife and drags it slowly across my cheek. I scream as my skin opens up and warm blood pours down my shirt.

"Take her away," Juan says as he turns his back on me. "Her answers will come more freely after more time in the dungeon."

As they drag me down the hall, a door opens. I hear a woman's voice before I see her. She stands in the doorway in a long gown, watching as I go by. There is pity in her eyes and something more. Alarm? Recognition?

Chapter 70

Dawn

We haven't reached the dungeons yet when I throw up for the first time. The guard jumps back as my breakfast splatters his boots. They quicken their pace and are glad to be rid of me by the time they throw me back in the cell.

I spend the rest next hour hovered over the wash bucket until there is nothing left of the extravagant breakfast in my stomach. Now I'm only dry heaving and spitting up stomach acid. My chest aches. My throat burns. My stomach growls. Lee tries to help me, but there is nothing he can do. At least I have stopped bleeding. I am a mess.

Boone returns the next day to swap out our waste bucket and bring us the tiniest bit of food. I eat slowly, afraid that it too will leave my stomach the same way it went in.

"Your food was laced with something," he explains. "Dehydration is a favorite torture around here. It drags out the suffering."

Boone has brought a lantern with him this time and the light is almost blinding, but comforting too. It feels good to be able to see Lee's face again. Boone pushes his shaggy blonde hair out of his eyes to stare at me closer.

"The good news is, your cut isn't infected," he says.

A laugh bubbles out of my chest before I can stop it. Good news in a place like this?

"Why haven't you asked our names?" I ask Boone.

"I figured spies would just lie anyway," he answers with a shrug.

"Did you tell us your real name?"

His head snaps up when he realizes what I'm insinuating.

"Yes," he says tightly.

"My name is Dawn Nolan," I say, ignoring his change in demeanor. "And this is Lee."

"Nolan?" Boone questions, his eyes widening, but he stops himself from saying anything further. "I need to go."

He gathers up the plate and bucket before rushing from the room in stunned silence.

Chapter 71

Gabby

"Come on!" I yell behind me. "We have to pick up the pace!"

"Gabby," Linc huffs. "We need to stop for the night."

"Like hell we do!" I yell in response.

"We're all exhausted Gabs," Jeremy adds.

"Then you guys stay here," Drew chimes in. "Gabby and I need to keep going."

"We all want to save Dawn and Lee," Linc pauses, "but what good will we be to them if we are dead tired when we get there?"

"He's right," Jeremy says. "If we stop now and get some shut eye, we'll reach the Moreno house by noon tomorrow."

"Fine," I say with a resigned sigh, taking a seat.

We've been pretty lucky over the past week, avoiding the Moreno patrols. There have been a few close calls, but the land has provided us with plenty of hiding places. Tonight is no different. It has been dark for hours now, but the sky is blocked from view by the trees that surround us. Most of the territory is flat and open so we've had to take the long way in order to stay out of sight.

I dig in my pack for the last bit of deer meat from a few days ago. Everyone takes some, but it isn't enough to fill us.

"So, do we use the same plan once we get there?" Drew asks. "We created that before it was a rescue mission."

In the darkness I can sense everyone staring in my direction hoping that I know the right call.

"Yes," I say decidedly. "Ana said the tunnels beneath the walls should take us right under the house."

"So, do we go in disguised as slaves?" Drew asks.

"Yes, but not you," I tell him.

He starts to protest, but I put my hand up to stop him.

"You could never pass for a slave Drew because you've never even met one. You ooze money and privilege," I explain. "Same goes for you Linc. You're too much the soldier. This is a two-man mission. Jeremy and I will go in and we may need some cover fire when we come out. Too many of us going in risks blowing our cover."

"Gabby ..." Drew starts again.

"No, Drew!" I command. "You aren't going in. That is an order. This is the best way to get Dawn out alive."

His face falls because he knows I'm right and there is nothing more he can say.

Chapter 72

Gabby

Saying the house that looms before us is big is an understatement. Its elaborate and dark fortress-like design stands in stark contrast to the sparse land surrounding it.

I don't have a good feeling about this.

We keep moving until we're south of the house, along the beach. Ana said the tunnels come out into a cave at the beach. I see many rocks, but no openings so we fan out.

A few minutes later, Linc hurries toward me whispering "Over here."

He leads us back along the beach and through some brush.

"You found it," I pant. As soon as I catch my breath, I start issuing orders. "We may be in there for a few days. Don't come after us until four nights have passed. Drew, I want you watching the cave for any signs of us or any Moreno men. Linc, I need you set up over on the ridge in case we need some cover fire," I explain. They nod and I turn to Jeremy. "I need you to hit me."

"What?" he asks, shocked, and takes a step back. "No way."

"Do it!" I command.

He hesitates, so I take a swing at him. He's too surprised to duck. He'll have a pretty nasty bruise on his cheek within a few minutes. He grabs my wrist and I all but force him to give me a fat lip.

"You know as well as anyone that slaves get hit all the time," I explain. "We need to look the part."

I rip the already fraying sleeves from my shirt and use my knife to cut up the bottoms of my pants and then to make a small cut on the back of my arm. I let the blood trickle free, while Jeremy removes his shirt all together and messes up his hair.

"Let's go," I say.

Drew and Lincoln watch as the light from our torches disappears into the dark tunnels. Ana said that you can get lost down here. She wasn't wrong.

Chapter 73

Dawn

"Lee," I nudge him as the door opens.

He returned last night in worse shape than the time before and he hasn't moved since. I can barely muster the strength to turn and see who has entered our prison. I assume it's the slave, Boone. His face isn't the one that greets me, however.

I squint as my eyes adjust to the light from a lantern and I see her. A woman hurries toward me, her long, dark curls whipping about her shoulders. Boone enters behind her.

"I'm here to make sure they eat," he says.

The two of them share a look and wait for the door to close behind them.

"I can't get you very long," a voice says.

I recognize it as that of Marco Moreno.

"Thank you brother," the woman says before the door groans shut.

Brother?

My eyes widen as I stare into the face of none other than Mya Moreno. She kneels beside me and lays down a bundle she has been carrying.

"Dawn Nolan," she whispers before motioning for Boone to help me sit.

I glance at Lee and his eyes are open and watchful.

"Boone, they need to eat," Mya says. "They have no strength."

Boone tips a cup of water against my dry lips. It's been two days since anything has stayed in my stomach...two days since I was poisoned. Mya holds out bread for Lee to eat and he moves slowly...like an old man afraid to jostle his brittle bones.

"I don't have much time," Mya begins. "I've been waiting for the General to send someone after the weapon."

"He said to tell you the time is now," I say.

"Well, now that you're here it is," she responds quickly. "I can't send any of my people after the weapon while Juan is still in power. He's sent Kearn to Floridaland to prepare to use it."

"What more can you tell us about the weapon?" Lee asks.

"It's old tech that the Texans have possessed since before anyone can remember. It's similar to the weapon they used to cause the collapse of the United States a very long time ago. It killed millions upon millions of people, and caused a great migration of millions more which set off a chain reaction of starvation and death that destroyed the already suffering nation," she explains. "Texas built the weapon as a threat to the British. When the Coles died, Kearn sold it and himself to the highest bidder, my brother. To him, it isn't just a threat. He's deranged enough to actually use it."

She stops talking for a moment before looking from me to Lee dubiously and asking, "are you the only people Nolan has sent to help?" The doubt on her face angers me.

"The rest of our people are coming for us," Lee says, irritated.

"Well, I can help you get out, but I can't get you to Floridaland," she says.

"That's enough," Lee replies, glancing at me to keep me from telling her about the Carlita cartel's aid that awaits us. We don't know this woman, so we don't know if we can trust her.

"What do we need to do?" I ask.

"I'm a prisoner here as much as you," she explains. "You will never get free while my brother lives. And my people will never be safe."

"Then what do we do?" Lee asks finally.

"We kill him," Mya answers, her eyes growing cold. "For years General Nolan has used the slave trade to put his people and mine in place throughout this household. We have the numbers to seize control, but only after Juan is no longer with us. I can't get to him, but you can."

When I don't say anything, she continues, "You will be summoned soon for further questioning. My brother does not want you to appear before him looking like a vagabond again. I have brought you proper clothing and you will join him for breakfast, but be warned that he'll use the puking potion again."

Mya pulls out a thin blade and presents it to me.

"I have sewn a hidden pocket into the dress for this," she says. "Your choice is simple, do this or live out the rest of your short life with the rats in these dungeons."

I hide the knife underneath me when the door opens.

"Mya, we must be gone," Marco urges.

Mya gets to her feet and dusts off her dress before leaving without waiting for my answer.

Once we're alone again, I scoot across the cold stone floor to sit by Lee, but he has no words of comfort or wisdom for me.

I harden my heart before I say the only thing that seems appropriate.

"I have to kill him."

Chapter 74

Gabby

We reach the garbage chute and noises from the house drift down toward us. I jump out of the way just in time to keep from being buried under a load of trash.

"Disgusting," I mumble with a grunt as I signal to Jeremy to put out the torch.

Trying not to breathe through my nose, I climb up into the chute, using the rough stones to haul myself up. It doesn't take us long before we emerge into the dark at the top. This is where the real plan begins, the slave quarters.

If only they realized how close they've been to their freedom all this time.

I find a place to tie the rope Ana gave me, and toss it down the chute. Climbing down may not be as easy as climbing up was. There are footsteps and voices just around the corner now. I motion Jeremy forward and we round the bend slowly.

"Remember," I say, "eyes on the ground."

He nods, and we step into the middle of a throng of slaves entering their quarters. We move slowly and awkwardly until we enter a room lit by only a few candles.

Cots line the walls, with buckets in between. There is nothing else. The stench assaults us, and only grows as we move further into the room. No one looks at us or anyone else. The people before us are emaciated, skeletal. Only a few of them have the dark hair that marks them as Mexicans.

"What now?" Jeremy whispers.

"We wait," I say. "We have to get to Mya Moreno first. She'll know where Dawn and Lee are and she'll definitely know where the weapon is. We'd never get past the guards at night, though. We'll wait until morning. Shift change is at first light, and Ana said the morning guards are loyal to Mya. Her quarters are on the top floor, near her brother's, so we need to be fully prepared."

The night is not an easy one. The other slaves ignore us because they are used to people coming and going, so no one gets attached to anyone else. This place is entirely different from the slave camp in Floridaland. It seems harsher, if that's even possible.

I feel a presence by my bed and open my eyes. The glow of a nearby candle illuminates the head of blonde hair that belongs to a man who's face is scrunched in confusion. I sit up cautiously, waiting for him to speak. He cocks his head to the side, examining me.

"I make it my business to keep track of every slave that comes in," he says. "Who the hell are you?"

"We came in yesterday," I lie, shifting my eyes away from his. "We've been sent from Floridaland."

"Bullshit," he says. "We haven't had incoming slaves from the British in Floridaland in ages. So, I'll ask again, who are you?"

"Chill dude," Jeremy says, standing behind him and putting a restraining hand on his shoulder.

"You were sent by the General weren't you?" the blonde slave whispers.

I weigh my words carefully. His eyes narrow and I know he is testing us.

What answer does he want? What answer will make him leave us alone?

"No," I say finally. "We're just here to work."

It's almost as if his eyes dim at my words. He's disappointed. He shrugs off Jeremy's hand before speaking again.

"Okay then. Well, I'm Boone," he says. "Tomorrow morning you will be put on breakfast service for Mya Moreno."

I look up sharply at the mention of her name, and he gives me one last long look as if he wants to say something else, but thinks better of it. He walks away and I don't get another moment of sleep the rest of the night.

Chapter 75

Dawn

My dress catches with every step as I'm pushed and prodded up the stairs. I fall forward twice and my guards are forced to catch me. They grunt and groan at my clumsiness when, in reality, it's weakness that dogs me at every turn. It's all I can do just to keep going.

With every movement, I feel the blade that Mya gave me. If Juan grabs me by the waist, he's sure to find it. And if he doesn't find it. I'm sure to use it.

We finally reach the door to Juan Moreno's quarters and enter. Once again, he is seated at the table, waiting for me. He stands and smiles when he sees me, nodding approvingly at my somewhat less grotty appearance. The dress is too tight and too long, but he seems to like it. Juan pulls out a chair and waves me forward. I sit reluctantly and he shoos the guards away.

"Eat," he commands.

I stare at the food and slowly pick up my spoon. Juan's too smart to provide me with a knife or a fork that I could use as a weapon. As I push the food around on my plate, Juan's eyes never leave me.

"Eat," he says again.

I take a small bite and chew, but I don't swallow. I bring my napkin up to my face to wipe my lips and discreetly spit the food into it. I repeat this process with every bite.

"I need to know how many of your people are going after Kearn," Juan says calmly, getting to his feet.

I stiffen as he moves closer.

"I don't know," I answer, the same way I have every other question, and his face twists into a frustrated scowl.

"I thought you would've learned by now that that isn't an acceptable answer," he growls.

In one swift movement, he dumps me from my chair. I hit the table on the way down, causing plates and silverware to crash down around me. My napkin rolls from the table and reveals the food hidden within. For a second I think he hasn't seen it because there is no reaction. Then suddenly, he grabs my hair and pulls me to my feet.

"What is this?" he screams. "You think you can fool me?"

His eyes are crazed as he pushes me up against the table. I can't move. I can't think. He stares at me for what seems like an eternity before reaching behind me and grabbing a fistful of food. One of his hands holds my chin in place while the other forces the poisoned food into my mouth. He holds my mouth shut while pinching my nose so that I can't breathe until I swallow. I punch and claw at his chest, but he doesn't budge. The food slides down my throat and I gasp for air when he releases me. The relief doesn't last long because he is ready with more.

I wipe my tears away violently and ready myself for it. The dehydration and starvation almost killed me the last time I ate from this table. I'm no longer fighting by the time he is satisfied. I've given up as I wait for more questions, but Juan silently takes a knife from his belt and walks toward me. I back away until my back hits the wall and I have nowhere else to go. He presses further still.

"There are still so many ways I can hurt you," he says. "The puking potion won't take effect for a while yet and I will have my answers."

He holds the knife up to my throat and then lowers it to my chest where he begins to cut away my clothes. Mya's dress falls to the floor in a heap. I try to cover myself with my hands and duck away, but nothing works. Juan holds my arms up behind my head and my tears come faster. I look to the ground where Mya's knife is hidden beneath the pile of clothes, out of my reach.

"Stop crying," he orders, but I can't.

"Do you realize what I could do to you?" he whispers. "You're going to wish you were dead."

Without thinking, I slam my knee into his groin. He winces and his grip loosens just enough for me to break free. I dart across the room, but I have nowhere to go. Juan is advancing on me once again, so I turn toward him with the table at my back. I stare at him with glassy eyes while my hand roams the table behind me, searching for anything I can use as a weapon.

He's screaming in my face as he presses up against me, waving his knife in front of my eyes. My finger is pricked by something sharp. A shard of glass from a wine goblet that broke when I fell.

It digs into my fingers as I grip it tightly and whip my arm around, burying the glass in Juan's throat. He screams in pain, but I don't give him time to come at me again. I pull the glass free before jamming it in yet again. The glass sticks in his neck and he stumbles backward.

I scramble to where my clothes lay on the ground and find the knife. Juan opens his mouth to yell for his guards, but I'm too fast. I stab upward, under his chin. His mouth opens, but only blood spills out. He stumbles toward me, grasping at my hand which still holds the blade. I stand frozen as he falls into my arms. As I let him drop to the ground, the blade slides out and his blood begins to pool at my feet.

I stand naked, covered in blood, and sobbing uncontrollably, waiting for the guards to enter the room. I have just murdered their leader, the most feared man in Mexico and Texas, Juan Moreno.

The door opens.

Chapter 76

Jeremy

Breakfast isn't the first duty of the day. No, the slaves are up hours before that performing other back-breaking duties. We're no different. Water spills over the side of each bucket I'm carrying as another soldier knocks into me, laughing. I reach the stables and set the buckets down for the horses to drink.

"Get back to work!" a soldier screams behind me after I've been standing still for only a few seconds.

I turn around, which is a big mistake. The soldier punches me and I stumble backward.

"Don't look at me, slave," he says.

I focus my eyes on the ground until he's gone and then lean against the wall and tremble.

I've done this all before... the chains, the beatings, and the forced labor. I squeeze my eyes shut and try to forget it all. A child works in the next stall over and I'm reminded of Claire.

I try to keep my head down, but every time I see a Mexican soldier, I can barely breathe, the chains zapping all the strength and courage right out of me.

"You need to keep working," Gabby whispers.

I open my eyes as she takes my hand in hers. She's ice-cold and there's fear in her eyes for the first time since we got to Mexico.

"Come on," she says, tugging at me, and I follow her to continue feeding the horses.

I don't let go of her hand until the stable-master enters and starts screaming at us.

"What is taking so god damn long?!" he yells.

Gabby and I stare at the bucket on the ground as he berates us. His voice has no Mexican accent, and when I catch a quick glimpse of him, I realize he isn't Mexican. He's an American who is working for the Mexicans.

"How could you?" I ask, unable to stop myself.

"Excuse me, slave?" he barks.

"How could you work for the Mexicans?" I yell. "You're a traitor."

Gabby doesn't even try to hold me back, because she's pissed too.

"You're just like the British in Floridaland," she growls. "Enslaving your own people."

A swift roundhouse from the stable-master sends me to the ground. I roll over and spit on his boots. He kicks me in the head and I taste blood as it pours into my mouth. After a few more snarls and kicks, he wheels around and leaves in a huff.

"Are you okay?" Gabby asks, kneeling beside me.

"No," I answer, spitting the blood from my mouth. "None of us are okay, Gabs."

I look up at her.

"Our plan has to work," I say. "We can't stay in a place like this. Not again."

Chapter 77

Gabby

We follow Boone to the kitchen to collect Mya's breakfast and then he leads us up an empty stairwell. My breathing is ragged by the time we reach the top floor.

"The shift has just changed," Boone informs us.

Does he know that's what we were waiting for?

We pass by two guards keeping watch outside an ornate door.

That must be Juan Moreno's quarters.

They don't acknowledge us as we pass. Jeremy and I trail after Boone as he enters a room and we set the trays on a table.

"One moment," Boone says as he disappears into an adjoining room.

He returns a few moments later with a woman. She's beautiful, but what strikes me most are her eyes. She's the only person here who will look straight at us.

"I need to know who you are," she says quickly.

I'm stunned by her directness.

"You're Mya Moreno," I say.

It's a statement more than a question, but she nods her head.

"I have a message from my father," I say.

Her expression sharpens.

"General Nolan says 'the time is now'," I tell her.

"I have already received that message," she says. "And I'm heeding his instructions."

"You've already received it?" I ask, but then it suddenly becomes so clear. "You've talked to Dawn? Is she okay? Is she still here?" I ask in rapid succession.

"She is here," Mya says cautiously.

"And Lee? Is he okay too?" I ask.

Before she gets the chance to answer, there's a commotion out in the hall.

"You stay here," Mya tells us before she disappears.

She is only gone a moment before she hurries back in.

"Come now!" she yells, her voice frantic.

I glance at Jeremy and we run after her. Mya's guards stand outside an open door with two unconscious guards at their feet. Mya quickly looks down as she steps over them and into the room.

The scene inside is chaotic. Dishes and food litter the ground near an up-turned chair. The table is marked with bloody handprints, as is the far wall. I slowly round the table to see what Mya is looking at. I almost trip over the dead man and fall into his blood before I see her.

My sister.

Dawny is naked save for the dark, red blood that covers her. She's standing still and makes no sound as she stares at us with wide, unblinking eyes.

"Get her some clothes!" I yell to no one in particular, only vaguely aware of Mya leaving the room.

Jeremy takes a blanket from the bed and hands it to me. Wrapping it around her, I squeeze her shoulders tightly. She finally looks at me, and the look in her eyes breaks my heart.

"Gabby?" she whispers.

"I'm here," I respond, hiccupping back a sob.

Using the corner of the blanket, I wipe the blood from Dawn's face and then Jeremy helps me get her into the clothing that Mya has brought. Not wanting to let go, I keep my arm around her shoulders.

"Where's Lee?" I ask Mya.

"The dungeon," she says.

"He… We…" Dawn stammers, trying to explain, but I stop her when I hear the quiver in her voice.

"Let's just get him out," I say and she nods gratefully.

"The dungeon is on the slave level," Mya says. "Take this."

She hands me an earring.

"Show it to the guard on duty. He'll know it's mine," she explains. "I will send a guard to get you there. Now go. You have to get to Floridaland and I have a mess to clean up."

We only make it halfway down the hall before Dawn starts to retch.

"Oh no," she says as she wipes her mouth.

We can't stop for long, so Jeremy helps Dawn walk a little further before he has to carry her down the stairs because she's bent over in pain.

The house is busy, with slaves and soldiers running about, so we pass through easily. Mya's guard keeps anyone from questioning us. Back on the slave level, I begin to feel more hopeful.

We're almost there.

The guard outside Lee's cell looks at the earring and then at me before he opens the door to let us in. I hesitate when I see him. He looks broken; fragile. They've beaten him half to death. He sees me and slides painfully into a sitting position. I look from Dawn to Lee and then back again.

"I want to kill every last one of them," I growl as I kneel in front of Lee and run my hands through his hair and down his cheeks.

"Lee," I whisper.

He winces in pain when I touch the bruise beneath his eye, but then recovers his composure and takes my hand in his.

"I knew you could do it," he says weakly as he tries to smile.

"I was so scared," I admit as I lean my forehead against his and close my eyes for just a second.

The sound of Dawn puking brings us back to reality.

"We need to go," I say, straightening up as Jeremy helps Lee out the door.

We pass through the slave quarters, and this time, I feel their eyes on us, nervous and bewildered. They watch as we disappear into the darkness of the garbage chute.

Chapter 78

Gabby

"Dawn," I say as I hold her hair back. "You can do it. You can keep going."

She stumbles forward, but doesn't respond. Every time she opens her mouth to speak, she convulses. By now, nothing comes out. Her chest heaves as she grows weaker and slower.

Jeremy lifts Dawn into his arms when she can no longer walk. Lee is struggling beside me, but all I can do is give him my arm for balance. He doesn't say anything. He doesn't have the strength.

Working together, we descend the garbage chute and make our way down the long tunnels that lead to the beach.

We see the light, but our relief doesn't last long because we hear Drew scream up ahead. Jeremy and I take off running, leaving Lee and Dawn hidden in the tunnels.

Blinded by suddenly bursting into the sunlight, we duck for cover as we look around frantically for Drew. He's on the beach ducking in and out and firing at the Mexicans coming toward him on horseback. In front of us lies Linc's mangled body on the ground at the base of the dunes, his sniper rifle still up top.

"Jeremy, get to Drew!" I yell.

"Where are you going?" he hollers back.

"I have to get to Linc's rifle!" I yell.

"It's too far!" he yells, grabbing my arm to pull me back into the safety of the cave. The horses are close now.

"Go!" I scream.

He gives me one last look before making a quick dash toward Drew. I dart out into the open and scramble up the hill towards Linc's rifle, zigging and zagging to avoid their shots. There are four of them. Two veer off from the others, dismount and come after me. The sand muffles the sounds of bullets hitting the ground as it is kicked up from the impact.

I reach Linc's rifle, dive and roll, and come up firing. I track the first one coming toward me and pull the trigger. He goes down quickly, but the second man keeps coming. He takes aim, point blank before I can get another shot off. He fires as I dive out of the way. I spring to my feet, bringing a handful of coarse sand with me as I do, and I throw it, blinding him, then thrust the butt of my rifle in his face as I swing my leg out to catch his knees. He falls to the ground, his rifle clattering over the edge.

I press the nose of my gun to his chest as he speaks rapidly in Spanish. He's young and afraid, but also loyal to Juan Moreno. He raises his free arm in surrender, and I look him in the eyes.

"Didn't you get the memo? Juan Moreno is dead," I say, pulling the trigger.

Down below, Drew and Jeremy have dispatched the other two attackers. I slide down the dune to where Linc lies still. He has no pulse.

"He's gone," I say when Drew walks up behind me with a now unconscious Dawn in his arms.

"They caught us by surprise," he says sadly.

I put my hand on Linc's shoulder and squeeze.

Another friend gone.

I smooth his hair and am still looking into his face when Drew asks, "Is Dawn going to be okay?"

"I think so," I pause, closing Linc's eyes and sighing. "I hope so."

I look out across the water and see something move. A small boat is rapidly coming into focus.

"It's okay," Drew says calmly. "They're our ride."

"The boat Carlos Carlita promised us?" Jeremy asks as he helps Lee over to us.

I go to them and offer Lee my shoulder to lean on. He takes my hand instead.

"Yeah. They're getting us out of here." Drew says. "They came ashore last night. They've been waiting for us."

After burying Linc and saying a few quick words, we walk across the beach to where the small boat has come ashore. Carlos' serious face greets us.

"Joseph Kearn and the weapon are in Floridaland," I inform him.

"Then we go to Floridaland," he responds.

Mexico disappears behind us as we motor out to the Carlita vessel waiting for us offshore. I watch the rocky beach where we left Linc until I can no longer see it. I find myself leaning back, an arm around my sister, the tension beginning to drain from my body, the salt water washing away the blood and sweat. Everyone is quiet and exhausted as we approach the ship that will take us to our final destination.

Chapter 79

Dawn

I open my eyes slowly to find Drew looking down at me. He grins, but I can't return the gesture because everything hurts. His smile fades as he sees me struggling to speak.

"Water," I mouth.

Drew slides his arm under my head to prop me up. He brings the cup to my lips and I start choking immediately. Water pours down my chin as he pulls away the cup and gently wipes my face.

"You're going to be okay," he says. "We're on a ship heading for Floridaland."

It all starts coming back... the Moreno house, the dungeon, the puking.

So much puking.

I thought I was going to die. I didn't, but Juan Moreno did. I killed him. I raise my hand to see if his blood is still on me. Tears leak from the corners of my eyes.

"Are we safe?" I ask weakly.

"For now," Drew whispers.

Brushing aside my hair and tears, he offers me another sip of water. This time it goes down a little easier and I drift off to sleep.

The next few days go much like that. People come to see me, but I'm not much good for conversation. Gabby sits by my bed for hours on end while I sleep. Between her and Drew, I'm never alone. Jeremy and Lee stop by every day. Lee looks about as bad as I feel, but he's up and moving.

Every bite of food gives me a little more strength until I can finally sit up in bed and then stand not long after that. I feel like I'm coming back to myself, like I have been missing for a long time and am finally me again.

"I want to go up on deck," I say to Gabby after lunch one day.

"Are you sure?" she asks.

"I need to get out of this room," I answer, preparing for an argument but, instead, my sister offers me her hand.

I take it and she pulls me to my feet. I wobble, but manage to keep myself from falling back onto the bed. Gabby wraps an arm around my waist and guides me towards the stairs. I take each step slowly and am proud of myself when I make it to the top. Gabby opens the door and the cool, salty air rushes in at me. I breathe it in and step outside. Carlos watches us as we walk to the rail and then he yells at his men to keep working.

I close my eyes and savor the feel of the sun on my skin, and enjoy the salt spray on my face. Gabby is about to say something, but then stops herself.

"I've been inside for so long," I explain. "From that dungeon to this ship." I pause when she looks at me and then say, "This just feels good."

"Carlos says we still have about two days," Lee says gruffly as he joins us at the rail. "It's good to see you up and about, Dawn."

I catch his eye and know exactly what he means. The two of us went through a lot together.

Lee's eyes shift to Gabby and I take that as my cue.

"Where's Drew?" I ask.

"Over there," Lee says, pointing him out to me.

"You need my help?" Gabby asks, worriedly.

"Not really," I say before winking at Lee and leaving them alone.

Drew isn't far. I walk up quietly behind him and wrap my arms around his waist, leaning my head on his shoulder. He grabs hold of my hands and turns to face me before pulling me under his chin and kissing the top of my head.

"I love you," he whispers into my hair.

"Ditto," I say with smile and squeeze him.

"I can't lose you," he says.

"You won't," I assure him.

"You can't promise that," he says softly.

"I know, but it felt good to say," I admit.

"I don't suppose you could let someone else step in and finish this mission?" he asks with a laugh.

"Not a chance. We need to stop Joseph Kearn. People are counting on us." I look up to meet his eyes, but they are fixed on the horizon. "Our countrymen are counting on us," I say.

"The first ships are probably already being provisioned," he says wistfully. "Your father called it the birth of a new tomorrow, a new England."

"Drew, what happens if Kearn sets off the bio weapon before we find him?" I ask.

"We can't let that happen," he answers.

Chapter 80

The General

"Any word from Mexico?" Adrian asks as he takes a seat in my office. He's just returned from a couple of weeks in St. Louis.

"None," I snap.

The question irritates me only because I wish I had a different answer.

"The Carlitas sent a ship to get them out of Mexico, but I haven't heard if they made it out or not," I explain.

"Well, shit," he says.

I look up sharply at the young Texan. He needs to learn how to speak like a leader. I've been trying to teach him, but he's been … reluctant to learn.

Texas is a powder keg waiting to blow. For so long, they had leaders they worshipped. They respected and feared the Coles. Adrian only has the name. He refuses to be their cult leader. I admire that, but dammit, this world still needs leaders.

"I've had word from England," I say. "The first evacuees will arrive in two months. They are going to land in east Floridaland and travel north from there."

"Why there?" Adrian asks.

"Ports," I say. "Docking facilities."

"Why not Vicksburg?" he asks.

"Because your damn Texans would think they were being invaded," I answer, irritated.

"Well, aren't we?" Adrian asks with a laugh.

I worry about leaving Texas in the hands of someone so young and inexperienced. I don't have a choice though.

"I leave for Floridaland in the morning," I say.

Adrian seems surprised by this, but he nods his head, allowing me to continue.

"And I'll need every truck you can muster in two months," I say.

"I understand," he replies, standing and extending his hand. "Good luck General."

"Adrian," I say, taking his hand.

"Yes, General?" he asks.

"If Gabby and her squad are too late, if Kearn sets off the weapon, all hell will break loose and he could very well turn back toward you and Vicksburg. Are your people loyal to you? Will they fight?" I ask.

Adrian tilts his head and looks me straight in the eye. "Let's hope we don't have to find out."

Chapter 81

Gabby

Lee's hand makes circles on my back while I sit next to him in the empty room. Drew, Jeremy, and Dawn are up on deck, giving us a rare moment of privacy.

"What are we going to do when this is all over?" he asks absently.

"Dawn says New Penn will need us," I say, not wanting to answer his real question. He wants to know what will become of the two of us. "We'll spend our days working rather than training. On laundry day we'll wash our normal clothes, because we won't be living in uniforms anymore."

"I'll hunt, and you can cook," he says, his voice as wistful as mine.

"Like hell I will!" I interrupt.

"Okay, you can hunt and I'll cook, or we both can hunt and Dawn will cook," he says with a laugh.

"That sounds more like it," I say. "We won't keep losing friends."

"No, that we won't," he says, growing quiet, and neither of us talks for a few minutes.

"There's still so much more to do before we get to all of that," I say, breaking the silence. "What if we're too late? What if Kearn unleashes the bio weapon on the evacuees?"

Lee doesn't answer because we both know where that question leads. He turns to look at me.

"I love you," he says.

He's said this a few times since he thought he was going to die in Mexico and he's never expected me to say it back. Instead, I close the small gap between us and kiss him deeply. If there's one thing we've learned from all of our dead friends, it's that anything can happen, and tomorrow, that anything will begin.

Chapter 82

Gabby

Floridaland.

I hate the sight of it. I hate the smell of it. I even hate the sound of the word. And yet, here I am back on its shore.

"You ready for this?" Jeremy asks as he steps next to me at the rail.

"No," I say honestly.

I don't have to look at him to know he feels the same way. Jeremy was born and raised in the Floridaland slave camp. He suffered more than most. His mother and sister died here.

I remember the day so clearly. Claire had just died from illness and Jeremy brought me here to the shore to mourn her. We watched the waves and talked and then he kissed me. In that moment, we wanted each other. We needed each other. Then they came. The British soldiers and their dogs. Jeremy was caught, but I made it back into camp.

I've been holding onto the rail so hard my knuckles are turning white so I loosen my grip. Dawn steps next to me so that helps. Her strength has been returning and she is almost herself again. I don't know if I could face all of this without her by my side.

Our local contact reported that Joseph Kearn and his men are at the plantation, so that's where we're headed. Carlos bids us farewell and good luck as we climb into the boat.

When we reach the beach, Jeremy bends down and scoops up a handful of sand only to let it fall through his fingers. "We shouldn't linger here," he says.

"You're right," I say, knowing what's going through his mind. "Let's go."

I lead the group toward the woods.

"Drew, I want you at the back to watch out for British or Mexican soldiers. Lee, up with me to do the same. Safeties off. Everyone stay on alert," I say.

I brace my arm in my gun sling, ready for anything, and keep going. The path begins to climb through the dunes and the thick underbrush.

"Stop," I whisper, holding up my fist when we reach the crest of the dune overlooking the camp. "The guard tower is empty."

"Maybe Kearn and his men took them out," Dawn says.

"Something isn't right here," Jeremy says in a hushed voice. "We need to get out of these woods and down there to find out what's going on."

"Lee and I are going to scout up ahead," I state. "The rest of you take cover and watch for us"

We slip silently down the path to the fence.

"Do you hear that?" I ask. "There's no electric hum."

"The fence isn't on," Lee responds.

We run silently to the tower. There's no one there. Moving back, we signal to the others who come silently to join us.

"The guards are gone and the fence is off," I explain, looking at each of them. "Time to go inside."

"We could get trapped in there," Dawn says.

After everything she's been through I don't blame her for not wanting to go there.

"Not everyone is coming," I say. "Some of you need to scout out the plantation."

"Gabs," Dawn begins, "If you're going in, we're all going in."

I open my mouth to say "NO" but she keeps going.

"This is bigger than any one of us," she says, putting both hands on my shoulders and looking me in the eye. "Let's go." She takes off in the direction of the fence.

I stare after my sister for a moment in stunned appreciation before catching up to her. We get to the strangely quiet fence and I cautiously reach out my hand. The cold wires bend to my will as I push them down so everyone can get through.

We round a cluster of huts and I'm lost in the scene around me when I run straight into Jeremy who has stopped dead in his tracks.

"What are you...?" I begin to ask, but then follow his line of sight.

There are bodies scattered across the camp.

Jeremy crouches down to examine the face of an older woman. No bullets. No sign of struggle.

"Everyone stop!" I yell, suddenly sure of the events that took place here. "Don't touch them!"

They all freeze as awareness comes to them as well.

"This was Kearn," Dawn says with certainty.

"Do you remember Raf's description of the attacks on Carlita villages?" I ask. "They tested their virus on them. Don't touch any of the bodies."

Jeremy is now kneeling beside another dead woman with tears rolling openly down his face. I move closer and see Amanda's still face. The woman who took care of me when I was here. The woman who practically raised Jeremy after his mother was killed. She was his last link to his past and his family. He looks up at me desperately as I drop down beside him and wrap my arms around his neck.

"I tried to get her to escape with us," I whisper.

"She wouldn't leave everyone else behind," he says, sobbing.

Forgetting myself, I reach out to wipe the dried blood from her face, but Jeremy catches my hand.

Amanda should still be here. Her and Claire. They were good. *How are the rest of us screw-ups still alive, but they're dead?*

Jeremy looks towards the sky. "It's a beautiful day," he says. "How is that right?"

"I don't know," I respond. "I don't think the sun cares about what's going on down here."

I think of all of my days in this place. The sky was blue and the sun was warm, but that didn't matter. All hope is now gone from this place. Maybe it was never here. Maybe it was just a figment of our imaginations. Something we made up just to keep us going. I got out, but the bad things don't end when you leave the camp. It's not that easy to just move on.

"We need to kill them all," Jeremy states.

"Every last one of them," I agree. "Starting with Joseph Kearn."

Chapter 83

Dawn

We leave the camp behind us as we head toward the plantation. The once beautiful lawn is overgrown and the well-kept flowerbeds are riddled with weeds. No one has taken care of this place in months.

"Why would they just abandon all of this?" Drew asks.

"I don't think they did," I say. "We know that the Rebels in England have been winning their battles for a while now. The troops here probably stopped getting reinforcements and supplies. They would've left a skeleton crew to guard the camp and make sure the harvests were done, but not to take care of the grounds."

We're about to cross the lawn when we hear the unmistakable sound of gunfire and bullets start penetrating the ground around us. We take off running toward the barn for cover. I'm the last one to dive in through the door, and by that, I mean actually dive. I land on my stomach and roll to my feet in one quick movement. The firing stops.

"Did anyone see how many there are?" Gabby asks, trying to catch her breath.

"I saw three," Lee replies. "All on the second floor of the main house."

"Do you think it's the Mexicans or the British?" I ask.

"My guess is Kearn," Lee says from across the barn. "The British are long gone."

"I think so too," Gabby says. "And Kearn's men will be here soon. Our top priority is to find Kearn. You can bet he's heavily guarded by Moreno men, and you can bet the weapon is here as well. We need to split up. Dawn, Drew, and

Jeremy, swing around front and create a diversion. I want you to pull as many soldiers out of the plantation house as you can and set up a kill zone. Lee and I will come from behind and clear the back hallways before we meet up with you all inside."

"We've got trouble!" Drew yells from his lookout point as three men sprint across the grounds, their guns drawn.

They burst through the door with wild abandon. The first one aims his gun at Gabby, but Lee takes him out. Jeremy surprises a second by jumping out from his hiding spot and burying a bullet in his belly. A third man knocks Drew out of his way and then backs away from Lee who has already finished off his fellow soldier. His gun is raised, but he is outnumbered. He starts firing wildly, but only gets a few shots off before he gets one right between the eyes, point blank.

No one moves. Out of the corner of my eye, I see Jeremy stumble backward and slide to the ground. He removes his hand from his side and stares at it in a daze. It is covered in blood.

Chapter 84

Jeremy

Strangely, there is no pain, just a dark circle closing around me. Dawn and Gabby are holding my hands and talking, but I can't make out the words.

"You guys will be okay," I try to say, but my lips aren't moving. "Hold on to each other."

And then I think, I'm going to miss kicking Joseph Kearn's ass, the bastard, and it makes me laugh. That only makes me choke, and the girls look frightened.

I hear a flurry of action and the distant sound of my name, as the circle continues closing around me, my eyes barely open.

And then the circle is complete and my sister, Claire, is reaching towards me.

Chapter 85

Gabby

I wipe my hand across my eyes and stand. No one has said a word in the time between Jeremy's last breath and now. My whole body trembles as I look down into his face.

They've taken another person that I care about.

"This has to stop," I say, steeling myself. "Joseph Kearn is within our grasp."

"We're hugely outnumbered," Lee says matter-of-factly.

"We are soldiers!" I bark, grabbing a rifle, and tossing it to Lee. "This, right here, is how we get our vengeance. This is how we mourn our friends."

I look at the brave faces around me and then down at Jeremy's blissful face as I swing the rifle off my back.

"Let's go," I say as I brush past Dawn and head for the door with Lee by my side.

He opens it and all four of us step outside.

Lee and I draw fire just long enough for Dawn and Drew to make it to the side of the plantation house. Pop goes a grenade into a window, and then another as Drew makes a run down the side. Now it's our turn to get around back. As I switch my clip, I place my hand on Lee's chest. He looks at me and smiles, just a little.

"Just so we're clear, before we do this, I love you," I say.

His smile fades and he runs his fingertips along my jaw.

"Say that again when all of this is over and we've made it. Say it when we're living that boring, normal life we dream of," he responds.

Pop! Pop! It's time to run.

My arms and legs pump as fast as they can. Dawn and Drew are laying fire on the Moreno men as they pile out of the house, bloodied and dazed from the grenades.

In seconds we're at the door that leads toward the prison cells. I run my palm over the bloody handprints before tossing in a grenade and barging through.

The hallway before us is empty except for the guard lying dead at the door. A second later, we're going room to room, shooting everything that moves. They're all running to the front of the house, not expecting us from within.

But where is Kearn?

Chapter 86

Dawn

Drew tosses his last grenade into the open window and scrambles back toward me as I empty bullets into the mess of soldiers coming out the front door. As I reach down for another clip, I squeeze my eyes shut for just a moment and hope that Gabby and Lee are okay.

"You good?" Drew asks.

"Yeah," I say as I open my eyes and empty another clip into the front of the house.

Drew motions to a truck parked behind us, mutters something about "Gabby's diversion", and takes off toward it. He flings open the door, puts a bullet into the chest of a stunned driver who has been hiding inside, and yanks him out.

Climbing in, drew starts the truck and careens toward the front porch into the group of Moreno men we had pinned down. He rolls out as the truck plows into the front door, sending gunmen flying in all directions.

One. Two. Three. I have become a killing machine. These are for Jeremy.

Drew calls me to the front door. A soldier pops up and then a shot rings out and he is dropped from behind as we scurry over the bodies and into the gaping hole made by the truck. The shot was Gabby's, no doubt. I only hope this is the diversion she needed.

Chapter 87

Gabby

What the hell was that?

I look down the hall and see a truck through the dust. A soldier turns and I drop him before running down the back hall again.

The smoke has entered the house, but that's the least of our problems.

"Where is he?" I scream. "Kearn! I'm coming for you!"

"Look," Lee says, pointing toward the back staircase. "He's probably up there. That's where the command center is."

A gunman appears at the top. He sees me and yells just as I pull the trigger. One more for Jeremy.

I duck back along the side of the staircase as another soldier comes running at me, firing. His bullets ping off the metal banister and past my head.

Lee darts out and drops him, then rushes up the stairs.

"All clear," Lee yells, motioning down to me.

At the top of the staircase is a long hall with the front staircase leading to what's left of the front door at the other end.

"I guess Dawn's diversion was bigger than we thought," I say.

Suddenly we both stiffen as the door next to us begins to creak open and then I'm staring down the barrel of a gun. Then the door flies open wider, and a hand pushes down the rifle aiming point blank at my face.

"Gabby! I almost shot you," Dawn says as she and Drew emerge from the room.

I put a finger to my lips. There's a sound as a door down the hall opens, and then closes. I head that way. Lee and I stand on either side of the doorway as

Dawn turns the knob. The door slowly swings open wide. No one is there. We enter the room, guns drawn.

As soon as we do, men pour in from an adjoining room. My rifle jams, so I grab my hand gun and pull my knife. I thrust my arm out and catch a man in the gut, while firing blindly in close quarters.

A female soldier has fallen in front of me and I have my gun to her temple when I see him coming through the door.

Joseph Kearn.

I quickly pull the trigger and jump over the woman's body toward him.

I grab him by the shirt and pull him toward me, as the others finish off his bodyguards.

"Where is it?" I scream. "Where is the weapon?"

"You're going to have to kill me," he answers, his eyes lighting up with defiance.

"Tell me where it is," I growl.

"Do you know what the virus does?" he asks, smiling like a man who knows he's going to die. "The worst part is the boils. They burn and there is no relief. They'll twist your pretty face into something grotesque. The fever comes and goes, but the hallucinations will persist. You will all die. And you won't even know your own face when you do."

I plunge my short blade into his leg and twist it. He screams.

"Where is it?!" I yell.

He doesn't respond because he has nothing left to lose and he isn't going to tell us shite. I pull the blade free of his leg and stab him below the ribs.

"That's for Linc," I spit.

He grasps for my arm as I do it again and blood splatters my face.

"That's for Shay," I say.

"Gabby!" Dawn shouts.

At this point, the fight is over and they're watching me in horror as I slay Joseph Kearn. Tears stream down my face as I stab him again.

"That's for Raf," I say, my voice growing quieter as it is invaded by sobs.

His eyes roll back into his head as I stab once more.

"And that one is for Jeremy," I say finally, letting his lifeless body fall to the floor with a loud thump.

No one comes near me. I look at my sister who's standing there in shock. Lee is leaning against the wall catching his breath, and Drew is on the ground. He's been shot in the calf, but he'll survive.

"We need to find the weapon," Dawn says finally, tossing me a rifle.

Lee and Dawn have Drew slung between them as we exit the room, guns ready.

Chapter 88

Gabby

"It has to be here," I say, tossing aside an empty crate.

"We've searched every damn room in this house," Lee responds.

"I have a question for you guys," Dawn chimes in. "Without Joseph Kearn, does the weapon really matter?"

"Of course it does!" I snap.

"But who's going to use it now?" she continues. "And maybe Kearn has hidden it so it can't be found. He might have been our only chance of finding it."

"He wouldn't have told us anything!" I snap defensively.

"We know that Gabs," Lee says passively.

"Let's stop for the night," Dawn says. "We can look with fresh eyes tomorrow."

"Shite," I say, my shoulders sagging in defeat, "okay."

I sigh and walk away from them. They don't follow me. There's only one person I want to talk to right now.

I climb past the demolished truck and out across the lawn strewn with Moreno corpses before slipping into the barn and walking on silent feet to where Jeremy still lies, or his body does anyway. I kneel beside him and take his cold hand.

"I'm so sorry, Jeremy," I whisper as the tears run down my face. "We started this together, you and me. Do you remember? In Floridaland? I wish you were here to help me now."

I don't say anything else for a while. I'm spent and lost in thought. When my eyes finally dry, I stand. "You were a good friend, Jeremy. You deserved better than this," I say.

I look around for something I can wrap his body in to take it out of this barn for burial.

I pull on a tarp that covers a stack of crates nearby. It comes free, and I'm about to bring it over to Jeremy's body, when I see the glint of a metal canister between the wooden slats. I reach in and pull out a cylindrical metal tube.

"My God, Kearn," I whisper. "Thank you, Jeremy."

I run out the door of the barn, screaming to Lee and Dawn.

"I found it!" I yell. "The damned thing was in the barn!"

I expect to hear Dawn respond in excitement or to see Lee run to me. Instead, I hear Lee scream.

"Gabby! Get down!"

Chapter 89

Dawn

They come in firing as soon as they see the smoldering house and Gabby running across the courtyard. Two truckloads of Moreno men send Gabby scampering back toward the barn. They pile out and surround the barn. There's a burst of gunfire and several of them storm in through the doors. Then there's more gunfire and shouting before everything is silent.

I look at Lee in terror and disbelief.

"It's Gabby. She'll figure out a way out of there," he says, but his voice isn't nearly as confident as his words.

We're no match for their truck-mounted machine guns, so we stay hidden.

After a few long minutes, the soldiers begin carrying crates from the barn and loading them. It doesn't take me long to figure out what's going on.

"They're taking the weapon," I say, drawing in a sharp breath.

"We need to do something and fast," Lee says. "Drew, how's the leg?"

"I can help," he says through gritted teeth. He's in pain and has lost a lot of blood.

"They'll be coming in here next. We need to get out of here and help Gabby," I say.

I help Drew to his feet and he winces as he puts weight on his shredded leg.

"I can run," he promises me.

I nod and open the door. Drew, Lee, and I make our way down the back staircase and into the brush. From there we wait and watch as some of the soldiers finish loading while several others cautiously make their way to the house.

Just as they approach the front door, an explosion rips through the first truck, sending truck and body parts flying across the lawn.

Dazed, the soldiers loading the other truck back away before being cut down by a machine gun and a second explosion slams the remaining truck.

A huge fireball envelops the grounds around the barn as the artillery shells holding the virus explode in succession. We're in shock until a few moments later when a troop of soldiers step out of the darkness to finish off the last of the Mexican men.

More troops, trucks, and then my father appear. His weapons are drawn and he's shouting commands. I can't wait another second. I spring up and go running for the barn, shouting my sister's name.

"Gabby!" I scream, but there's no answer.

The soldiers take aim until Drew shouts, "General Nolan! It's Dawn, Drew, and Lee!"

"Gabby!" I yell again as I approach the barn. "Where are you?"

I fling open the barn doors and plead into the darkness.

"Gabby, are you in here?" I ask.

A muzzle flashes and Lee drops one last Mexican hiding inside.

I don't turn around as I yell, "Someone get me a light!"

Lee appears beside me, torch in hand, and we enter together. Jeremy's body is lying where he fell, against the far wall half covered in a tarp. We step closer and that's when we see her. My sister's lifeless, bloody body is sprawled in the dirt in front of the last crate of biological weapons.

"No," I stammer, trying to remember to breathe. "No!"

I take Lee's hand as we kneel beside her. There is no pulse.

"You can't leave me, Gabs," I say, reaching for her hand.

Suddenly there is more light around us, and soldiers are coming in the barn, but they don't make a sound.

"You found the weapon," Lee says to Gabby, leaning down to look directly into her face. "You did it. You saved your people."

He kisses her forehead and flattens her hair as I sit motionless.

"I love you," he says, sobbing, "so much."

I reach out to cup her chin and then wipe away the slow trickle of blood streaking down her beautiful face.

"What am I supposed to do without you?" I ask her finally.

I lift my teary gaze to the weapon Gabby died to find.

"She completed her mission," I say to Lee.

"Of course she did," Lee responds. "Was there ever any doubt?"

We're surrounded by a reverently silent group of Rebels, to whom Gabby is now a legend. They bow their heads and move back as Drew limps forward. He wraps his arms around me and I bury my face in his chest and sob.

"Your father is here," he says softly.

I lift my eyes to his and then get to my feet.

I grab Lee's torch and scan the faces surrounding me.

He steps out of the shadows, tears streaming down his face. He holds his arms out to me and I start to cry all over again as I run to him and he holds me tightly.

"Shhhhh," he whispers into my hair, rocking me gently. "Shhhhh."

Chapter 90

Dawn

We buried Gabby and Jeremy the next morning.

How do you say goodbye to someone you loved with every inch of your being?

They called her and Jeremy "heroes," but that doesn't make it any easier.

I miss you, Gabby, terribly. And I wish you could be here to see the results of your sacrifice.

Chapter 91

Dawn

We've been in New Penn for about two months now, and everywhere I go, people ask me about my sister. They want to know the tale of the girl who led an unlikely group of people to save everyone.

The weapon was destroyed, leaving the way clear for the English to come here, and come here they did. They've been arriving in droves and I've been told it's going to take over a decade for the English migration to be complete. Everyone is working hard to get them set up in their new lives. Hell, we're still working on our new lives. I wish Gabby were here to help. I talk to her daily.

I tell her all about this new world we're creating, the one that she made possible. I tell her about what it's like to have a father again instead of just a general. How he spends his days working in the garden or in the smoke room. I've found him cooking in the kitchen and once he was even doing laundry. Riley is the unofficial leader here, and my father has gladly ceded all power to him.

"Jerky!" my dad calls as he enters the house, balancing a platter of meat.

I can't help but smile when he's in a mood like this. He sets the plate down as Drew and I sit with him.

"Hope you like jerky," Dad says, winking at Drew.

"Again?" Drew and I say simultaneously before laughing.

Jerky was our first meal together as stowaways aboard that British transport plane. We weren't too fond of each other then.

"Hey guys," Lee pops his head in. "Jerky! I love Jerky!"

He sits down and helps himself. This is how most evenings go. We pick up our meals from the kitchen and then we end up here, eating together, a family.

Lee doesn't talk about Gabby much, but I know it still hurts. We have an unspoken agreement that we don't ask each other how we're doing. We already know the answer. It's going to take time.

Ryan and his kid sister Emily wander in next. Ryan was already here when we arrived. His family lost their fight in Cincinnati, but the survivors were allowed to leave. They came to New Penn for a fresh start.

Corey drops by most nights as well, and tonight is no different. He never had much of a choice in becoming a Rebel after his parents were killed in their Texas home. He could never bring himself to go back. He says that none of us are Rebels now. He says we're not even British, or Texan, or American now. Colonials maybe? I don't know. We have a lot to figure out in this new world.

I catch my father's eye and he gives me a sad smile. We're both missing the people that will never come through that door.

"Who's up for hunting tomorrow?" Ryan asks.

That's the turn the conversation takes. Although we joke and laugh and smile, none of our thoughts are ever far from everyone who isn't here at this table. After losing so much, we're all trying to figure out how to go on, together. We will never forget the people that got us here, but, one day, maybe it won't hurt so much.

Chapter 92

Epilogue
10 years later
Dawn

"How's the expansion going in the west?" I ask Lee as we pour over a map of the rapidly growing New Penn.

"Everything is on schedule," he answers.

"Good," I respond. "We need to come up with a name for the new town."

"I'll get some people on that," he replies, scratching his head. "Storm season is coming and the northern silos are a bit low on grain."

"The southern fields had a great crop this year. See what they have to say down there," I tell him.

"Yes ma'am," he says, turning to leave.

"Lee," I say, irritated. "Can you please stop that?"

"You've been elected," he says, a glint of humor in his eyes. "I'm just showing you the respect our leader deserves."

He bows and I swat at his head.

"Just go," I say with laugh.

"Will I see you tomorrow at your father's?" he asks.

I nod and he gives me a small hug before heading out to complete the tasks I've given him. Lee's my resource manager, in charge of food stores, energy, and water, and he's really good at it. He seems content.

I sit in my oversized chair in my oversized office and lean back with my feet on the desk. *How did I get here?*

New Penn has branched off into other towns as more and more people have immigrated. We're expanding as fast as humanly possible and our population has reached the thousands.

Peace has been the name of the game for the past ten years, so people are having children and carving out lives for themselves. It took me a while after Gabby's death, but I eventually moved on as well.

I play with the bracelet on my wrist that I still wear most days. Gabby stole it, for me. That's how I got here. I laugh at the absurdity of it all, and then sigh as I focus on the report in front of me. I crumple it up and toss it in the dustbin as there is a knock on my door.

"Yes?" I answer.

Drew pokes his head in and smiles.

"Hi," he says. "Can we come in?"

"Of course," I answer as I stand and move around my desk.

Drew comes in, hand-in-hand with the most precious girl I have ever seen.

"Hi Gab," I say as I reach down to pick her up.

She grins and wraps her chubby arms around my neck.

"Hi mommy," she says as I kiss her head and smile at Drew.

He gives me a quick kiss before saying, "I wanted to do that before I give you news that will keep you from coming home to us early tonight."

I groan. If I could, I'd leave with them now.

"What's happened?" I ask, bracing for bad news.

"Nothing bad," he says quickly. "Adrian Cole, Mya Moreno, and Carlos Carlita have arrived for the trade summit."

"Oh," I say.

We weren't expecting them until two days from now.

"I guess I better go welcome them to New Penn," I say.

"Your dad wants to know if we're coming over for dinner tomorrow," Drew says before I go.

"Tell him I wouldn't miss it," I say, pausing. "And I'll bring Adrian with me."

"You know what tomorrow is, right?" he asks.

I sigh and nod my head. I've been doing my best not to think about it.

"It's my sister's birthday," I answer, my voice coming out quietly.

Before coming to the colonies all those years ago, Gabby and I always did birthdays together, just the two of us. She'd be thirty tomorrow. We still celebrate it every year even though she isn't here to join us.

Sensing my mood change, Drew takes our little girl from my arms and gives me another kiss before heading for the door.

"I'll see you at home, Mrs. President," he says before closing it behind them.

The End

Thank you for reading!

Readers are why we do what we do. Please take a moment to post what you thought of this book on Amazon.

What about a free book? Visit http://michellelynnauthor.com/ to pick up your copy.

Books by Michelle Lynn

Legends of the Tri-Gard (Written as M. Lynn)
Prophecy of Darkness
Legacy of Light
Mastery of Earth (2018)

Dawn of Rebellion Trilogy
Dawn of Rebellion
Day of Reckoning
Eve of Tomorrow

The New Beginnings series
Choices
Promises
Dreams

The Invincible series
We Thought We Were Invincible
We Thought We Knew it All

Standalone
Lesson Plan

About Michelle

M. Lynn has a brain that won't seem to quiet down, forcing her into many different genres to suit her various sides. Under the name Michelle Lynn, she writes romance and dystopian as well as upcoming fantasies. Running on Diet Coke and toddler hugs, she sleeps little - not due to overworking or important tasks - but only because she refuses to come back from the worlds in the books she reads. Reading, writing, aunting ... repeat.

See more from M. Lynn
www.michellelynnauthor.com

Lightning Source UK Ltd.
Milton Keynes UK
UKHW041849250221
379413UK00008B/471/J